"You're in ⌷⌷⌷⌷ ⌷⌷⌷ ⌷⌷⌷⌷
cowb⌷

Abby's mouth dropped⌷ ⌷⌷⌷⌷⌷ ⌷⌷⌷⌷⌷
wouldn't come. She co⌷⌷ ⌷⌷⌷⌷⌷⌷⌷⌷
tenderly rocking the ⌷⌷⌷ ⌷⌷⌷⌷⌷⌷⌷
whimpers disappeared. "I don't want to talk about it,
Donna."

"Yes, you do. But *I'm* not the person you need to talk
to."

Abby looked away from the truth in her friend's eyes.
"What's the matter with me, Donna? I thought all this
was behind me."

Donna squeezed her arm. "Why do you think Tom
would be scandalized by something that happened ten
years ago? Something you had no control over?"

Abby swallowed. "Tom wouldn't condemn me, but he
wouldn't understand. Women in his world don't—"

"Then you need to begin distancing yourself from that
family, Abby. For all your sakes."

Abby closed her eyes. "I know," she said softly. "But
knowing doesn't make it easier."

Dear Reader,

While working as a feature writer for a newspaper, I interviewed families dealing with loss brought about by murder, suicide and domestic violence. While this book is purely fictional, as are its characters, I owe these courageous people a debt of gratitude for opening my eyes to the "ripple effect" of violence in our society. Daily, hourly, lives are turned upside down by violent crime. Victims' advocates can and do help families caught in the cross fire put their lives back together. Real-life support groups—such as the one now called Footsteps at the St. Agnes Medical Center in Fresno, California—help young people deal with the repercussions of tragedy and loss through facilitated peer support. I also learned that in some cases "doing the right thing" can be accomplished with style and grace, humor and love—the mark of a true hero.

This is my first published book and I need to thank all my family members and friends who have stuck by me for the long haul, rewrite after rewrite. I am also indebted to Barbara Hale for patiently teaching me an editorial concept that often escaped me: less is more. And a special thanks goes to Patti, who insisted on a "storybook" ending.

Within these pages you'll run across my personal credo: "If you are open and receptive, good things come to you." I'm living proof it works. May only good things come your way!

Debra Salonen

THAT COWBOY'S KIDS
Debra Salonen

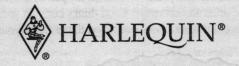

TORONTO • NEW YORK • LONDON
AMSTERDAM • PARIS • SYDNEY • HAMBURG
STOCKHOLM • ATHENS • TOKYO • MILAN • MADRID
PRAGUE • WARSAW • BUDAPEST • AUCKLAND

ISBN 0-373-70910-2

THAT COWBOY'S KIDS

Copyright © 2000 by Debra K. Salonen.

For my mother and father,
who gave me time to dream.

For Paul, who gave me time to write.

CHAPTER ONE

"How much longer, Daddy?" Heather asked plaintively.

Tom Butler stifled a sigh. "Five more minutes, punkin," he said without consulting his watch.

"That's what you said five minutes ago," Angela grumbled, her words muffled by a thick wad of long dark hair.

Tom glanced at her. His twelve-year-old daughter, a spooky mixture of limbs and emotions, sat folded into a tight ball up against the passenger door of his pickup truck. With artistic finesse she winnowed out one ebony strand from the rest of the waist-length tresses and threaded it between sullen lips.

Grazing on hair, he thought, one more thing no one had warned him about.

"Don't worry, Thomas. You're doing just fine," Janey Hastings had told him at dinner last night after Angel stormed off in a huff over some imaginary slight. Janey and Ed, who were more surrogate parents to Tom than mere employers, had been his lifeline these past four months, his tether to sanity. Sadly, next Monday the Hastingses would be off fighting demons of their own. Janey's last mammogram showed a questionable spot, and her doctors had ordered her to Stanford.

"It's a phase," Janey had said sagely. "Just love 'em—that's all that matters. Don't sweat the small stuff.

After all," she'd said with an understanding smile, "it's every teenage girl's goal to drive her father crazy. My granddaughters were the same way. I was sure Peter was going to send them back here to live with me until they were old enough for college."

Tom knew how much Janey missed her sons—Edward lived on the East Coast, Pete and his family in Colorado. Ed missed them, too, but he had Tom to fill the gap—a surrogate son to run the Standing Arrow H, the ranch and orchard operation that was Ed's passion.

Angela sat up suddenly and jammed the inch-thick soles of her ugly black boots against the truck's already cracked dashboard. "Why do we have to do this, anyway? It's stupid."

"Feet down, please," Tom said, keeping his tone level. It had occurred to him more than once these past few months that dealing with a teenager was like breaking in a two-year-old colt—you do everything slow and careful and keep body parts out of kicking range. "It's what the judge wants, honey, you know that." They'd been over the issue a dozen times in the past two days.

Her feet didn't budge. "Well, I ain't gonna talk to no therapist. I ain't crazy."

Tom leaned across Heather, who seemed to shrink from the cross tone of her sister's voice, and gently tapped Angela's shin. "Don't say 'ain't.'"

"Don't hit me," she bristled, pulling back.

Tom sighed wearily and gazed out the cracked windshield of his half-ton Ford. Angel's moods changed faster than the weather. Some days she was Little Miss Homemaker, fixing tuna casseroles or macaroni and cheese on Tom's two-burner hot plate; some days she sat glued to his small, black-and-white television watching whatever crap the talk shows aired. Tom hadn't been too pleased with Judge Overman's edict that Heather and Angel see a counselor, since it meant prolonging the bureaucratic umbilical cord wrapped around his neck, but a therapist might help.

"Daddy, I hav'a go potty," Heather said in a tiny voice.

His heart lurched painfully. Poor Heather. No mood swings for her. His bright little poppet had changed from a bubbling, fearless five-year-old at Christmas to a shadow person afraid of the wind.

"We're going right in there, sweetie," he said, pointing to a low white stucco building with a small, discreet sign beside the door. "I'm sure they have a bathroom. Can you hold it?" She'd been wetting the bed ever since her mother's death five months earlier.

Heather's head bobbed tentatively. He put his arm around her and pulled her tiny body close. He'd have given ten years of his life to turn back the hands of time. Maybe if he could have talked Lesley into staying with him, she'd still be alive.

Why, Les? Why didn't you stay? He knew the answer. The love they'd shared had been enough to produce two daughters but not strong enough to close the huge gap in their dreams and ambitions.

Despite their divorce, Tom always respected the way Lesley set goals for herself and met them, goals that didn't include horses, cows and everything else that went along with being a cowboy's wife. At first, he'd hated her for taking away his children, but she'd made sure Tom always had contact with his daughters. Even after she married Val, she'd invited Tom to spend the holidays with them.

Thank God for that, Tom thought. At least he wasn't a stranger to his daughters. Bad enough he was a single parent who didn't know the first thing about raising little girls.

"She's late," Angel complained.

Tom checked his Timex. "One minute to go."

A maroon Honda sedan drove into a parking place two spots away and stopped.

"Maybe that's her." Tom fished a scrap of paper out of the pocket of his jeans.

Angela snatched the paper from his fingers. "Abby Davis," she said, reading the name on it aloud. "Abby. Probably short for Abigail. What a dorky name! Sounds like an old-maid schoolteacher."

"You'll hold your tongue, miss, and I mean it," Tom said, his voice sharp. Beside him, Heather trembled like a wet pup. Tom gave her a comforting squeeze. "She's a victim's advocate. She helps people. The judge seems to think we need some help, and I think maybe he's right."

Angela's eyes filled with tears, making Tom instantly contrite. She was a great kid, she just had too damn much on her plate.

"Besides," he added, trying to lighten the mood, "it's not her fault about her name. Look what your grandma did to me. Thomas Richard Butler. My dad used to say Mama tried to name me after all her boyfriends—every Tom, Dick and Harry, only Harold wouldn't fit on the birth certificate." His mother, the shyest, most self-effacing woman he'd ever known would blush like a schoolgirl when Walt Butler teased her, but Tom knew they both enjoyed the banter. Tom was happy to see his effort earn a weak smile from Angela, but the strand of hair went back into her mouth. He swallowed a sigh. One battlefield at a time.

"DECISIONS, DECISIONS," Abby Davis muttered softly, willing herself to get out of her car when every instinct in her bones told her to put it in reverse and drive.

Abby eyed the unremarkable postwar bungalow that housed VOCAP, the Welton, California, Victims of Crime Advocacy Program. Her home-away-from-home for the past seven years. "Go or stay?"

Without meaning to, Abby took in the large, mud-splattered truck parked nearby. Normally, she might have wondered about its three occupants. It was impossible not to notice the solemn expressions of a family in trouble, but they weren't her problem, she told herself.

She had enough problems of her own. Like turning thirty and realizing her dreams were withering on the vine.

Daniel had left her with few options.

"It's a lack of *dinero,* Abby," her boss, Daniel Kimura, had told her over pasta primavera at the upscale downtown restaurant where he'd taken her for a birthday lunch. "You know how much we need you. You're the heart and soul of VOCAP, but I fully understand your position. You're intelligent and ambitious, and we're guilty of exploiting your goodness and humanity without fully compensating you in either money or title. But my hands are tied thanks to those greedy, short-sighted bastards in Sacramento."

His ebony eyes flashed contempt, making Abby wonder whether the rumors about his own political aspirations were true. Well, why not? A third-generation Asian-American with an admirable record as a district attorney, he had good face. And the camera loved him.

"You deserve better, Abby. It hurts me deeply that I can't give you what you need."

''What are you going to do if I quit?''

''Weep.'' Whoever called him a cold fish—probably Melina—hadn't shared garlic cheese bread and two glasses of Chablis with him. By the time they split the obligatory brownie sundae, listened to off-key waiters and several curious diners singing her the birthday song, Abby was almost feeling sorry for him.

Almost. Daniel would return to his desk, a highly polished cherry-wood model dwarfed by the size of his office. Abby, on the other hand, was expected to swallow the party line and return to her closet-size cubicle from which she ran the agency that helped victims of crime rebuild their lives. Her modest salary was capped because she didn't have her college diploma, which she'd missed by one semester when she'd pitched in to help after her predecessor got pregnant. Her one-semester job of acting supervisor—the title of supervisor being reserved for the fully accredited—turned into a seven-year stint.

Stay or quit? Abby loved her job, but lately she'd begun to feel as if it was taking over her life. Maybe it was time to go back to college and take a stab at law school.

Ruefully acknowledging that any major decision would have to wait until she could take stock of her finances, Abby opened the door and climbed out. Besides, she had a one o'clock appointment. Some guy whose ex-wife had been killed in a robbery five months ago. The file arrived that morning and, although she'd only had time to glance at it, she'd noticed the court-ordered counseling for two minors. Well, maybe she'd assign the case to someone else because it was time for Abby Davis to move on with her life.

''No more Ms. Nice Guy,'' she muttered. Lifting her

chin, she marched ahead, forgetting about the labyrinth of busted concrete distributed in her path courtesy of a massive root from the shady but messy mulberry tree that was allowed to grow unimpeded in VOCAP's front lawn. The lawn-service budget was an early casualty.

The heel of her left pump disappeared into a San Andreas–size crevasse; the right one snapped out of sympathy and down she went.

"Damn it all to hell," Abby said under her breath, dusting off the quarter-size hole in the knee of her panty hose.

Torn between tears and a temper tantrum, she didn't move until a deep, polite voice asked, "Are you okay, ma'am?"

Abby looked up to see whom fate had designated to share her humiliation. A cowboy. Even if he hadn't been wearing formfitting jeans, dusty boots and a turquoise and pink canvas shirt, she'd have pegged his profession. Blame it on the slight bow in his legs, the Clint Eastwood squint of his sky-blue eyes shaded by a pearly white hat or the Yosemite Sam handlebars framing tight, serious lips.

"Anything broken?" he drawled. Not a southern drawl, more of a western-music sound. Not that she was all that familiar with either; it was a gut feeling, and it did weird things to her gut.

"Nothing worth suing over. Unfortunately," she muttered, twisting the heel, which made a 180-degree turn but remained attached to the shoe.

"I've been nagging Daniel for months to get this sidewalk fixed," she said, more to herself than him. "Tight budget, he says." She snorted. "Tight something else if you ask me."

His very faint chuckle made a rift of gooseflesh break

out on her arms, thankfully hidden by the plum-and-cream plaid suit, which undoubtedly would now show scuff marks on several unbecoming places.

"May I help you up?" That he even asked put him in a class of men Abby had heard of and read about but assumed was extinct: the gentleman.

"Um...sure. Thanks."

He didn't touch bare-skin, just the clothed arm below her elbow. It seemed to be enough for him to levitate her to an upright position. Abby was pretty sure she had nothing to do with the process since her knees suddenly had as much substance as the whipped cream on her brownie sundae.

"My heels," she explained, in case he was inclined to put a different spin on her wobbliness.

He nodded, just a bit. An economical motion that probably made dogs round up whole herds of cattle and women whip up batches of biscuits and gravy.

"Thank you," she said formally. "I'm not usually this clumsy but it's my birthday." *Aargh, how lame is that?* "I had wine at lunch." *Nice, Abby. Now he'll think you have a dependency problem.* "With my boss." *Shut up, already.*

Her hero was saved from trying to make a polite response to any of her ramblings when a young voice asked, "Are you Abby Davis?"

Abby fought the blush that engulfed her. It was one thing to be a klutz anonymously, but now her humiliation was public. "That's me." Under her breath, she added, "Unfortunately."

The cowboy apparently was blessed with better than average hearing since the hanging-down parts of his mustache twitched.

"My dad's here to see you, and my sister needs to use your bathroom."

For the first time, Abby noticed the two little girls standing in front of the pickup truck. The older child's coloring was darker than her father's, almost Mediterranean, but the family resemblance was borne out in the eyes—old beyond her years. Abby guessed her to be eleven or twelve; she would be a beauty some day soon—probably too soon to suit her father. The younger girl, maybe five or six, was a miniature angel with a halo of white-blond hair and big blue eyes that looked everywhere but at Abby.

Abby's embarrassment evaporated. Children in need were her special weakness.

"Then let's go," she said, taking a wobbly step forward. "Our rest room has green and purple fish on the walls." She bent down to the younger girl's height and whispered, "With orange lips."

The child looked up at her father, who scooped her into his arms like a feather on a breeze. "Let's go see," he said in a gentle voice that made Abby's heart flutter as if touched by the same breeze.

Abby led the way. After three toddling steps, she kicked off her shoes. The shredded panty hose would be next. "If you know my name, I should know yours, but I'm at a loss," she said over her shoulder.

"I'm Angela Butler. My dad's Tom Butler," the older girl said, joining her at the lead. "He has an appointment with you at one o'clock. Some old-fart judge ordered it."

Aah, Abby thought, the name from the file.

"Is your real name Abigail?" the girl asked with a challenging look at her father.

"Nope. Abner," Abby joked, sensing some undercurrent between the two.

"What?" the girl squawked, nearly losing her balance on a hunk of sidewalk.

With youthful nimbleness, she regained her equilibrium before Abby could grab her arm. "Just kidding. That's what Gabe Calloway called me in fifth grade until I popped him in the nose." She caught the sudden movement of Tom Butler's mustache—a frown, she assumed, and tried to make amends. "Not that I condone violence, of course, but in this case, he, um, well, anyway, to answer your question, my father wanted to name me Abigail after his grandmother, but my mother said that sounded too much like an old-maid schoolteacher, so they settled on Abby, instead."

The older girl flashed her father a smug look that left Abby baffled, but she pushed the matter aside when they reached the building's metal-reinforced door. No matter how many times she walked through this portal, she always shivered, remembering one very close call two years earlier.

"Are you cold?" the little girl asked, catching what few adults ever saw.

At eye level in her father's arms, Abby could see the remarkable blue of her eyes and the sadness that left smudge prints under each eye. Poor baby, Abby thought, but she smiled reassuringly and opened the door wide enough for the family to file past. "No, sweetie, but thank you for asking. This door just gives me the willies. It used to be a pretty glass door, but one day a very angry man came and broke it."

Tom Butler's mustache quivered again. Another frown, she sensed. He waited politely for her to enter.

Yep, a gentleman.

Abby scooted past him and paused in the small foyer beside Angela. The original foyer had been twice as big, with a picture window and two couches that gave it a homey look, but added security measures, including video cameras and electronic passkeys, meant less room for the people they were supposed to serve.

"Why'd he do that?" Angela asked. "I thought you helped people."

Abby stifled a sigh. A big part of VOCAP's focus was helping victims of domestic abuse. The man who took out their door—and very nearly Abby's head—wanted his wife and family back. When Abby wouldn't give him either, he took his anger out on her. She'd managed to get away and call the police. The door wasn't so lucky.

"We do. But sometimes people aren't ready to be helped." That her chipper tone, meant to shore up her own flagging morale as much as reassure her new clients, came off sounding like a cheerleader on the Mickey Mouse Club was confirmed by the girl's look of scorn.

She won't be easy, Abby thought, but who could blame her? Trust isn't easily given by someone whose world's been shattered by violence.

AFTER SETTLING HIS DAUGHTERS in the cheerful waiting room, Tom followed Abby Davis into her office. "Make yourself at home," she said. "I'll be right back." Tom lowered himself carefully into the square upholstered chair squeezed into a niche opposite a cluttered desk. Perched precariously to one side of the desk was a computer screen.

While the entry and hallway of the building sported large posters proclaiming the rights of victims, particularly women and children, this office revealed an attempt to promote serenity. A climbing plant with variegated leaves framed the room's single window, which faced the parking lot; two watercolor paintings of unstructured seascapes lessened the impact of metal bookshelves crammed with textbooks and stacks of files.

Tom was becoming a bit of an expert on mid-level bureaucratic office decor—he'd seen more than his share over the past five months. This had to be one of the smallest, yet classiest, offices yet. He particularly liked the hubcap-size, self-sustained waterfall that muffled the sound of the computer.

The machine's drone reminded him of what lay ahead: another retelling of the story, bringing to mind images safely stuffed in the recesses of his head—until fatigue or sleep brought down his guard.

Why even bother? What can these people do? Can they bring back Les? Can they take away Heather's nightmares or make Angel smile again?

Fighting off a wave of despair, Tom reminded himself why he was here—the court order. It might be a hopeless waste of time, but he didn't have any say in the matter. His rights had pretty much vanished the minute some junkie looking for drug money had put a gun to his ex-wife's head and pulled the trigger.

With a hoarse cough, he swallowed the gagging sensation in his throat.

A moment later, Abby Davis entered the room. Barefoot. She'd discarded her broken shoes and damaged hose. She seemed flustered, as if the lack of shoes somehow diminished her professional armor, leaving her vulnerable.

Tom studied her. Clear skin, pale from her indoor job.

A few tiny lines starting around the eyes. She wore no makeup, except for a ruddy lipstick.

She was a nice-looking woman, even if her taste in clothes didn't appeal to him. The severity of the cut and length of the jacket pretty well hid what looked like a trim rear end and shapely waist; the color was something he'd have buried once he made sure it was dead.

"Okay," she said, sliding into the upholstered desk chair. She folded her hands primly on the desk between them and asked, "How can we help you?"

Help. A word he'd come to deplore. He stifled a jolt of anger, reminding himself, as he had Angel, this was the way it had to be.

"This ain't—isn't—for me. I'm here for my girls," he said with as much civility as he could muster.

He looked away from the sympathy he saw in her greenish-gold eyes. He didn't need sympathy; he needed someone to tell him how he was going to make a life for his daughters without screwing things up. He only knew one way to live his life, and it hadn't been good enough for their mother, how could he expect it to be good enough for them?

If she read deeper implications into his response, she chose to ignore them. "The girls will be fine in the waiting room. We've got the hottest video games around, and Becky Barton's great," she said, mentioning the young black woman she'd introduced to him in the waiting room. "She's a student volunteer. She works with victims all the time."

Victims. Tom swallowed hard. Not a word he ever thought would apply to him.

"I apologize for not being more prepared, but your file just arrived this morning." She picked up a piece of paper from her desk and studied it.

He knew how to save them both some time. He'd repeated the story so often it was beginning to sound like a fairy tale. A bad fairy tale. "My ex-wife, Lesley Ahronian, Heather 'n Angel's mom, was killed January 7." His mouth filled with a rancid taste. The finality of saying those words never failed to get to him.

"A robbery?" she asked, her voice businesslike, detached.

"She was getting money from an ATM machine. The guy who did it got a hundred and eighty dollars. They found one of the twenties under her body along with the receipt for two hundred bucks."

Val told him the bank's security camera provided a horrific record of the event. Although the image wasn't perfect, it produced a suspect, a drug addict with a long history of violence. Whether or not it would be enough to convict him of murder remained to be seen.

"Heather was in the car when it happened," he added gruffly, trying to keep that horror from engulfing his last bit of sanity.

A grimace of anguish flashed across her face.

"She was asleep. The guy tried to steal the car, too, but the alarm scared him off." Even saying the words made his stomach work closer to his throat. What if...?

"Where was Angela?" Her matter-of-fact question put him back on safe ground.

"At a friend's house. Val, Lesley's husband, picked Angel up after the police told him about Lesley. There was some initial confusion because the car was registered to their business and Lesley didn't have any ID on her. The police took Heather into protective custody," he said, recalling the terrible anguish of that weekend.

The attack happened Thursday night, but because of

his stupidity, Tom didn't find out about it until late the next morning. One of Ed's friends flew Tom down south, but by then Tom was too late to see the judge and no one would let him near Heather without a judge's decree.

"You do have legal custody." Tom could tell she tried to keep it from sounding like a question, but it still irked him.

"They're my kids," he snarled.

She glanced up at his tone. "Sometimes when a woman remarries, her new husband adopts the children." Her voice sounded soothing, the way he'd talk to a skittish colt.

She had no way of knowing what a sore subject this was, especially after his recent trip to court. "It was suggested. Once," he said pointedly.

Valentino Ahronian was a decent guy who made every effort to be friends with Tom but Tom just couldn't get past the idea that Val had something that belonged to Tom—his family. Of course, he would have hated the breakneck pace Val and Lesley had chosen, but that didn't stop him from resenting the man who'd married his ex-wife and who saw Tom's children on a daily basis while Tom was relegated to the background—a shadow father trotted out on special occasions and for two weeks in summer.

"Are there any custody issues I should know about? Is Mr.—" she consulted her page in a quick nod that set her blunt-cut pageboy dancing near her jawline. Her hair was thick and shiny, about the color of his favorite roan mare "—Ahronian out of the picture then?"

"No," Tom answered, wishing he had a better handle on his feelings where Val and the girls were concerned. "He calls. The girls still have feelings for him."

Compassion deepened the gold in her eyes, as if she could feel the torment he went through every time Val called. Tom forced himself to look away. "But, Val's got his hands full trying to keep his business running. Lesley was the guts of their operation."

She kept reading and Tom sensed when she came to the most recent entry. She didn't make any outward sound or sign, but Tom felt her flinch, inwardly.

"Last month, Lesley's mom filed for custody," he said, trying his best to keep his tone level. "Ruby Pimental's got a few problems of her own, and Les's death hit her hard. Somehow, Ruby got it into her head I killed Lesley and she wasn't about to leave her grandchildren with a murderer. She found some crook of a lawyer to take her case, and we had to go to court." Tom would never forget that horrible scene in court when Angel rushed to his defense, calling her grandmother every name in the book.

"It got thrown out, but the judge decided the girls might need some help coming to grips with their loss." Court words. He'd heard them so often they almost made sense. Sense. How could anyone make sense of something like this?

She looked at him, her eyes dark with emotion he couldn't interpret. "Violent crime is like a bomb going off in your world. Pieces fly every which way. Survivors wander around in shock, wondering how or if they'll ever get back to the place they'd been in before it happened."

She wasn't saying anything Tom didn't know, but her empathy touched him in a way he hadn't thought possible. Chubs and Johnny Dee had tried to console him; their wives had sent casseroles and cakes. But Tom didn't want sympathy or food. He wanted to know if this pain would ever get easier, but he wasn't brave enough to ask. What if it didn't?

"Some people call what we do here 'triage,'" Abby said, making an encompassing motion with her hand. "We patch you up so you can start to pick up the pieces of your life and move forward. For some, it means walking them through our convoluted judicial system. For others, it's a matter of finding the right resources to rebuild their lives. Violence marks you, but it doesn't have to destroy you, or define the way you live your life from that point on."

Something inside Tom reached out for the invisible lifeline she was offering. After months of slogging through the guilt and shock that were weighing him down, he felt as if he might have found a way out of the pit.

"Trust me, Mr. Butler, things will get easier. You have to take it one day at a time." She spoke slowly, as in prayer. "And if that's too overwhelming, then one hour at a time. If that doesn't work, one second at a time.

"You keep breathing," she continued, "even though it hurts like hell. You make yourself eat, even though every bite tastes like dirt, and you sleep when your body can't stay awake any longer."

Something about the way she spoke made Tom realize she was speaking from personal experience. This woman knew loss; she knew grief.

She took a breath and added softly, "You and your daughters are facing some big changes. Painful changes."

She reached out and touched Tom's hand, taking him by surprise. He hadn't even realized his right hand was gripping the laminated desktop. Her fingers were cool and soothing like an evening Delta breeze after a scorching summer day. "We can help...if you'll let us."

Something pulsed inside Tom's heart. Hope. A stranger was reaching out to help him shoulder the fearful responsibility of raising daughters who barely knew him and came from a strange world that he didn't know at all.

Tom's daddy had taught him not to expect something for nothing. "What's it cost?"

She withdrew her hand and reached into a side drawer of the desk, giving Tom time to regain his composure. She smiled brightly. Had he only imagined her dark memories? "Our service is free, Mr. Butler. The citizens of California got fed up with criminals walking around after serving a few days or weeks for their crimes, while the people they hurt took years to get their lives back together. They told the courts to impose stiffer fines and put that money into a fund to help victims and the people who witness crimes."

She blinked twice and cleared her throat. "Judge Overman has ordered counseling for Heather and Angela. The first thing we have to do is find the right person to help your daughters get past this horror."

We. God, it felt good to share his burden with this stranger.

"I have someone in mind. Donna Jessup. She's great with kids, but counseling is a highly subjective matter and not everyone connects with the same person, so we can try several. With your permission, we'll try Donna first."

Tom nodded. He felt as if he'd made the first forward motion since that January morning when he woke up in his truck with a highway patrolman knocking on his window.

While Abby made the call, he rose and stretched. He wondered how anyone could stand to be cooped up in a four-by-five cubicle five days a week on a regular basis. He didn't understand it any more than he understood why Lesley had chosen the hustle and bustle, smog and crime of the big city over clean air and open spaces.

"Done," she said, reaching across the desk to hand him a piece of paper with a name, address and phone number all set out in neat, loopy penmanship. "Donna will see you at four this afternoon."

He nodded. "Thank you."

She deflected his gratitude with a casual wave of her hand. Reaching beneath the lip of her desk, she pulled out a sliding table holding a keyboard and mouse. "Now. Let's get you into our system."

Tom shuddered. The last four months had proven how suffocating the octopus arms of the "system" could be, but his peaceful anonymity was a small price to pay for his daughters' welfare.

She typed diligently for a few minutes, glancing between her faxed copy and the screen. She seemed engrossed in her work, her lips pursed in a half frown. Tom recalled that she'd mentioned today was her birthday. Thirty, maybe? Lesley would have been thirty-five in September.

"How are you doing for money?"

Her question took him by surprise. "Excuse me?" he said stiffly.

A blush engulfed her cheeks. "I'm sorry. I've been doing this so long I sometimes let my agenda get in the way of good manners."

She took a deep breath then said, "What I meant to ask in a more sensitive way was, has this been a terrible

financial drain on your resources? We have some dis-
cretionary funds available and state programs such as
food stamps that can help.''

Tom knew she was simply doing her job, but she
hadn't grown up with Walt Butler's prejudice against
the dole. Tom turned sideways to look out the window.
In the parking lot his ancient truck stood out like a mule
among thoroughbreds. This was going to be the year he
bought a new one. Was.

''My daddy always said the dole is what ruined many
a good man, and we Butlers do it ourselves or we do
without.''

She typed and talked at the same time. ''I can appreciate that sentiment and I don't mean to sound conde-
scending, but if you need to spend your days making
sure your daughters feel safe and loved, how can you
be out doing whatever it is you do? What do you do,
by the way?''

''I manage a ranch, 'bout twenty miles south of here.
We run a few head of cattle and have a couple of hundred acres of almonds. My boss, Ed Hastings, covered
for me when I was getting the girls moved up here, but
now I'm back full time,'' he said.

Finances were tight, but when weren't they? So far,
he hadn't had to sell any of the broodmares he and his
friend, Miguel Fuentes, were raising on the side, but
he'd damn well do that before he accepted a handout
from the government. Miguel would understand. He and
Maria were pinching pennies, too, what with the new
baby coming.

''Okay, fine,'' she said, pushing the keyboard back
beneath her desk. At that moment a printer sitting atop
a gray plastic shelf to Tom's right came to life. ''But if
it happens that you can't manage as well as you'd like,

I hope you'll let me know. We have a wide array of programs, including low-interest loans for things like remodeling or adding rooms to homes. Sometimes when you add a couple of new bodies to a house, space becomes a problem. So just keep it in mind.''

She had to stretch across the desk to reach the paper ejected from the printer. Tom reached for it, too. Their fingers met momentarily, and she jerked her hand back as if scalded.

A moment of stiff silence was shattered by a scream, piercing and high-pitched like a small wounded animal caught in a trap. Heather. Tom bolted through the doorway. Too many nights he awoke to the bloodcurdling horror of that cry. He raced down the corridor, almost taking the waiting-room door off its hinges.

Heather was seated on a worn, oval carpet between a low wooden table capped with children's books and a lumpy couch where Angela slouched, a handheld electronic game loose in her fingers. Becky Barton, the young volunteer, was kneeling beside Heather trying to comfort her.

Tom dropped to his knees beside them and scooped Heather into his arms, babbling nonsense words in a tone that always soothed a frightened horse. ''Shh, baby love, it's okay. Your daddy's got you, and nothing bad can happen.'' He rocked her back and forth until the cries wound down to hiccups. Keeping up his monotone he made eye contact with Angel, who shrugged her shoulders, indicating she didn't have a clue about what had upset her sister.

Becky gave him a sympathetic smile, but appeared as bewildered as Angel.

When Heather's sobs subsided, he used his cuff to

wipe the wet tracks streaking her chubby red cheeks. She blinked as if not sure where she was.

"Hey, sweetness, what happened?"

Her bottom lip shot out, trembling.

"You got scared?"

She nodded then buried her face in his shoulder.

Right or wrong, Tom had been running on instinct. Like a wounded animal, he'd taken the girls and gone to ground. He'd protected his daughters the only way he knew how, by isolating them from the world. Maybe that had been a mistake. Instead of getting better, Heather seemed to be sinking deeper into a pit of despair.

He rose, Heather's warm little body plastered to him like a bandage. "Maybe we should see that doctor right away."

Abby nodded. "I'll call ahead and see if she can take you earlier than four."

But will it do any good? Tom's frustration weighed heavily on him.

As if reading his thoughts, Abby said, "Believe me, Mr. Butler, it won't help Heather to keep things bottled up."

She laid a gentle hand squarely on his daughter's little back. She probably didn't feel Heather's sigh, but Tom did.

Abby led the way to the exit, pausing at her office to give Tom her business card. "My home number is there. Feel free to call if you need anything." She smiled. "Please don't give up on us," she said softly. Whether to him or Heather, he wasn't sure.

"ARE YOU READY for a good time, birthday girl?" a voice called, echoing in VOCAP's empty hallway.

Melina Orozco, Abby's best friend and co-worker, had two missions in life: find a man to make her mother happy and have a good time to make herself happy.

"Just give me a minute. I have one more call." Abby smiled as she dialed the number.

Since it was after normal office hours, Donna picked up. "Hello."

"Hi. It's me. How'd it go this afternoon?"

"You mean with the handsome cowboy and his two darling daughters?"

Despite the light tone in her friend's voice, Abby knew Donna was a complete professional. She'd been Abby's therapist at one time, and they were still close. "Did you connect? Are you going to continue seeing them?"

"Abby, dear, you know I can't discuss my patients with you. Besides, one hour with two traumatized little girls and a worried father pacing just beyond the threshold didn't give me a lot to work with. I've suggested therapy twice a week and participation in Rainbows." Tomorrow's Rainbows was a ten-week peer counseling session in Fresno.

"And he went for it?"

"Yes. With some reservations. Apparently the logistics are tricky—the new Rainbows session will be on Thursdays at six-thirty. Not the best time for him, I gather, but he said he'd work it out."

"Great!" Abby had sensed Tom Butler's reluctance to reach out for help.

"Interesting man, isn't he?" Donna asked conversationally.

Abby knew the ploy. "I called because I was concerned about the children. Not the father."

Donna laughed. "So you think. But I know you, dear

heart, and you want to help them all. You're the queen of fix-it.''

''That was the old Abby. From now on, it's me first. I'm thinking about quitting to go back to school this fall to get my law degree. Earn the big bucks.''

Donna was silent a moment then said, ''You have to do what's right for you, Abby. Just be sure it's for the right reasons. Thirty is not old.''

After saying their goodbyes, Abby considered her friend's words: the ''queen of fix-it.'' ''Not this time,'' she muttered. She'd do her best to help Tom Butler and his daughters get back on their feet, but if they were still in the system by the end of summer, she'd arrange for another advocate to take over. She couldn't afford to keep putting the needs of others before her own happiness.

''DON'T START READING without me, Daddy,'' Heather said, scooting off the double bed she shared with Angel.

Angel rescued the bottle of nail polish that almost tipped over when the mattress jiggled. ''Damn it, Heather, you're gonna make me screw up,'' Angel snarled, ignoring the look her father gave her. She knew he disliked swearing, but she didn't care. She had a right to swear. Her whole damn world got turned upside down and she was supposed to like it? Not even.

Frowning, she concentrated on applying a second coat of polish to her toenails. Cat-puke green, her father called the color. Like she cared what he thought; he didn't have a clue about what was cool. He was just a cowboy, living in this shack out in the middle of nowhere. Angel liked it okay when she came to visit in the summer—it made for great stories to tell her friends.

But summer was one thing, actually living here was something else. And she was pretty sure she hated it.

"Whatcha need, punkin?" Her father called as he dropped into the spot Heather had vacated.

Angel rescued her polish a second time, growling under her breath.

"A drinka' water," Heather answered, skipping out the door like the little kid she was. She'd started wetting the bed right after the police gave her back. The week-end-long ordeal must have scared Heather pretty bad because she was acting more like a three-year-old than a kid who'd turn six in August. Angel felt bad for her, but it was hell sharing a bed with a bed wetter. "Why don't you just put her in a diaper?" she grumbled.

She felt her father's warning frown.

"Go ahead and get your drink, sweets," he told Heather, who stuck her tongue out at her sister. "Remember what Dr. Jessup said? This'll get better soon."

Angel pictured their encounter with the therapist that afternoon. Right at first Angel thought the woman looked more like a hippie bag lady than a doctor. She had more beads resting on her broad bosom than some department stores had for sale.

"How long will this take? A couple of weeks? A month?" her father had asked, pacing like a cat stuck in a doghouse.

Angel actually liked the room; there was a "safe" feeling about it. In a way, it reminded her of her mother's office back home.

"There's no credible timetable for grief, Mr. Butler," Dr. Jessup told him. Her voice was kind, it made Angel feel warm inside. "There is, of course, a recognized grief process, a pattern of predictable steps we go through toward healing, but no formula that says you should be done with stage one by week three. It just doesn't work that way. It would make my job so much easier if it did."

When she smiled, Angel saw something she liked. Honesty. Nobody was ever honest with kids. They all act like we're a bunch of babies who can't understand what's happening.

Angel understood most of what had happened. Her mother and Val had a fight. Angel had tried eavesdropping but they'd stayed in their bedroom, which was half a flight higher at the end of the hall. When her mom came and got her, Angel had seen tear streaks on her face, but Lesley had refused to talk about it. All she said when she'd dropped Angel off at Caitlin's house was, "It's grown-up stuff, honey. It'll be all right."

Well, it wasn't "all right." When Val came and picked Angel up early the next morning, he said her mother had been attacked when she stopped at an ATM machine. Angel didn't believe him at first. Her mother was such a stickler for safety. How could she have been that stupid? Angel wondered for the millionth time.

Now, not only was her mother gone, but so was their life—their real life. And Angel was pissed as hell.

"Angel-babe, please try to cut your sister a little slack," her father said softly. "She's doing the best she can. We all are," he added under his breath.

Angel knew that. None of this was his fault. He was a good guy who tried real hard to make things okay for them. And things had been going along pretty good until her crazy grandmother decided to sue for custody. Damn judge. Angel knew how hard it was on her dad's pride to have to go to that victims' place today—even if the lady there was nice enough, and sorta pretty.

"I know," she said, regretting her rotten humor. It

wasn't Heather's fault she was having bad dreams. Angel had a few, too.

"Like the lady said, we just gotta take this one day at a time," he said, reaching out to touch her shoulder.

Angel closed her eyes to keep back the tears that seemed right on the verge of coming out nearly every minute of the day. She wanted to scream and hit things. Hurt things. She wanted her old life back. She wanted to go home, but she was stuck in this valley forever.

Angel shrugged off his touch and didn't say anything. Her mom always told her if you can't say something good, then don't say anything at all. The way things were going, Angel figured she'd never have to speak again.

CHAPTER TWO

ABBY CLOSED the refrigerator door on the last of her groceries. Saturday mornings weren't what they used to be in Welton. Traffic in the once-sleepy central valley town was beginning to rival the Bay area—quite different from when she first moved into Billy's house on Glendennon Court.

Actually, the three-bedroom bungalow had belonged to Billy's mom until she passed away, and Billy had left it to Abby in his will. Janice Eastburn, Billy's mother, had been a neighbor when Billy and Jarrod, Abby's brother, were classmates and best friends in high school, but once Billy joined the marines, she'd sold their house in Fresno and moved to Welton, where she took a job in a dentist's office. She lived alone until diagnosed with lymphatic cancer, then Billy moved home from Hawaii to help her. He wasn't back three weeks before she died.

Billy, Abby thought, pausing before the open cupboard, a box of Grapenuts in her hand. A familiar buzzing sensation bloomed in her chest like the beginning of a cold. Her memories of him were so jumbled—some good, some horrible—she was tempted to lock them out, but Donna had taught her to accept any memories that came. "Shove them in a black hole and they'll fester like pond scum," Donna warned her patients.

Resigned that she was having a "Billy moment," Abby set down the cereal and picked up her new

"Thirty Isn't Old—I'm just 21 with 9 years' experience" mug and poured herself the last of the morning's coffee. After taking a sip of the aromatic brew, she pulled out a stool at the counter and sat down. Tabby, her overweight cat, rubbed against her ankles, hoping no doubt for an après-breakfast snack. Abby ignored him, focusing instead on the past.

Poor Billy, she thought wistfully, he didn't really stand a chance where I was concerned. I put him on a pedestal not even a superhero could keep from falling off.

She tried to picture herself back in 1988, when Billy came home from Hawaii. A nineteen-year-old college coed, fifteen years his junior, Abby doubted if she'd recognize that silly, naive girl who didn't know the first thing about love...or grief. She learned fast.

Abby, who was just a baby when Billy and Jarrod were in high school, had grown up on Billy stories, from his bad-boy image in high school to his heroism in Vietnam. Jarrod called him "G.I. Bill," since all Billy ever wanted to do was be a soldier. According to Jarrod, Billy's greatest fear was that Vietnam would be over before he got there.

Taking a sip of coffee, Abby pondered the start of her hero worship. Honors English, she thought, bracing her chin in her palm. Each student selected someone local who had made a significant personal sacrifice for someone else. Since Billy lost a leg while helping to evacuate civilians at the close of the war, Abby felt he qualified.

Jarrod gave her Billy's address in Hawaii. Abby wrote him twice, but he didn't write back. So, Abby interviewed Billy's mother, instead.

If Abby had been older and less idealistic she might

have been able to separate truth from wishful thinking, but as it was she drew a picture of Billy in her head and so it stayed. When he returned home to help his mother, Abby was already halfway in love with him, even though she never really knew him.

And she wasn't disappointed when she accompanied her family to Janice's funeral. Hawaii had given Billy a sort of "Baywatch" mystique: tan and weathered, a sun-bleached ponytail and wide, muscular shoulders from using crutches—he was the embodiment of a hero. Someone with a more experienced eye might have caught the jaded look in his eyes, the lines of dissipation from ten years of drinking and carousing.

Abby sat back on the stool and looked around her bright, cheerful kitchen. *It's so weird that he's gone and I'm still living here. What would my life have been like if he had returned my letters? What if he'd told her his story the way it was, not the way his mother had perceived it?*

Instead of a heroic amputee who lost his leg through a selfless act of bravery, Billy had stumbled out of a bar into the path of panicky citizens trying to flee their dying country. Knocked to the ground, he was too drunk to get out of the way of an army truck that backed over his foot, crushing his ankle. Chaos and confusion resulted in less than perfect medical treatment, which led to a series of infections and months of hospitalization. When gangrene set in, Billy agreed to a partial amputation of his foot. Unfortunately, a staph infection resulted from the operation and he nearly died. By the time he woke up, still in pain despite heavy medication, he discovered three-quarters of his leg had been removed to stop the infection from claiming his life.

Bitter and addicted to painkillers, he accepted a disability settlement and hooked up with two ex-Marine buddies in Hawaii who needed some capital to open a bar. Billy drank most of his share of the profits, but his disability income kept him solvent and he tended bar just often enough to hit on lovely young ladies eager to ease his pain.

Abby believed his mother's death was an epiphany for Billy. As their relationship evolved, Billy told Abby about his life in Hawaii—the drugs and alcohol and the women. He insisted on being tested for AIDS before he would consider making love to her, and even then he always used a condom. Billy said he wanted to put the past behind him and straighten out his life. Who better to infuse him with energy and hope than an idealistic college student?

Who better, indeed? Abby thought ruefully, tracing the printing on her mug. Maybe he'd have succeeded in turning his life around if she hadn't been so full of hero worship. How could any man live up to that, especially a man who felt his whole life was a sham?

"Abby? Are you home?" a voice called from the front of the house.

Another voice from the past. "In the kitchen, Landon," Abby said with a sigh.

Landon Bower, her ex-boyfriend of eleven months, had a habit of dropping by for advice on his new relationship with the beautiful, if difficult, Deirdre.

Dancer lithe, boxer light, he made his usual flamboyant entrance, sliding across the terra-cotta floor tiles on stocking feet. He always took off his shoes inside a house, claiming it his birthright since he was born in Japan. Abby believed it was because he never had to wash his own socks.

"Hi, beautiful birthday girl." Gallantly bowing, he

offered her a thick bouquet of white daisies, pink carnations and yellow spider mums.

"My birthday was last week."

"I know. I forgot." He flashed what his mother called his "guaranteed-to-make-women-love-me smile." She'd sent Abby a birthday card, much to Abby's surprise. When Abby and Landon broke up, his mother told her, "You'll regret this someday, Abby. Landon is a wonderful person." Abby wasn't sure if she was trying to convince Abby or herself.

"I'm sorry, girly-girl. You know how I am about dates. Hence the blooms. When we were living together, I always got away with murder if I brought home flowers." He frowned. "I wish that worked with Deirdre."

Abby rolled her eyes. Sometimes she couldn't believe she'd cohabited with him for as long as she had. Donna called it Abby's self-imposed penance. "I told you at the time, a dog would have accomplished the same thing—companionship and utter dependency, but no, you had to bring Landon home," Donna liked to tease.

"Why can't Deirdre be more like you, Ab?" Landon asked.

Abby moved to the sink, ostensibly to tend to the flowers. She liked Landon, but she was tired of being his sounding board for his new girlfriend. Another area of my life that needs work.

"Don't blame Deirdre because she's not a pushover like me." Abby tried to keep her tone light, she'd been wallowing—at least, wading—in self-pity too much the past week.

Landon gave her an inquiring look. "I prefer to think of you as a softhearted person," he said, sounding as though he meant it.

Abby smiled for real. Landon could be very sweet

when he wanted to be. They'd lived together for almost four years. But their feelings for each other never blossomed into the real thing. Not that it surprised Donna.

"He doesn't engage your emotions—the ones you locked up after Billy," Donna told her. Abby wasn't sure such a man existed, or that she would want to meet him if he did.

"So, how's work?" Abby asked, changing the subject.

Landon walked past her to pull out the stool she'd been sitting on. As he passed, she could smell his cologne. Canoe. The one she'd picked out for him at Macy's. Did Deirdre know it was Abby's pick?

"Abby," he groaned, dropping his face into his hands, "my life sucks. I think it started going down the toilet when I left you. Is it possible we made a terrible mistake?"

One small part of her danced in triumph. Yippee. Somebody needs me and worships me and wants me. The adult part of her, the thirty-year-old, groaned. "Landon, our breakup was mutual. Granted, you had someone waiting for you, but I needed you to leave. I needed the space to find answers about myself."

"What'd you find out?" His tone seemed sincere, not skeptical like her mother's.

"Lots of things." *Liar.* "I know I let people take advantage of me." *Most people. Except for certain cowboys who have too much pride to ask for help.* One silly little part of her had expected a call from Tom Butler all week. When it didn't materialize she was oddly deflated.

"But, no more," she said, pounding her fist on the counter for emphasis. "I've made up my mind to stop being so...accommodating."

He fought a smile—she could see him trying—but eventually it burst through. "Abby, you don't have a prayer. You're the kindest person I know. Maybe you are too nice for your own good, but you don't have it in you to be any different."

Before Abby could respond with an infuriated retort, the phone rang. She snatched up the receiver, glaring at Landon—to his obvious amusement. "Hello," she snarled.

The voice on the other end was not the one she'd been hoping for. She listened mutely, before saying, "I'll be right there."

TOM CAREFULLY CLOSED the screen door of the bunkhouse behind him. Heather was napping—for how long was anybody's guess. Every time she closed her eyes, her little body drooping like a wilted flower, Tom prayed she'd sleep for hours, but so far no luck. Sometimes, only minutes later, she'd wake up shrieking from dreams too terrible to remember.

As far as Tom could see, their initial three meetings with the therapist had been as productive as milking a bull, but Dr. Jessup did have a special way with kids. Tom had sat in on Friday's session. Angel had chatted easily like the self-absorbed teenager he remembered from last summer. She described in detail the outfit she wore to her mother's funeral—Tom couldn't even recall whether or not he wore clothes that day. Heather snuggled into a comfortable spot on Dr. Jessup's lap and silently fingered the woman's chunky wooden beads.

On his way out, Dr. Jessup told Tom, "I think it might help if the girls felt more connected to their home. Maybe a little decorating, hang up their posters or pictures, rearrange the furniture."

Before Tom could explain about their living condi-
tions, she added, "Angel told me things are a bit
crowded at the moment. Why don't you give Abby Davis a call? She can work bureaucratic magic when it
comes to remodeling."

Like a seed from Eve's apple, the temptation was
planted. And grew.

"Angel," he called softly through the paint-splattered
mesh, "come here."

It took her two minutes to cross the twenty-foot room,
but she came.

"It's a beautiful day. Don't you want to do something? I could saddle Jess. You haven't ridden since you
got here."

She shook her head. "I'm reading." She held up a
paperback novel, then turned away and plopped down
on the lumpy couch before he could say anything.

The frenetic chatter of cartoons erupted from the
small, snowy screen of his television set. "Still only
black and white?" Angel said that first night back at
the ranch, after her mother's funeral. "Daddy, those
were around in like the Stone Age, for heaven's sake."

Her complaint went no further...yet, but it was only
a matter of time. Nothing about his humble abode, once
the ranch's bunkhouse, came close to matching Lesley
and Val's two-story, 2,800-square-foot home.

"Did you finish your social-studies paper?" he
called.

The words "Of course" accompanied a deep sigh of
disgust.

Angel was a good student. Her accelerated class,
which was part of a year-round school system, was due
to go off-track two weeks after Lesley's funeral, so her
teachers were not concerned about her absence. They'd

passed her without a second thought. The local principal
suggested letting her make a fresh start in the junior-
high program that fall, instead of putting her into a
sixth-grade class where she would be bored. Tom
agreed, but he adamantly opposed giving her an addi-
tional five months of vacation, so both girls were enrolled in an independent study program.

So far, Angel's only complaint was the lack of a lap-
top computer, apparently a tool she used to borrow from
her stepfather. Last week, the young woman who
brought the girls their lessons suggested the possibility
of doing homework ''on-line.'' Tom, who'd heard horror stories about on-line predators, squashed the idea.
His daughters could make do with pen and paper. Besides there was no extra money for expensive electronic
equipment.

Rosie and two of Tom's cow dogs suddenly started
barking. Tom squinted toward the road. The walnut
trees that backed up all the way to the highway cut into
his line of vision, but he spotted a dust devil whirling
out of the gravel as a vehicle raced down the driveway.

The ranch, some 650 acres, was divided into irrigated
pastures for grazing, and three sections of almonds. The
advent of drip irrigation made it easier and less expensive to plant uneven terrain, and Tom knew it was only
a matter of time before ''cowboying'' was a thing of
the past. Ed loved his cows, but he was a practical busi-
nessman, too. Tom figured if he learned anything from
the last four months it was: nothin' stays the same. Tom
kicked up a little dust as he walked out into the drive
that separated his place from Ed and Janey's newer
ranch-style home. The Hastingses' home sat on a slight
knoll, offset by a nice green lawn and flanked by an
almond orchard on three sides. Tom's house was set in

what amounted to a pie-shaped hunk of land between the driveway and the permanent pasture. His place faced the barn and corrals, but an ancient mulberry and semicircle of straggly lawn kept it from being too austere.

"What now?" Tom muttered, feeling an all-too-common burning in the pit of his stomach.

The rumble of a truck engine gave Tom a face to put with the sound. He shoved his hands into the front pockets of his jeans and waited to direct the driver away from the house before the dozen young horses in the paddock beside his bedroom window took it in their heads to get excited. He didn't want anything to wake Heather.

A bevy of barking dogs raced alongside the vehicle as Tom pointed toward the shade of the barn. The truck rolled to a stop. John Dexter Moore—Johnny Dee to his friends—killed the engine and climbed out of the '94 Ford half-ton.

"Hey, Tom. How's it goin'?"

Tom made a "so-so" gesture. Johnny motioned for him to follow him to the back of the truck. He lowered the tailgate and hopped up, dragging a small plastic cooler to his side. When Tom sat down beside him, Johnny reached inside the cooler for a beer and offered one to Tom.

After their last get-together—the night Lesley was killed, when nobody could find him at home because he was passed out cold in his truck—Tom couldn't bring himself to accept the offering. He shook his head.

Johnny was a Hulk Hogan kind of guy with receding blond hair and a heart of gold. He and Tom had been friends since childhood. He knew Tom as well as anybody and apparently had no trouble guessing what he was thinking. "It wasn't your fault, man," Johnny told him. "You didn't know. None of us did."

Tom would have liked to use his friend's solace as it was intended: to let him off the hook, but guilt had its own plans for him—slow torture.

"Hell, you didn't even want to go with us. Chubs 'n me had to twist your arm."

When Tom bumped into his old friends that fateful night in January, he was on his way home from a week in the mountains. Ed leased a thousand acres of range-land in the foothills. Since things were slow on the farm, Tom had combined a little fence repair with some fishing. Maybe he'd been hungry for social contact as well as real food, because it didn't take much arm-twisting to get him to the bar.

"You only stayed 'cause of what was happening with me and Beth," Johnny said, kicking the gravel.

Tom caught something different in his friend's tone, and realized sheepishly it had been three weeks since they'd talked. "How's that working out?"

Johnny lifted his substantial shoulders and let them fall. "She moved home, but we're not sleeping together. She's calling it a cooling-down period. Like I was some overheated stud. Like we even had sex often enough before she left to get worked up about."

Tom understood exactly where Johnny was coming from. His own first reaction to Lesley's departure had been nine-tenths bravado and one-tenth paralyzing fear. If he kept up the bravado long enough and made it real loud, he'd thought, maybe no one would see his pain.

"That's a start. At least you can talk face-to-face instead of long distance."

"The kids hated Fresno. All their friends are here."

Johnny crushed the empty can and tossed it on top of

a pile of greasy tools in the pickup bed. He cracked open another. "How're you fixed here? Beth said to tell you she's sorry she hasn't made it over, but if you need a woman's touch to give her a holler. I think she meant in the kitchen. She'd better've meant in the kitchen."

Tom grinned at his friend's tone. "That's Angel's domain. We may eat quesadillas more often than I like, but I wouldn't want to hurt her feelings. But, as to that other kind of touching..." His teasing ended when Johnny's elbow connected with his side.

"Need a TV? We got an extra. It's a twenty-four incher."

Rubbing the tender spot on his rib cage, Tom shook his head. "Ed and Janey offered one, too, but things are a little crowded with all the girls' stuff, and we don't get enough stations using rabbit ears to make it worth it."

"That reminds me—how's Janey doin'?"

Tom looked away. Squinting, he could make out the snowcap on the distant mountains. It wouldn't last long—last week had three days over ninety degrees.

"Hold that thought, I gotta pee," Johnny said, hopping down to scurry toward the back of the barn.

Resting against the side of the truck, Tom closed his eyes and thought about Janey. It broke his heart to see her ill. More than anyone else, throughout this whole ordeal, she'd remained a rock, always positive and frank. She was the one person he could trust with his despair, his self-doubts, his fears.

Janey's illness brought back memories of his mother—fit and spry one week, hospitalized the next. Gone before he knew it. The doctors never did figure out what took her; a viral infection was their best guess.

Tom read all the breast cancer pamphlets the doctors

gave Janey. The disease sounded treatable if caught early. He sure as hell hoped she could beat it. Not only did he love her, but the girls thought of her as a surrogate grandmother. He wasn't sure any of them could handle another loss so soon.

"Janey's gonna make it," Ed told Tom yesterday when he returned home for some of Janey's personal belongings. "They did a lumpectomy, and now they want her to take chemo and radiation to make sure they kill everything."

The late-afternoon sun had cast harsh shadows across Ed's face, emphasizing the lines of worry and fear. Tom saw a vulnerability he'd never seen before. "Janey says she can beat it and I believe her," Ed continued. "But I also know we're going to make some changes around here. Big changes."

Tom's heart lurched. He'd seen more changes in the past four months than he thought he could handle. He craved stability but knew he had to respect Ed's wishes. Tom owed him more than he could ever repay. After all, Ed had backed him when Tom broke his arm and couldn't rope, and Ed and Janey had been there to pick up the pieces of his heart after Lesley left, too.

Ed's face twisted in pain, as if picturing his wife in the hospital room. "Janey never complains, but I know she had it in her mind to do some traveling when we retired. Go visit her sisters. See the boys." Ed's voice faltered over the last.

Tom knew how disappointed Ed had been that neither of his sons wanted anything to do with the ranch he'd spent his entire life building. Edward, an architect in New Jersey, rarely called or visited. Peter, an advertising executive in Denver, kept in touch and visited at least once a year, but his relationship with his father was always tempered by disappointment and hurt feelings.

"I'll only say this once, Tom. You know you're like a son to me. You 'n me think alike when it comes to the land. I'd feel real good about selling this place to you on a contract to deed." When Tom started to say something, Ed placated him. "Don't get your back up about the money, boy. That'll work out in the wash."

Tom's heart swelled from the compliment Ed was paying him, but he wasn't sure he could accept. "Ed, we've both got a lot on our plates right now. You took care of the whole show when I needed you, helping out now's the least I can do. Let's focus on getting Janey well before we worry about anything else, okay?"

They'd left it at that, but Ed was adamant about making some changes, starting with remodeling Tom's place to give the girls more room. "Janey's been harping about that for months. If that lady at the victims' place can help, then give her a call and start the ball rolling. I'll pay for everything. Just get it done."

When Johnny returned, Tom told him, "Janey's doin' up pretty good. Next week she starts chemo or radiation, I can't remember which, but she told Ed to get me started on remodeling. We're supposed to add another bedroom and bath to the bunkhouse before she gets back."

Johnny nodded enthusiastically. "Good idea. Believe me, you can't have enough bathrooms when there are women around. And any girl over the age of four constitutes a woman when it comes to bathrooms."

Tom cleared his throat and spat onto the dusty ground. Another bad habit to break. "You ever hear of a place called VOCAP?"

Johnny thought a moment then snapped his fingers.

"Sure. The victims' place. They helped out after Maria's cousin got killed, right?"

Tom nodded. "I talked to one of the advocates last week," Tom said, picturing Abby Davis's reassuring smile. For some reason, he'd found himself drawing upon that smile more than once this week for a little comfort and reassurance. "She set the girls up with a grief therapist, and she said she could help us out with other things, like remodeling."

"Great. How are the girls doing?" Johnny asked.

"Heather's still having nightmares, but Angel's doing okay." At least, she didn't bite my head off when I asked about her homework. "But they miss their mom."

The two were silent a moment, then Johnny said, "I still can't believe she's gone, Tom. So young 'n pretty."

Tom's throat began tightening up, the way it did whenever he pictured Lesley's funeral. "Funny thing about death—you know it's real. You say all the words and watch 'em lower the coffin into a hole, but she's still alive in your mind. Laughing, arguing, being pissed off." He forced a chuckle. "And nobody could be more pissed off than Les."

Johnny nodded so emphatically he spilt beer in his lap. "Remember the time you an' me was coming back from that roping in Elko and she thought we stopped off to gamble? Hell's bells, man, I thought she was gonna take off your head before you showed her the check for your winnings."

"She was mad a lot back then," Tom said evenly.

"She was a beautiful woman, Tom, and I know you're not supposed to speak ill of the dead, but I remember thinking it was awful cold of a person to move out on a guy when she was carrying his kid. Although

in all honesty, I never pictured Lesley Pimental settling
for anything in or around this valley.''

Tom's thoughts went back to the summer after his
mother died. He'd had three successful years on the roping circuit and had managed to make a name for himself. He took time off to help his father settle her estate.
He'd met Lesley, who was working as a receptionist in
the lawyer's office handling the probate. Although Tom
had known Lesley in high school, she was three years
his junior and he hadn't seen her in years. His knees
almost buckled when the tall, slim beauty got up from
behind her desk and walked over to him, telling him
how sorry she was for his loss. A quick hug cinched
it—he was in love.

They were married in late September. That winter
Tom's father gave him money from the proceeds of the
estate to buy Hall's Golden Boy—Goldy—a quarter
horse Tom had had his eye on for several years. It had
baffled both husband and son that the quiet, demure
woman they thought they knew so well had somehow
hoarded a modest sum and invested it in gold. Tom
knew his mother would have appreciated the poetic
irony of using the money to buy a roping horse named
Goldy.

''When I heard you two was getting hitched, I figured
it was because you were a big-name roper.'' Johnny
wiped a spot of condensation on his beer can. ''You
were doin' pretty good till you busted your arm.''

Johnny was right about some of it, Tom thought.
Their first couple of years of marriage were great, cud-
dling together each night in a single sleeping bag on the
sweet hay in the horse trailer. Then, the year after Angel
was born Tom fell off the tailgate of his truck and

landed wrong—a silly misstep that fractured his arm in three places.

The doctor told him there was a good chance he'd never rope professionally again. When his sponsors found out about his arm, they pulled out. Tom would've lost his truck if not for the kindness of his old boss, Ed Hastings, who made him foreman of the Standing Arrow H.

The arm healed, but by then Tom had lost his taste for the constant travel, competition and pressure. Lesley hadn't; she kept after him to start roping again. "You haven't even tried, honey," she'd say. "How do you know you won't be good again? You don't lose a skill like that."

Tom watched a shiny blue fly march up his sleeve and sighed. "Life's funny, Dee. If I'd kept on roping, I might still be married, and Lesley would still be alive. I sure as hell would have more to my name than a four-teen-year-old truck and a few head of breeding stock."

"You got the house on Plainsborough Road. The one Miguel's rentin' from you."

"You know I bought that house for Les. I bought it with the money from Golden Boy."

Both men sighed.

"Man, that was a horse," Johnny said. "Musta killed you to sell him."

Tom shrugged. "I figured just because I didn't want to rope no more didn't mean he had to quit. When that guy from Calgary offered cash, I snapped it up." Tom started to spit but changed his mind and swallowed instead, almost choking. Johnny pounded on Tom's back until Tom held a fist up between them.

"So, why don't you move over there instead of fixing up this place? It's three-bedroom, ain't it?"

Tom hesitated, recalling with photographic clarity the look on Lesley's face when she realized the little farm-house, with its covered porch, white picket fence and row of primroses—his midnight effort—wasn't a rental like all the others. She looked at him with tears in her eyes and whispered, almost like a prayer, "Not Goldy?" Tom's heart felt as if it had been squished by a truck tire. But she made an effort and put on a good face. For a couple of years, anyway. Long enough for him to fall in love with one daughter and make a second.

"I can't just kick those poor kids outa there. Maria's got a baby comin'," he said. "So I guess we'll give remodeling a try. Maybe give Abby Davis a call."

ABBY SLIPPED through VOCAP's back door, locking it behind her. Her mind was reeling as she headed to her office.

At Daniel's unexpected call, she'd raced over to the district attorney's office, anticipating a change of heart—but not this kind. Her illusions of a pay raise and a promotion came to a screeching halt the minute Daniel told her about his imminent divorce.

Knees weak, Abby sank into her chair, replaying their conversation in her head.

"Hi, Abby, thanks for coming. Have a seat."

She selected a butter-soft leather armchair she se-cretly coveted. "No problem. What's up?"

His handsome, squarish face showed signs of stress. He heaved a long, portentous sigh. "This is a bit awk-ward for me, and I want you to know you're the first person within the office I've told. I didn't want to say anything during business hours. You know how the tax-payers are about public servants conducting personal business on their time.'' His laugh sounded fake, his tone held an edginess that made her uneasy.

''This isn't business business, then?'' Abby asked, oddly unnerved to be alone with Daniel in his office on a bright, cheerful Saturday morning. To calm her nerves she focused on the Kimura family portrait, which hung prominently to the left of his desk. In it, Daniel stood behind his wife, Marilyn, who was seated between their children, Robert and Rebecca.

''No, it's not. But what I have to tell you will, inevitably, affect our business relationship,'' Daniel said, pausing dramatically. ''But it's my hope that the news will have a positive effect on our...friendship.''

Friendship? Daniel was her boss, not her friend. They'd had shouting matches over budgets; they constantly argued about protocol; they vied for turf where judicial interests overrode the interests of her clients, but the bottom line always came down to power. Daniel had it; Abby didn't. Did that constitute grounds for friendship? She didn't think so. She held her tongue and waited. What he told her next nearly blew her out of the leather armchair. ''Marilyn and I are getting a divorce.''

Since Abby's mouth dropped open, Daniel probably thought she was going to speak, but any words she might have wanted to say were lost in utter shock. After a minute, he went on. ''This has been a long time coming, but we kept things quiet until after the election and Becky's wedding. Robert's back at Stanford. Becky and Troy are still on their honeymoon. Marilyn thought this was as good a time as any. She filed yesterday. It's public record now.''

Still not sure why she was being made privy to this, Abby's grip on the soft leather arms tightened when

Daniel rose and walked toward her. He paused before her, his expensive cologne following like a well-trained dog. He rested his hip on the edge of the desk and gave her a long, meaningful look. "Abby, you and I have always had a strong working relationship. I didn't realize how much you meant to me—personally—until you started talking about leaving," he told her.

Since her mind couldn't process this totally unexpected turn of events, she stalled. "Daniel, if I'd known you were going through such a rough time, I wouldn't have mentioned anything. It's not like I'm turning in my resignation tomorrow. Even if I do decide to leave VOCAP, it won't be right away."

The intensity of his stare made her squirm.

"Besides," she said, her voice catching in her dry throat, "a new case fell into my lap last week. A man whose ex-wife was killed and a judge decided his daughters needed…"

Daniel's eyes narrowed. "You always go for the hard-luck cases, don't you?" he said, interrupting her.

"It's my job," Abby said, hating the defensive tone in her voice.

Daniel leveled an inscrutable look at her. "But you do it with all your heart, Abby. That's what makes men fall in love with you."

The strangled sound that came from her throat was part laugh, part cry. "You make me sound like a real femme fatale." His ridiculous assertion was made all the more ludicrous by her outfit: faded gray leggings, scuffed deck shoes and one of Landon's discarded J.Crew sweatshirts.

Even in jeans and a polo shirt, Daniel looked professional. And attractive. She and Melina had always joked about Daniel's political sex quotient, but that was when he was safely married and off the market.

Confused and unnerved, Abby beat a hasty retreat, sprinting across the parking lot to the safety of her office. As she rocked back and forth in her chair, one part of her wanted to laugh—could a woman whose sexual history included just two men be considered a heartbreaker? Another part wanted to weep—how did she always manage to attract the wrong type? First a depressive, then a womanizer. And now, her boss—and the ink wasn't even dry on the check to his divorce lawyer.

The blinking light of her answering machine caught her eye. Out of habit, she pressed the play button and received another shock.

A masculine clearing of the throat preceded, "Um...Ms. Davis. This is Tom Butler. I was in last week to see you. With my daughters." There was a pause. Abby could picture the man, his discomfort wearing hard on his soul. "You mentioned something about helping out with home improvements. I think maybe I might like to take you up on the offer. The sooner the better, I guess. I'll be waiting to hear from you."

Abby sighed. Damn. What was it about that man's voice that made her want to do the two-step? She didn't even like country-western music.

CHAPTER THREE

ABBY TOOK her eyes off the road to glance at the basket of goodies on the passenger seat. She felt like Little Red Riding Hood. Home visits were an integral part of her work, but a first visit was always awkward.

For reasons she couldn't quite discern, she was more nervous than usual. She'd worked with hundreds of families and usually managed to maintain a certain level of detachment—you needed it to keep from going crazy—but something about this family touched her more deeply than she cared to admit.

Maybe it stemmed from witnessing poor little Heather's anguish. Maybe it was because she could identify all too easily with twelve-year-old Angela's loss. Abby had been eleven when her grandmother died. Grammy had lived with them since the day Abby came home from the hospital, and her death rocked the foundation of Abby's life.

Abby's mother had returned to work when Abby's older brothers were eight and thirteen. Two years later, when Abby came along, Grace Davis's decorating career, which she'd put on hold to stay home with her sons, was just taking off. The boys didn't need a full-time mother at home, but a new baby did. Fortunately, Grace's recently widowed, impoverished mother-in-law, Agnes, agreed to move into their home and care for Abby.

Abby had adored her grandmother with all her heart. She'd been utterly devastated when Agnes died, suddenly, after exploratory surgery. No, Abby had no trouble empathizing with Angela Butler's pain.

That, Abby told herself, was why she wanted this to go smoothly. Which was why she'd called her sister-in-law, Robyn, that morning. When Abby asked Robyn for the scoop on her kids' likes and dislikes, Robyn laughed out loud. "You want to know what's in with preteens? Why? Are you in the market for a couple? I'm taking offers."

Abby explained about Tom Butler and his daughters, trying to downplay the depth of her own interest.

"What kind of bribes are you looking for?" Robyn asked, her tone teasing. Robyn and Matt constantly razzed Abby about letting her work take the place of a real life.

"Not bribes—gifts."

"Whatever. Well, listen, candy never fails, but you have a single father who may not remind them to brush every night, which might lead to cavities. Stay away from healthy stuff, they'll think you're a real tweek."

"Is that anything like a geek?"

"You got it." She paused. "How 'bout videos? You may not have noticed, but my two are so evolved they can watch a video and do homework at the same time. Charles Darwin would have been impressed."

Abby chuckled, adding the word to her list. "Like what? Disney?"

"Good for the little one. Kiss of death for the teen. How 'bout *Little Women?* Winona Ryder's hot."

"What if they don't have a VCR?"

"Good grief, where do they live? The backwoods of Tennessee?"

"On a ranch."

"If they have electricity, they have a VCR. Trust me. No parent can function without one."

Abby made a note to take along the TV from her bedroom. It had a built-in VCR. She'd tell Tom, who probably wouldn't accept it as a personal loan, that it was a standard VOCAP practice.

Abby was about to make her goodbyes when Robyn said, "I talked to Grace this morning."

Abby's breakfast flip-flopped in her belly. She loved her mother—in the abstract, Hallmark kind of way, but the two couldn't be in the same room for a minute without Grace saying something or doing something that left Abby feeling "lacking."

"That's nice," Abby said noncommittally. "I guess that means they're back from their cruise. Did Dad hate it? He was sure he'd die from golf-withdrawal."

"I talked to him, too. He said it was fun, but he was glad to get home. Grace said she tried calling you on your birthday, but no answer. Hot date, perhaps?"

Abby had listened to her mother's message—a slightly off-key rendition of "Happy Birthday"—on her answering machine when she returned home from her celebration with Melina, but hadn't gotten around to calling back. "Melina and I went out. We had key lime pie margaritas. Can you imagine such a thing?" Abby asked with forced cheer.

Robyn made a gagging sound. "I can imagine barfing them up. Yech! Your mother's right, girl. You don't have a social life." Before Abby could mount a defense, Robyn said, "Grace is worried about you, kiddo, and so am I. I keep picturing you home alone with only that obese cat for company."

"Tubby is not just any cat. He's a thirty-pound feline

sumo wrestler.'' Robyn's snort did not sound amused. ''Besides, Landon drops by off and on.'' Whoops. Tactical error.

''Jesus, Abby, does he bring his new girlfriend along, too? Are you a masochist or what?''

Abby toyed with the plate of stale birthday cake she intended to feed to the birds. Robyn was right; Abby needed to get on with her life in more ways than one.

''Listen, Abby, I know you hate it when I try to fix you up, but there's a guy I want you to meet.''

Abby groaned, wetting her finger to pick up German-chocolate crumbs.

''Don't do that,'' Robyn scolded. ''He's really neat.''

''That's what you said about Garvin.''

''Gavin. Forget about Gavin. He was a mistake.''

''Yeah, a genetic mistake.''

''Hush. You're going to like Adam. He's not a computer droid, he's a headhunter.''

''Oh, there's a lovely image. Is he four foot six with a bone in his nose?''

Robyn laughed. ''He's over six foot and very cute. Just wait. You'll see. I've invited him to the Memorial Day barbecue.'' Abby groaned. She'd have tried to come up with some creative excuse, like sudden-onset leprosy, but right now she was anxious to get on the road. ''Well, pal, I'd love to hear about your little matchmaking business, but I gotta run. Duty calls.''

''That's another thing your mother said,'' Robyn told her, not taking the hint. ''You're letting that job take the place of a real life. This is Sunday. You should be doing something fun—bike riding, in-line skating, sharing the comics with some handsome hunk.'' Robyn paused, then giggled. ''Dang, I'm starting to make my own life look like hell. I was on my way to clean the toilets when you called.''

Abby laughed, grateful she didn't have to muster her usual defense. She wouldn't admit it to Robyn, or any other member of the family, but lately her life did feel empty, devoid of passion. If it weren't for the Butler case, she might have spent the whole afternoon weeding her garden and watching videos. Alone.

CALL IT WORK, Abby thought fifteen minutes later as she turned off the main highway onto a traffic-free side road, but at least this way I'm driving down a country road on a beautiful late-spring day to spend time with a family that needs my help.

She pushed a button on her armrest to lower the window. Warm, fragrant air filled the car. Alfalfa, she thought, confirming her guess when she spotted a recently cut field of green. Although Abby grew up in Fresno and attended a parochial high school, she had friends involved in 4-H and Future Farmers of America. Her best friend, Kate Petersen, lived on a ranch that bordered the San Joaquin River. Some of Abby's fondest memories were of riding horses along its tree-lined banks and flirting with the cowboys who worked for her dad.

As the road turned southeast, toward the foothills, Abby tried to work out what was bothering her most: her family's interest in her affairs, or the knowledge they might be right. Again. Her sweaty hands slipped on the steering wheel. She wiped them on her jeans and pushed up her sunglasses. She fought the urge to speed up since she wasn't familiar with this part of the county and didn't want to end up in an irrigation ditch.

The directions she'd scribbled on the sticky note had

seemed pretty straightforward when Tom dictated them to her last night. She'd deliberated about returning his call on a Saturday night, but, in the end, curiosity won out. He didn't seem at all surprised that she didn't have anything better to do than return phone messages on a Saturday night. She would have been annoyed if not for the honest pleasure she heard in his voice. Her heart had done the funniest little back flip.

Nervously chewing on her bottom lip, Abby consulted her sketchy map. "This has to be more than four miles," she muttered.

The flat, agricultural land, leveled to allow flood irrigation of tomatoes, corn and peppers, had given way to undulating land that sported green shafts of bunch grass and scattered groups of black and brown cattle. Interspersed in the mixture were orchards of almonds, walnuts and pistachios.

"Oh, here we go," she said, spotting the names on two large, steel-gray mailboxes. The bigger of the two bore the word "Hastings" stenciled on the side; the smaller wore the tag "Butler."

She turned off the paved road and slowed down to accommodate a washboard of ripples. On either side of the hard-packed road ran a strip of natural grass, already turned its summer gold. Parallel to the road were two irrigated pastures, home to several dozen head of cattle. Beyond the pastures, Abby spotted silvery-leafed almond trees and, in the distance, a newly planted orchard laid out in precise rows with white, milk carton–like boxes protecting the young saplings.

The driveway curved to the right and appeared to circle back at the top of a slight rise. A grove of mature walnut trees on the left obscured her view. A scouting party of four or five dogs raced between the stout, mottled trunks to meet her. She hastily rolled up her window, muting the raucous furor that might have scared her off if Tom hadn't declared the dogs friendly but barky.

As the driveway completed its S pattern, she looked for Tom's yellow pickup truck but couldn't spot it. An expensive-looking silver-and-blue truck was parked cockeyed in the driveway of a long, low California-style ranch house to her right. An artsy steel sign set amid the riotous glory of red, white and blue petunias defined the owners as "Hastings," with an arrow making up the left-hand upright of the H.

With her foot barely touching the gas, Abby scanned the area. Her impression was of neatly organized obsolescence. No high-tech vehicles or fancy implements in sight, just well cared for tools of the trade. A tractor, its huge tires caked with mud, stood to one side of a massive, weathered red barn. A small group of horses vied for a front-row view in a corral attached to the narrow, faded redwood shed to her left.

"Well," Abby said, trying to decide where to go.

A movement at the door of the shed caught her eye. A wave. She hoped. Either that or the glint of the sun off a gun barrel, she thought sardonically. After all, the building would have been right at home in an Old West movie where tired ranch hands bunked down for the night after a long day of fighting off rustlers.

The door opened all the way and Abby saw Angela Butler step out. No gun in hand. Abby pulled into the graveled, semicircular driveway, parking beneath a brutally trimmed mulberry tree. As she turned off the engine, she saw Angela motion the dogs away. Abby opened the door and got out, taking a deep breath of pure, country air. The distinctive smell of horses and recently irrigated soil made her smile.

"Hi, Angela," Abby said, not bothering to close the car door. She left the basket of goodies, including her pan of hastily prepared Rice Krispie treats, on the seat. Donna had warned Abby to proceed with cautious diplomacy on Angela's turf. "I wasn't sure this was the right place. Where's your dad's truck?"

Angela, barefoot, in baggy jeans and a cropped T-shirt, didn't budge from her spot on the crumbling concrete stoop. Her thin shoulders lifted and fell. "A neighbor called. Some cows got out. He tried calling you, but you'd already left."

"No problem. It's a gorgeous day and I'm happy to be out of the house. Is Heather here?"

"She pitched a fit when he started to leave so he took her with him."

Abby understood the disgust she heard in Angela's voice. On one level Angela probably would have liked to be able to pitch a fit of her own, but as an almost-teenager she had a certain image to maintain.

"Five is pretty young to have to face something like this, but in some ways it's even harder when you're twelve. People don't expect a five-year-old to cope, but when you're older..." She didn't fill in the rest. Angela's quick, probably involuntary nod showed the girl agreed.

"I brought some things I thought you might be able to use. Want to help me carry them in?"

Angela's tentative smile was cut off by an epithet so explicit it made Abby gape. The girl exploded off the stoop like an Olympic sprinter. "Rufus," she screeched, "if you ruined anything, I swear I will kick your skinny ass. Go home, you good-for-nothing son-of-a-bitch. Ed's gonna put a leash on you if you don't stay home.''

Abby spun around, following the girl with her gaze. With athletic grace, Angela dived for the car door and reared back with a wriggling armful of puppy. The dog, a black Lab almost half her size, slithered out of her hold and dashed away.

Abby hurried to check the damage.

''They weren't brownies, were they?'' Angela asked, her voice low and tense, holding up an empty pan. ''Chocolate ain't good for dogs. I'd rather kill him myself.''

Abby stared at the pan, too surprised to quite make sense of what had happened. ''No. Rice Krispie treats.''

''Goddamn it!'' Angela swore. ''I really like those. Why does everything have to get ruined?''

A quiver in her voice made Abby look up in time to see tears tumble over the rims of Angela's eyes. Without thinking, Abby put her arms around the slim, shuddering shoulders and drew her close. It was on the tip of her tongue to offer to make more treats, but she knew the root of these tears couldn't be fixed by a trip to the store.

How well she knew! A wraith, older than Angela but just as anguished, hovered peripherally, breathing life into memories too well hidden to be anything but ghosts.

TOM WAITED beside Abby's Honda while she leaned inside to grab the clipboard she planned to use to make notes about everything that was wrong with his living accommodations. He'd jokingly suggested she'd need more than one pad, but Abby had smiled serenely and replied that her forte was getting more from less.

Tom could believe it, too. By the time he and Heather

returned from a hasty fence repair, Abby and Angel were measuring the interior of the bunkhouse with a broken tape measure he kept in the kitchen drawer. Before he knew it, Abby had Heather holding one end and Angel the other, somehow turning the process into a game that had both girls laughing.

Now his daughters were happily ensconced in front of the nineteen-inch color television with built-in VCR—on loan from VOCAP, Abby told him—watching the movie *Babe*. She'd given the video to the girls claiming it was an old one she'd grown sick of, but Tom spotted the telltale cellophane wrapping on the floor of her car.

"Got it," she said, returning to an upright position.

Tom liked her better that way. It took too much willpower to keep his gaze off her shapely rear end, which looked every bit as good in blue jeans as he thought it would.

"I make myself these detailed lists so I won't forget anything, then I go off and forget my list," she said, brushing her hair away from her face. "I must be getting old."

"That's my excuse," Tom said, thinking he really liked her hair. The style fit her face and the color picked up highlights of copper he'd missed that day in the office.

Her smile wavered. "Thirty is not all that young, by today's standards."

"Lesley would have turned thirty-five in September," he said without thinking.

He regretted his words when he saw a dark shadow pass across her face. She was much too gentle and caring to have to deal with all this horror. From the first moment he saw her stumble in front of her office, he'd felt a need to reach out and sweep her away to some-place safe. It was a foolish notion since she seemed perfectly happy in her job and able to juggle other people's problems with a magician's finesse.

"She was lovely," Abby said, her tone somber. "Angela showed me her picture."

For reasons he couldn't explain, Tom felt the need to make her understand his feelings toward his ex-wife. "Les and I split up before Heather was born. She hated this life. Wanted action and went looking for it.

"People are like horses. Each one's got a certain nature and there's no changing that. I knew when I married her what she was like." He sighed and looked across the irrigated pasture to the foothills muted by the afternoon haze. "I guess maybe she thought she could change my nature."

"You were both very young," Abby said softly.

"I guess. She was full of dreams. Her only mistake was thinking I could make them come true," he said, unable to keep a smattering of bitterness out of his tone. "She tried hard when Angel was little, but it just got to the point where she wasn't happy no matter what..." He left off the words "I did." No use making it look like it was all Lesley's fault. He'd played his part by being bullheaded and inflexible.

"So she moved to the city," Abby said. "Did that make her happy?"

"I guess. She made good money. Had a big house, nice things." He chuckled wryly, looking over his shoulder at his home. "Heck, this place could fit in one of her bathrooms. She even had a TV in the master bathroom. Can you imagine watching television in the tub or on the—whatever?"

She smiled but didn't say anything. Maybe she had

one in her bathroom. He felt himself flush. Maybe everybody but Tom Butler had a television set in the toilet.

Consulting her notepad, she asked in a professional tone, "Do you own or rent?"

"Neither. Ed Hastings owns this place, and I'm his foreman. We have a sort of lease-option arrangement. His sons aren't interested in the ranch, and he doesn't want to see it broken up after he passes on."

She nodded, which made the sunlight dance off the rich shiny texture of her hair. "How does he feel about remodeling?"

Tom recalled his conversation with Ed half an hour earlier at the mailboxes. Ed was returning to the hospital.

"I saw a car go by earlier," Ed hollered over the drone of the diesel. "That the gal from VOCAP?"

"Yep," Tom said, hating the despondency he heard in Ed's voice. Ever since Janey's diagnosis, Ed seemed tired and distracted.

"Good," Ed said, mustering a little enthusiasm. "I talked to Ralph Miller this morning." Tom recognized the name of the lawyer he and Miguel had used to set up their partnership agreement. Ralph was an old friend of the Hastingses. "He says we should set up a limited power of attorney so you can run things when I'm not around. I'll be back Thursday to settle it."

"Whatever you want, Ed. Just keep us posted on Janey."

Ed nodded, his lips tight. "Tell that VOCAP lady to pull out the stoppers and get going on the addition. It'll give Janey something to look forward to."

To Abby, Tom said, "Actually, Ed would like to see us get started as soon as possible."

"Great. I'll send a contractor out next week. He'll be

able to come up with some plans and a dollar figure, then I'll find the money.''

Tom cleared his throat. He hated talking money with her, but the subject always seemed to come up. ''Ed plans to cover the building costs.''

Her eyes lit up with a smile. ''That's wonderful, but...'' She hesitated, looking at the sheaf of forms on her clipboard as if searching for some hidden answers. ''If you don't need a low-interest loan, you don't really need me, do you? I mean, I'd be happy to help, but—''

''Well...'' It wasn't in his nature to ask for help, but Tom didn't know what else to do. ''I've never done this before and I don't even know where to begin.''

There was understanding in her sudden smile. ''I have,'' she said, leaning back against her car. She folded her clipboard against her chest, innocently enhancing the shapeliness of her breasts against her plain white shirt. ''I completely remodeled my house four years ago. Talk about a learning experience!''

Her lips pursed thoughtfully. Tom couldn't help noticing how full and attractive they were. Had he noticed that before?

''You said you're going to be running the ranch alone while the Hastingses are at Stanford, right?'' Tom had been forced to explain about Janey's cancer treatment when Heather blurted out earlier, ''Janey's real, real sick and her doctor lives in a big city so she had to go there. She might have to buy a wig.''

He nodded.

''Well, I doubt if that will leave you much time to oversee a project like this, will it?''

Before he could answer, Abby put out her hand and touched his arm. Her fingers barely skimmed his skin, but Tom felt the contact all the way to his toes. ''I think this is where my famous 'interceding on your behalf' comes into play,'' she said, her tone sounding faintly amused. ''I'll call a contractor friend of mine tomorrow. Okay?''

Tom nodded, more relieved than he could imagine. Until that moment, it hadn't even crossed his mind how he was going to handle the myriad aspects of remodeling, from subcontractors to design. Thank God, Abby Davis had offered to take this on.

Impulsively, Tom asked the question that had been on his mind ever since she called him back to set up this meeting. ''Do you do this for everybody? Make a home visit on a Sunday afternoon?''

A rosy color flashed across her features and she lowered her head to scribble something in her notebook. ''I had the time and it seemed like a good idea to get the ball rolling.''

''Why?''

She looked up, confused. ''Why is it good to get going?''

''Why do you have the time? Why aren't you spending it with your family?''

She shrugged. ''My parents live in Palm Desert and my brothers and their families live—''

He didn't let her finish. ''Why aren't you married?''

She looked stunned for a second then threw back her head and laughed. The sound made the horses scatter edgily. ''Wow, you cowboys don't pull any punches. My father asks me the same thing all the time, but you kind of expect that from a dad.''

Tom waited.

She lifted one shoulder and let it fall. ''I've lived with two men.'' She grinned wickedly. ''Sounds scandalous, doesn't it? But one was too sick to marry and the other too flaky." She sighed and looked toward the field beyond the barn. "Donna says one was darkness, the other light. Too much of either isn't healthy. I guess I just haven't found that perfect balance."

Tom knew all about balancing acts. At times, he felt like a man juggling land mines on a tightrope.

Abby made a few more notes then opened the door of her car. "I'll call you as soon as I have a meeting set up with the contractor." She cocked her head as if listening for something. Tom heard the sound of a movie sound track. Abby seemed pleased. "Tell the girls goodbye for me. I always hate being interrupted when I'm watching a movie."

"Thanks," Tom said seriously. "For everything—the movie, the TV—"

She waved off his gratitude. "No problem. I'm glad to help. And I'm excited about the addition. Remodeling gets in your blood, you know."

Tom watched her drive away. It wasn't his nature to take to people right off—his mother called him a watchful owl, but he liked Abby Davis. He liked her cheerful candor, even if he sensed a somber undertone.

Humming under his breath, he went inside, intending to start supper. Sunday was his night to cook. So far the girls hadn't complained, but he'd stretched his culinary repertoire about as far it went—quesadillas, egg sandwiches and macaroni and cheese. Tonight, he planned to make chili. From a can.

As he headed for the kitchen, Heather sat up from her sprawled position on the couch and motioned for him to come over.

"What is it, baby-love?"

"Sit with me."

Grinning, he plopped down beside Angel and hauled

Heather into his arms. She giggled and squirmed for a few seconds before quieting.

"How's the movie?"

"Okay," Angel said, her tone filled with ennui. "We saw it at the Cineplex near our house."

"I like Ferdinand," Heather said. "He's a duck."

Despite himself, Tom found his gaze drawn to the bright, clear picture. He was curious about the movie Abby had selected.

Angel passed him a bowl of popcorn.

"She's pretty cool, you know," Angel said.

"Ms. Davis?" Tom asked, his voice neutral.

Angel rolled her eyes. "You're so old-fashioned, Daddy. She said to call her Abby."

"Oh."

Angel kept her eyes on the screen. "She said her mother is an interior decorator, I mean, designer. That's what they call them now. She's going to get us some magazines and books so we can design our bedroom. Cool, huh?"

Tom didn't want to burst her bubble, but, despite Ed's largesse, there were finances to consider. "We'll see. It's a ways off, sweetheart."

"I know," she said with a petulant frown. "But Mom always said it doesn't hurt to dream."

Tom closed his eyes. Lesley was dead, and he had a ranch to run and two children to raise. He didn't have time to sleep, much less dream.

MONDAY MORNING Abby raised the cup of aromatic herbal tea to her nose and inhaled, hoping the cinnamon-apple scent could soothe her jangled nerves. She'd spent the last several hours on edge, worrying about what to say to Daniel if he suddenly called or, worse, showed up.

He was an attractive man, but Abby knew the risks of getting involved with a boss, not to mention someone going through an emotional upheaval. Daniel was neither light like Landon nor dark like Billy, but he was stuck in a gray area that he wouldn't be clear of for months, maybe years.

"Wow!" Melina exclaimed, popping her head around Abby's door. "Did you hear the latest? Marilyn booted Daniel out. She's keeping the house and the Mercedes. God, he loved that car."

Abby flinched. Gossip was one of the least attractive parts of working in a small office.

Melina's perfectly waxed eyebrows shot up like parentheses turned sideways. "You knew this, didn't you? He told you Friday, and you didn't tell me." Her tone was hurt and accusing.

"No. He didn't say a word," Abby said honestly.

"Then how'd you know?"

Abby stifled a sigh. "He called me Saturday and asked me to meet him in his office. I guess he wanted me to know before the gossip hit the fan, so to speak."

It sounded plausible to her ears, but apparently Melina heard something different. She stepped into Abby's office and closed the door. Taking the seat across from Abby, she said, "Oh my God."

"What?"

"He has the hots for you."

Abby smiled at Melina's dire tone. "Don't be silly. He's at a vulnerable point in his life, and I'm a reliable associate. Everybody cries on my shoulder, why should Daniel be any different?"

Melina shook her head, making her thick, wavy hair

dance across the black suede lapels of her red-and-white checkered suit jacket. "No, Abby, it's more than that. Otherwise, why didn't he meet you at a coffee shop or someplace public? He wants more than your shoulder for comfort."

Abby took a deep breath. "Forget it, Mel. Even if that were the case, I'm not getting involved. I know a dangerous proposition when I see one. I'm sticking to my original plan."

"You're leaving." Her friend's tone was so downcast, Abby reached across the desk and squeezed her hand. They'd hit if off the minute Melina interviewed for the job of associate counselor. Daniel had lobbied for a man with a bachelor's degree in human resources. Abby had insisted they needed someone bilingual, as Melina was, but secretly she wanted another woman on staff and she liked Melina's bubbly personality.

"Eventually. Not right away," Abby reassured her friend.

Melina pursed her lips—theatrically red today. "I wanted to ask you about that. Roy told me about your new case—a cowboy and his kids. He said you're handling him personally."

Melina's choice of words made Abby blush, so she took a swig of tea to hide her face. "You and Roy both have full loads, and your cruise is coming up pretty soon, right? I figured I was the logical choice since the Marshall case just closed."

Abby gazed at the pale liquid in her cup. If she was serious about changing her life, now would have been the perfect time to start downsizing her caseload instead of volunteering to oversee a three-to-four-month-long remodeling project. But the look of desperation she'd seen in Tom Butler's eyes had robbed her of the ability to think straight.

Melina frowned. "Does this have anything to do with the fact that he's a hunk?"

Abby laughed. "Tom Butler is many things, Mel, but I don't think he considers himself a hunk. He's good-looking…in a country kind of way, but plain. No frills. No vanity or pretensions."

Abby watched Melina's facial expressions as she weighed Abby's reply. The young Hispanic woman was prone to drama, always seeking deeper motives for someone's actions. "Would you say he's the exact opposite of Daniel?" she asked.

"Pretty much. No suit and tie in Tom Butler's closet."

"And he's nothing at all like Landon."

Abby frowned. She didn't like where this was leading. "You could say that."

Melina took a deep breath. "Abby, my friend, my mentor, my mother's idea of a role model, I know I don't have to remind you of this. You are the consummate professional, the standard-bearer for all advocates, the Saint Joan of—"

Abby snorted. "What are you getting at?"

Melina sat forward. "Abby, you can't get involved with this guy. It's unethical."

Abby jerked her hands free. "Who said anything about getting involved?"

Melina rose and put one hand on Abby's shoulder. "You did." Her tone held a Mother Superior quality.

Abby gaped. "I did not." Her own tone sounded just like Angela Butler arguing with her sister.

Melina sighed. Although four years younger than

Abby, she was vastly more experienced in the ways of romance. "Abby, I know you. I can tell you like him."

"So? He's a nice man. He cares about his kids. He doesn't kick dogs. What do you want from me?"

With a gentleness she'd seen Melina employ with children who came to her broken and bruised, her friend said, "I want you to be careful. I know you'll work yourself to the bone for this man—this family, but in the end, they will heal and move on with their lives. They always do."

The truth of her words sunk into Abby's flesh like acid.

"This is what we do, remember?" Melina said as she prepared to leave the office. "We help them get their lives together so they can go forward, then we disappear into the past, like old friends who moved away. You're the one who told me you have to hold something back, otherwise this business eats you up inside."

For several minutes after Melina left, Abby gazed out the window. Her grandmother always said the truth was hard to swallow, but it was better than a bellyache from a lie. The truth was she *was* attracted to Tom Butler...and his daughters. But Melina was right about something else as well. Abby was a professional and she could do her job without breaking her heart in the process. She had to—three other hearts were at stake.

CHAPTER FOUR

TOM HURRIED into Ed's office, a small, cluttered room at the back of the ranch house. He caught a scent of stale coffee and looked at the coffeemaker sitting on the file cabinet—gray globs floated atop an inch of black goo.

A glance at the Caterpillar clock above the room's lone window told him he had forty-five minutes before Maria Fuentes returned with the girls. When she'd picked them up at eleven, he'd given her a grateful hug. "You have no idea what a lifesaver you are. Your husband and I are going to be up to our knees in mud all day."

In typical Maria fashion, she'd waved off his gratitude. "My niece's school sponsors this festival every year. I'm hoping the girls will meet some kids their own ages. I grew up on a ranch, I know how hard it is to make friends, but I had eight brothers and sisters to keep me busy. Besides," she said, ushering his daughters to her '87 Toyota wagon, "you've done so much for Miguel and me."

"Maria," Tom said, uncomfortable with the praise. No matter how many times he told the young couple they were doing him a favor by renting his house on Plainsborough Road, they insisted on treating him like a hero.

Tom had known Maria's family most of his life. He'd

played football with her older brothers in high school, and there wasn't a man around he respected more than Ernesto Garza, Maria's father.

Maria, the second to youngest of nine, met Miguel Fuentes on the sorting line at a local cannery the summer after her high-school graduation. Although, at the time, he barely spoke English, Miguel had ambition and drive. When Maria introduced him to Tom, Tom felt an immediate bond. Ed agreed to give him a chance, and Miguel had proved his worth every day for the last four years.

Maria scolded Tom with her eyes. "Miguel and I can never repay you, Tom. When other landlords were afraid to rent to us because of our...little problem, you handed us the key to your beautiful little house—no first and last months' rent, no deposit."

Their problem was an arsonist who had never been caught. The police theorized that whoever set fire to their duplex was a hired torch courtesy of Boyd Johnston, who was in prison, serving a life sentence for murdering Maria's cousin, Adelina.

It was during the sentencing hearing that Maria's family turned to Abby Davis for help. Thanks to her impassioned plea, Adelina's baby daughter, Celeste, went home to her mother's family instead of to Boyd's parents. Two months later, Maria and Miguel returned home from work one day to find their house reduced to ashes.

At first, Tom had worried that opening his and Lesley's house to the Fuenteses would stir up old ghosts, but Maria had redecorated in her own style, and it filled Tom's heart with pleasure to see horses grazing in the pasture behind his small white barn. Collaborating on a shared dream, Tom and Miguel pooled their resources to buy three broodmares. By trading horse training for stud fees, they were now into their second year.

Tom yanked on the back of Ed's oversize desk chair. He heaved himself into its tweed padding. When he shuffled aside a mound of unopened mail, Tom noticed an envelope from an insurance company. He'd promised to look into group policies for Miguel. Ed paid top dollar but didn't offer benefit packages.

The phone beside his elbow rang. Its partner attached to the fax machine across the room echoed in unison.

"Tom Butler."

"Tom? I tried the house, but Angel didn't answer so I thought I'd leave a message on the machine."

Abby! Tom rocked back in the chair and kicked out his legs, hooking his boots on the corner of the desk.

"Maria took the girls to a school function this afternoon. I didn't even ask about it." He frowned, stroking the coarse, comforting texture of his mustache. "Does that make me a bad father?"

Her light, melodic laughter eased some weight inside him. If he closed his eyes he had no trouble picturing the smile that went with that laugh. "Yeah, right," she said dryly. "Maria Fuentes could take those kids to a biker bar and they'd be safe."

"I forgot you know her. From her cousin's case, right?"

"Yep." The lightness went out of her voice. "One of the hardest cases I've ever worked, but Maria was a rock, even when it looked like the judge was going to award custody to Boyd's family. But the good news is— Celeste is doing great."

Tom stared at a cobweb arching from the file cabinet to the overhead fluorescent-light fixture. He needed to hire a housecleaner before Janey got back, but he was too tired to think about it. "It was an awful time for Maria. She and I have talked about the parallels of what happened to Adelina and Lesley. Two mothers. Both murdered. Maria even suggested I come see you, but I thought I could handle things myself."

"Tom, you need to remember that it's okay to ask for help. You had nothing to do with the violence that created this situation. You're a wonderful father, but even the best parent needs a break now and then. I think it's terrific that Maria has the girls. It'll be good for them, too."

Tom closed his eyes. The praise felt good, even though he didn't want to admit it. "I'm a little worried about Heather," he told her before he could stop himself. "She had a really bad dream last night—worse than usual. It took hours to get her back to sleep."

"Good," Abby said, catching him off guard.

"Good?"

"Believe it or not, that may be a sign of progress with Donna. Be sure to mention it when you take the girls in tomorrow. Is that why you sound so tired?"

She can tell? "That, and I was up at four. Miguel had some problems with one of our irrigation pumps. Out here, water is money."

"So you raced out to the field in the middle of the night with practically no sleep and fixed the pump. Sounds like a job for SuperCowboy."

The humor in her tone made him smile. "I didn't fix it. That's P.G.&E.'s problem—well, it will be once I get this fax off to them. That's why I'm in the office. I hooked up a temporary unit and diverted the water to another field so it wouldn't go to waste and we were back in business."

"Then you went home and took a nap, right?"

Involuntarily, Tom hooted. "What planet do you live on?"

"I was being facetious." She paused, and Tom could picture a serious look settling on her face. He'd noticed her habit of taking a few seconds to compose her thoughts before delivering a serious message. "You know, Tom, sleep deprivation is a dangerous thing. For one thing, you could be too tired to cope with the girls."

Before he could protest, she asked, "You operate heavy machinery, right? Tractors? Farm implements? The kind where one slip could cost you life or limb?" When Tom didn't answer, she continued, "At the very least, when you get run-down, you enhance your chances of getting sick. And that wouldn't do any of you any good, either." He could hear the concern in her voice.

He started to answer, but she beat him to the punch. "Tell you what—why don't you let that fax wait until tomorrow? Just rock back in that big comfy chair of Ed's and close your eyes for a few minutes. A catnap's better than nothing at all."

The suggestion caught him off guard and he had to admit he felt as tired as he could ever remember. His eyelids drooped; his arms felt too heavy to hold the phone. "Wait a minute," he said, surfacing above the waves of fatigue that were pulling him down. "How do you know Ed's chair is comfy?"

Her musical giggle made him smile. "Quit procrastinating. Angel and I used the fax to send my mother a rough sketch of the floor plan yesterday. That chair could house a family of five. I almost stole it. Just close your eyes and let go," she coaxed. "I'm hanging up."

"Wait," he feebly protested. "Why'd you call?"

"It can wait till tomorrow. I'll meet you at Donna's

when you take the girls to their session. Sweet dreams.''
She hung up.

Tom put down the receiver with a deep sigh. As fatigue carried him into a black, dreamless state, his last thought was of Abby, a sweet-voiced siren who cared about tired, lonesome cowboys.

No maroon Honda.

Tom scanned the parking lot one more time, but clearly Abby wasn't waiting for him at Donna's as planned. He swallowed his disappointment and parked the truck, letting his children's chatter wash over him without hearing a single word.

He'd gotten a fairly decent night's sleep—only one mild nightmare for Heather—and he'd been looking forward to telling Abby how much the nap she'd suggested had helped him. Twenty short minutes had been enough to put a smile on his face when Maria brought the girls home. They'd actually played Chutes and Ladders after dinner until bedtime and he'd still had enough energy to tackle paperwork. All in all, it was a nice evening and he wanted to thank her. He wanted to see her.

Donna met them at the door. As usual, she had her hands behind her back and a grin on her face. ''Hello, my young friends. Which hand today?''

Tom didn't know if this was part of their therapy or just a ploy to get in their good graces, but she always had some small treasure or goodie waiting when the children arrived. As usual, Angel let her little sister pick first, a generosity that both amazed Tom and made him very proud. As always, Heather chose the left hand.

Donna produced two perfect Bosc pears.

''Thank you,'' the girls chimed in unison.

''You're most welcome. Now settle down at the table

and I'll be right there." She waited until they were seated, then partially closed the door. "Tom, Abby called a minute ago. She tried to reach you at home but you'd already left. Something came up and she couldn't meet you here."

"No problem."

Donna studied him a second. "Are you getting enough sleep?"

He smiled. "Almost enough. Abby helped."

Donna's eyes showed surprise. "She did?"

"She told me it's okay to take a nap when you need it and to let other people help with the kids."

Donna's smile looked less reserved. "She's right, of course. And it is important that you look after your health during this difficult period. Your daughters need you to stay healthy. If you were a woman, I'd tell you to treat yourself to a trip to the beauty parlor for a little pampering." She let out a small sound of impatience. "What a sexist remark! Tom, go find a beauty parlor and treat yourself to a little pampering. That's an order from your health-care professional."

Chuckling, Tom left the building at a loss as to how to fill his time. He was childless and off duty for the next hour and a half. He usually spent the time running ranch errands, but since he'd planned to meet Abby, he'd left his paperwork on Ed's desk.

Idly choosing the path of least resistance, he wandered along the sidewalk of the small, shady strip mall. A striped barber pole at the far end of the complex caught his eye and he headed toward it.

Angel had been threatening for weeks to trim his hair in his sleep. His eagerness slowed as he neared the doorway. The original barbershop had metamorphosed into a beauty parlor. Outlined in brightly painted flowers, the rose and gold printing on the front window promised Glitzing, Acrylic Nails, Perms, Facials and Aromatherapy. Tom lowered his chin and started to pass it by when he noticed a hand-scribbled sign that read "Walk-Ins Welcome."

The scents that assailed his senses were far more caustic than anything his barnyard produced. His nostrils twitched and he almost turned around but braved the threshold. If this was aromatherapy, those New Age people needed their noses examined.

"Hey, sugar, come on in. My name's Jackie. We don't bite unless you ask us real nice." The person attached to the throaty drawl was a caricature composite of Mae West and Lucille Ball. A good two hundred pounds, the red-haired woman wore shiny pink bicycle pants and a baggy top sporting two dancing purple poodles with pink polka-dot bow ties. "What can we do you for, honey?"

"Haircut," Tom croaked, glancing around the room in case he needed a weapon or quick escape. The shop's other two occupants consisted of a matronly-looking woman with a helmet of skinny blue plastic rollers who was receiving a manicure by an elfin Asian woman of incalculable age.

"Well, hand over your hat and park your butt in that royal-blue throne, cowboy, and we'll give it a go."

Tom cringed when she tossed his good, white felt hat carelessly on a magazine-strewn coffee table, but he obediently walked to the indicated chair. He eyed its reclined back wedged up tightly to a sink with an indentation about the right size for a neck, and said, "Just a haircut, ma'am. I washed it this morning."

Grinning, the woman chomped on a wad of chewing

gum with enough snap to mimic gunfire. "Indulge me. It's all part of the price—sixteen bucks."

Tom lowered himself into the chair and leaned back. With a speediness that amazed him, Jackie secured a plastic bib around his neck and aimed a tingly spray of warm water at his head. Tom closed his eyes, relaxing to the feel of her fingers massaging his scalp. The apple-scented lather smelled good.

"Nice, isn't it?" Jackie said. "Men don't know what they're missing at barbershops and I can tell this is your first time in a beauty parlor, right?"

Tom was too lethargic to answer. He grunted.

As she worked some apple-scented lather into his hair, she asked, "So what brings you to these parts, stranger?"

"My daughters see a...doctor in the building across the way."

"Oh, really? I know one of the doctors over there. Her name is Donna Jessup. She's cool. She helped out my son when he was nineteen. Had a little drug problem."

"Is he better now?"

"Yep. Goes to Narcotics Anonymous faithfully and finished college. He and his girlfriend just had a baby. I told him if he didn't get off his duff and marry that girl, I was sending him back to therapy, but he said people don't get married for the same reasons these days. A kid isn't a reason enough? Who knows? Maybe he's right. I married his father for that reason and look where it got me—bruised, battered and divorced."

She squeezed the excess water from his hair and dried it briskly with a big fragrant towel. Her touch held a mothering quality he liked.

"You married?" she asked, pushing a lever that sat the back of the chair upright.

It took Tom a minute to get his bearings. "Not anymore."

"Over here, doll." She led him to a silver-flecked padded plastic chair on a hydraulic lift.

He sat down warily and eyed his wet image in the mirror. Surrounded by an oval of round white bulbs like in the movies, the image of a wet-dog cowboy in the silver-flecked chair looked ridiculously out of place, yet something about its air of glamour made him relax, as if he were preparing for some unannounced play.

"You share custody with the mom, huh?" Jackie asked.

Tom looked at her in the mirror. Kind eyes were hidden beneath an outrageous layer of mascara and black eyeliner. She was real, he decided, even if the color of her spiky locks wasn't.

"No. She died. The girls are getting some counseling to help them deal with it."

"Well, good for you," she said, grasping his shoulder in a supportive way. "What a smart dad you are! I lost my mama when I was nine, and my daddy sent me to live with my aunt. She was a good woman but she had four kids of her own and I didn't make it easy for her. I was mad at my mama for getting sick and dying, mad at my dad for sending me away, just mad at the world, I guess. I think my life would have been a lot different if I'd had someone to help me see it wasn't anybody's fault."

She straightened up, suddenly all business, and spun Tom around to face her. "Now, what are we doing here, son? Way I see it is we have two choices—same ol' same ol' or something a little radical. Which is it gonna be?''

''I could probably stand a little change.'' Even as he said the words, Tom had a feeling he was going to regret his choice.

She rewarded him with a big smile. ''Then close your eyes, honey, and let Jackie go to work.''

Tom lost track of time. When Jackie suggested losing the mustache he'd groomed and pampered since the early days of his marriage, he shrugged with cavalier ease but drew the line at glitzing, whatever that was.

''Okay, honey,'' Jackie said with a flourish, spinning his chair to face the mirror. ''Open your eyes.''

Tom did. He searched the mirror for a familiar visage but found a stranger sitting in the chair with silver stars. He blinked. So did the man across from him. Oh my God.

''Well, what do you think? Am I a genius or what?''

Jackie's infectious triumph helped take the edge off the severity of the change. This person didn't look like him, but he didn't look bad. In fact, he looked younger and more...current.

''I think my twelve-year-old will love it.''

Jackie winked. ''So will your twenty-five-year-old and your fifty-year-old. Trust me, Tom, you're a hunk.''

The other two occupants voiced their approval. The grandmother went so far as to volunteer for a date, if her husband of fifty-one years gave his okay. Tom let the knot in his stomach relax. What would Abby think?

As FAR AS Abby was concerned, Al Carroll was a god. Or the next thing to it. Fifty-five. Bald. Built like a bull terrier with suspenders, he made miracles happen. She'd seen his work dozens of times over the years, starting with the remodeling of her home. He'd transformed her dark, moody ranch-style house into an open, sunlit bungalow.

She couldn't wait to turn him loose on the Butler house.

Originally Abby had planned to meet Tom to go over some remodeling ideas, but when Al had called and said he had a couple of hours free, she'd jumped at the chance to meet him on-site.

"Not good," Al said, kicking his booted toe at the crumbling foundation. "Why do people build without footings?"

"How bad is it?" Bad meant money.

"I've seen worse. We'll just make sure not to involve the county suits in that part of the process. This newer stuff is acceptable."

Abby trotted along, trying to see what Al discerned in the weathered plank siding and moss-covered shingles. "I'd suggest putting gutters on the whole building when we do the addition. Saves some settling and might help shore up this area. Landscaping helps, too."

Abby scribbled notes while swatting flies. "He's going to have to move the horse pen, right?" she asked, more prayer than question.

"Makes sense. That area is already level and if you go the other direction you run into septic problems."

Good. She had a feeling that Tom had agreed to this addition out of both a sense of doing the right thing for his daughters and a dire need for privacy and space, but she knew he wasn't crazy about the changes it would entail.

She glanced at the slim watch on her wrist. The family should be back from Donna's any minute.

"What about this area?" Al called, catching Abby staring at the road.

She hurried around the corner of the building, nearly stumbling over a pile of firewood debris. A huge ax protruded—Paul Bunyanish—from a circle of wood. An image of Tom chopping wood on a cold morning, muscles taut beneath his worn flannel shirt, caught her off guard.

Al gave her a moment's scrutiny. "You okay? You oughta get some boots if you're gonna be out here in the country."

Abby looked down at the beige heels that accented her outfit: off-white Liz Claiborne silk and wool–blend suit with sculpted shell and nude hose. Not quite Eva Gabor in *Green Acres,* but close. She'd only been here twenty minutes and already there was a paw print on her skirt and some sort of vegetation on her sleeve.

At that moment, the thunderous roar of a diesel engine combined with a cacophony of barking filled the air. The faded yellow pickup rolled to a stop around the corner from where Abby and Al were standing. Angel appeared at Abby's side almost before the sound of the engine died.

"Wait till you see Dad," she whispered breathlessly. "You won't believe it."

Abby caught her breath. Angel's impish grin could be read as good or bad, you just never knew with girls this age. Abby leaned around the corner and nearly lost her balance again. Heedless of slivers, she anchored one hand on the rough siding.

"Ohmygod."

The mustache was gone. He'd left his hat in the truck, and his hair—what was left of it—was short. And wavy. And gorgeous. The shorter locks were full of rambunctious waves, which glinted like tempered bronze. This new look, even with a strip of slightly lighter skin tone above his upper lip, was more mature, more polished. Except for the faded denim shirt and scuffed blue jeans, he could have been a *GQ* magazine model. He should have been. "Wow."

"Cool, huh?" Angel enthused. "Do I have the, like, most with-it dad in the whole world, or what?"

"Absolutely. He gets my vote. Doesn't your daddy look great, Heather?" Heather, who was in Tom's arms, hadn't taken her eyes off her father's face, as if she expected him to turn into someone else while she watched.

"Daddy lost his mistash," Heather told Abby. "He went for a walk while we were at Dr. Donna's and some genie stole it because it was so pretty the genie wanted it for his wife."

Abby laughed and couldn't resist throwing her arms around the pair of them and giving them a hug. "Well, I'm glad I'm not married to that genie. Can you picture me with a mistash?"

Heather giggled and wiggled to get down.

Abby dropped her arms and backed up a step, suddenly self-conscious.

"Daddy says I get to pick a kitty from the new ones that were born in the barn. Wanna help me pick one?" Heather looked up at Abby expectantly.

Abby was grateful for the diversion. "I'd like that a lot."

Tom leaned down and planted a kiss atop the springy blond curls. "Mama cats sometimes hide their babies, punkin. Why don't you go find them and Abby'll catch up?"

"Okay, Daddy."

As Heather trotted off, Abby eyed Tom more circumspectly. "I do like it. But I have to admit I'm a little jealous. I go into the beauty parlor and come out the same, every time. You go in Tom Selleck and come out..." She searched for the right celebrity's name. "Tom Cruise."

Angel shook her head. "Naw. Too smooth. How 'bout Nicholas Cage?"

"Too extreme. Sean Connery?"

"Too old."

Tom coughed. "Would you like to introduce me to your friend?"

Abby's cheeks heated up as she realized Al was watching this exchange with bemused puzzlement. "Oh, sorry. Tom, this is Al Carroll, the best remodeling contractor in the business. Al, Tom Butler, homeowner."

"And movie star," Al said dryly.

Tom shook his hand. "Not exactly. I knew there was a reason I always went to the same barber all these years."

"Me, too," Al said, passing a freckled hand over his bald pate. Everyone laughed.

All awkwardness behind them, Tom and Al set off around the building with Angel at their heels, discussing the project. Abby started toward the barn but gave herself a moment to compose her scattered sensibilities. It was only a haircut, for heaven's sake.

TOM LIKED Abby's favorite contractor. The man knew his stuff and had some excellent ideas. In fact, talking to Al Carroll energized him. This project underscored the realization that the girls were here permanently and it was up to him to make a home for them.

Abby will understand, he thought. When Al Carroll left, Tom headed toward the barn.

As he walked, he thought about the look on Abby's face when she saw his haircut. To be honest, Tom had to admit her reaction hadn't hurt his ego. Donna had been reserved about his new look until she saw how the girls responded. Tom had been a little worried about what Heather might think, but she'd stroked his smooth cheeks and kissed him without reservation. "Where'd your mistash go, Daddy?"

He invented a story that made her laugh and she was fine with the change. Donna told him, "I'm pleased. I see this as real progress. She's comfortable that you're here for her and nothing about that is going to change. This is very good." Then, before he left, she winked and said, "Not to mention it looks great. Very debonair."

Tom entered the barn quietly. He didn't want to disturb any important girl talk. He was also curious about why Heather had included Abby in the choosing of a kitten.

He heard a quiet murmur of voices and stepped closer to the yellow glow of the light he'd suspended over a stacked pyramid of hay bales.

"I used to have lots of kittens of my own when I came up here to visit Dad in the summers," Tom heard Angel say.

He peeked over the railing of the empty horse stall. Abby was perched on the edge of a bale beside the two kids, who were sprawled on their bellies trying to see inside a hollowed-out area between the stacks.

"Those summers alone with your dad must have been very special," Abby said, trying to peer over their shoulders without losing her balance. "My brothers were ten and fifteen when I was born. My grammy told me they thought my being born was the worst thing that could have happened, that I'd ruin everything.''

Tom smiled.

''Did ya? Did ya ruin everything?'' Heather asked, ignoring the nudge from her sister.

''Just the opposite. Turns out I was a built-in babe magnet. The boys took me everywhere. All the girls would come around and 'ooh' and 'aah.' Nothing like a cute little toddler to break the ice.''

''Didn't you have any sisters?'' Heather asked.

Abby shook her head. ''Not until later on when my brothers married. Robyn and Patrice are my sisters-in-law and I love them like sisters. Matt and Robyn have two kids, Megan and Patrick—you're right between them in age, Angel. And Jarrod and Patrice just had a baby, Chloe, right before Christmas.''

Angel sat up, cross-legged; she eyed Abby intently. ''Dr. Jessup says you have great mothering instincts. How come you don't have any kids?''

Tom's pulse jumped. He almost interceded to admonish Angel. He was stopped by a curious flash of pain that crossed Abby's face before she camouflaged it by poking at a piece of moss on the sleeve of her prissy off-white suit.

Her tone seemed artificially bright when she said, ''I have a cat. His name is Tabby, but I call him Tubby. He thinks he's in charge of my house.''

Tom cleared his throat to announce his presence and joined the little conference by squatting beside Angel. ''Hello, ladies. Have you picked out a kitten?''

Heather shook her head. ''The mama hided them way back there, Daddy.'' To Abby, she said, ''Mama cat hides the babies so the papa won't eat them.''

"Oh, gross," Angel exclaimed, shooting to her feet. "I'm outta here."

Tom caught her hand, not wanting her to leave this warm, friendly closeness. "Where're you goin'?"

She flashed him a dark look that made him flinch. "Nowhere. Of course. I just want to be alone. Is that all right?"

Tom felt his cheeks heat up. What did he know about the needs of a girl on the brink of womanhood? He could understand the need for private time, but ever since he'd run across a pamphlet on teen suicide at Donna's office, he'd become very cautious. Maybe overly cautious. He let her small tense fingers slip from his hold. "Sure."

She raced toward the rear of the barn.

As if sensing his worries, Heather held out her arms to him. "Is the daddy cat mean, Daddy?"

Tom scooped his younger daughter into his arms and settled back against the stack of bales opposite Abby. "Not exactly, honey. Just forgetful. He forgets those are his babies and thinks some other cat planted kittens in his territory. The mama keeps the babies safe until they're big enough to look after themselves."

Abby made a small sound.

He caught a puzzling flash of some dark emotion cross Abby's face before she glanced at her watch. "I should be going."

She stood up quickly, brushing off her skirt. "It's my night to help at the women's shelter. Tell Angel I said goodbye. I'll call as soon as Al's got the plans ready."

Tom looked at Heather, who seemed oblivious to the sudden shift of mood. "Wait a sec," he said, rising to one knee. "We'll walk you to your car."

Abby paused by the gate. "No. Stay. You have a

kitten to choose. These are important moments in a girl's life.''

Puzzled by both her cryptic words and sudden somberness, he sat back down. She flicked her hand like a wounded butterfly and hurried away.

Heather reached up and laid her small, soft hands on either side of his face and directed his attention to her. ''Can we pick the kitty later? My tummy says it's time to eat.''

ANGEL SETTLED BACK against the makeshift couch she'd created from hay bales. The soft fleece lining of the old sleeping bag she'd found in the storage room below the loft helped protect her from the scratchy building material.

Just last week she'd remembered the hideaway her father had created for her a couple of summers ago. He'd called it a fort, but she and her friends, Brandi, Laura and Trudy Gills, called it the Hidey Spot. Her dad hadn't been so busy then and had time to cart her friends out to the ranch to play. Angel didn't know if any of the girls still lived around here. Last summer, Angel only spent a few days with her dad because her mother enrolled her in a computer camp, a gymnastics camp and a stupid, three-week leadership camp.

Shortly after the funeral, her father had suggested they try calling some of Angel's old friends, but, so far, she hadn't wanted to. Sometimes it just seemed too hard to explain to people about her mom.

Angel tilted back her head and studied the dust particles floating in the shaft of sunlight coming through a hole in the roof of the barn. It was quiet up here, peaceful. She knew her dad worried about her. He didn't understand why sometimes she wanted the television on as loud as possible and other times she'd want absolute silence, like now. She didn't understand it, either. Maybe she'd ask Dr. Donna. *Maybe she'll tell me I'm going crazy.*

Sighing, she reached for her new purple clipboard. "Imperial plum," Abby called it. The clipboard, complete with drafting paper and mechanical pencil, was a gift from Abby. Angel ran her finger along the surface of the blue-lined paper. It had a clean, professional feel.

"Measure your furniture," Abby told her. "Your end tables, dressers and beds, and then figure out what that comes to in scale—one foot equals one square. Then cut out the shapes so you can come up with designs."

Abby didn't go into big long explanations. She seemed to know Angel was smart enough to figure things out on her own.

Too bad Dad doesn't understand that, Angel thought bitterly.

Angel knew he was trying, but lately he'd been trying too hard. She felt like one of the colts he was training. He'd play out so much leader, letting the colt think he was free, then snap the line to show him who was boss.

This morning, Angel woke up early and started making oatmeal. The instant kind. Boil water—add the stupid oatmeal. Any idiot could do it. But she'd gotten sidetracked by Heather, and when she turned back to the pathetic hot plate that was supposed to pass for a stove, the oatmeal was bubbling like one of those volcanic pits she saw on the Discovery Channel. A big old glob spurted out and landed on her arm.

It had burned like hell, and she'd shouted a few swearwords, which made her dad jump off the couch, where he slept, and race to the kitchen. By then, Angel had everything under control and she'd smeared butter on the nickel-size blister the way her mother taught her.

"Oh, no, Angel-babe, that's an old wives' tale. Using butter on a burn can actually lead to infection," he'd said. "Go rinse that off and we'll put some antiseptic ointment on it."

Like he was a mother. How did he know?

Twelve was a sucky age, Angel decided. People expect you to be "responsible" but they don't give you any responsibility.

On the way home from Dr. Donna's that afternoon, she'd asked her dad to drop her off at the mall to do some shopping. "The mall?" he'd croaked in this frog-like voice.

"Yeah, that big place north of town with shops in it. Remember?"

"Alone?" His voice turned dark and serious. Not a good sign.

"Well, it's not like I have a whole lot of friends to hang out with."

He pretended to be too busy driving to look her in the eye. "Dr. Donna told us Abby and her contractor friend are at the house, remember?"

Angel knew an excuse when she heard one. She sulked in the corner, sucking on a hunk of hair.

"Maybe Maria could take you shopping next week," he suggested, a few miles later.

Like Maria wanted to hang out with a twelve-year-old at the mall. Angel liked Maria a lot, but she had a baby on the way. Angel didn't think she'd be up for any serious shopping in the near future.

"Forget it," she snarled with enough volume to make Heather squirm even closer to their dad. Out of sheer spite, Angel pinched her sister on the meaty part of her thigh. The little twit howled like a puppy caught in barbed wire.

For a second, Angel thought her father might raise his hand to her, something he'd never done before. Her heart pounded so loud she couldn't hear the damn country-western music on the radio. But he didn't. His knuckles were white against the cracked black steering wheel, but they relaxed after a minute. He ruffled Heather's hair and told her, "Grumpy people aren't much fun, are they? Sorry you got caught in the middle of our disagreement, punkin. Your sister will apologize, too, right after she gets done mucking out the foaling stall in the barn."

Remembering, Angel grimaced as she nibbled on the grainy eraser of the mechanical pencil. So far, her dad hadn't mentioned the chore again, but that was probably because Abby was here.

I wish Janey were home, Angel thought. Dad listens to Janey. A twinge of guilt made Angel frown. Janey was in the hospital fighting breast cancer. Angel's mother would have scolded her for worrying about her own problems when Janey was fighting for her life. Lesley took breast cancer very seriously. Every October, Angel and her mother ran in the annual Breast Cancer Awareness marathon at Pismo Beach. They did the short run, but still, they made lots of money for a good cause.

Angel thought about this coming October. Who would take her this year? Dad? Not likely. He hated jogging and seemed to get embarrassed if a woman in a bra ad showed up on television. Val? He always told her mother his idea of helping was writing a check. Janey? Angel knew two women from her mother's aerobics class who were breast cancer survivors, but they told her it took them a full year to get back on their feet.

An image of Abby crossed her mind, but Angel brushed it away. Abby was temporary—here for the short term, like Dr. Donna. Once Angel and Heather were better, Abby would move on to the next family in need. That's what Abby herself said when Angel asked about her work.

"I help people get back to the business of living, then I slip into the background so they can get on with their lives," she'd said, frankly.

"You never see them again?"

Abby seemed to read some concern into Angel's question where there was none. Angel was just curious, that was all. "I still get Christmas cards from some of my old clients. I bump into others from time to time and we catch up a little, but it's hard to keep track of all the people I've worked with over the years. It's just the nature of the job."

We're just a job to her, Angel reminded herself as she picked up the sheet of paper with measurements scribbled on it.

Two nights ago, she and Heather and their dad went to Janey and Ed's to measure a set of twin beds. The maple headboards looked boyish, but Dad said he would paint them any color she and Heather wanted.

"I want purple," Heather said.

Angel pretended to gag. "You have absolutely no taste. Nada. Zero. Zip."

The little twit started to cry as if her heart was broken. "I can too taste," she said through her sobs.

Their dad kinda laughed, but he told Angel sternly, "She's only five, Angel-babe. You probably didn't have the greatest taste in the world either when you were five.''

''Maybe not, but the only person we can ask about that is dead, isn't she?'' Angel had no idea what made her say that.

Her dad looked stunned, but she didn't hang around for him to say anything. She threw down the measuring tape and ran back to the house. Later, when he carried Heather to bed, Angel pretended to be asleep, even though she wanted to crawl into his arms and cry. She stayed rigid, knowing even one movement would be her undoing.

CHAPTER FIVE

"IT'S A FINE LITTLE MACHINE, Tom," Maria said, closing the door of his new microwave oven—that morning's Wal-Mart purchase. She pushed the appropriate buttons and the unit began to hum. A gleaming white mini-iceberg in a sea of rummage-sale castoffs, it was the result of her very gentle nagging. "I'm so glad you bought it. Now the girls can heat up my tamales without so much fuss and bother."

Tom and Miguel were seated at Tom's kitchen table, waiting to sample nachos. The table, with its fake gray-marble top and molded aluminum sides and tubular legs was a long-ago hand-me-down from his parents. Janey told Tom she'd seen one just like it wearing a two-hundred-dollar price tag at an antique store.

"Your tamales are the only reason I bought the machine," Tom said. Maria had promised to keep his freezer stocked if he'd move into the twentieth century.

Tom took a deep satisfying breath. The aroma of chilies, cilantro and tomatillos stewing together with chunks of pork made his mouth water. Chili verde bubbled on the hot plate—the next archaic monster to go, if Maria had her way. When she called Tom that morning, she'd promised him a little "fiesta." Tom was still waiting to hear the reason for the celebration. Although he'd tried several times throughout the day to pry it out of Miguel, the young Hispanic man was the most close-mouthed person he knew.

"Well," Tom said, leaning across the table, "when are you going to tell me?"

Miguel, his dark eyes twinkling, said something to his wife in Spanish—too fast for Tom to catch.

Maria left her preparations and joined them. A petite five foot two inches, she carried what looked like far too much baby. Tom pulled out a chair for her, and she sat down with a sigh.

A moment later, after some silent signal from her husband, she said, "Miguel has a job offer in Modesto. In the city parks department, where his brother, Gonzalvo, works. It's union, Tom. Full benefits and holidays." She delivered the news solemnly, for she knew, as Tom did, this good news for the Fuentes family was sad news for him.

He reached deep to find the enthusiasm they deserved. "That's fantastic, amigo. You won't have to run out in the middle of the night to wade through irrigation ditches and hassle with foolish cows and ornery horses. Is there a place for me, too?"

The young couple laughed, all tension gone. Tom wanted the best for them and this sounded like a terrific opportunity.

"This way I'll be able to go back to junior college sooner and finish my degree," Maria said, wiping her hands on her calico-print apron. "We have tons of family around there to help with the baby.

"Miguel's uncle has a place for us to rent. The tenants are moving to Idaho. It's not as nice as your house, and I'll miss my garden, but you can't have everything."

Tom toasted with his can of Tecate. "To good fortune

in Modesto. May you only know success and happiness.''

Maria jabbed the hem of her apron to her eyes as she rose and hurried back to the cauldron. Tom discovered his appetite gone.

He rose and walked to the sink where Maria stood staring out the small square window. A hint of twilight filtered through the walnut trees. He touched her shoulder. "I'm happy for you, Maria. Really. We'll miss you, but…''

"Just my cooking.''

He turned her around to face him, moved by the traces of tears on her smooth cheeks. "Your wisdom and patience and girl talk and womanly touches.'' He pointed to the cheerful rose-print curtains she'd made for the window. "You've helped so much. We'll miss much more than your cooking.''

"It's not that far,'' she said in a rush. "And Miguel will be back to help with the horses.''

The horses. Tom and Miguel's breeding program was still in an embryonic stage. Miguel handled the halter breaking and early-stage training—some of which required almost daily attention. "It'll work out. Don't worry. We'll come see you all the time. How else will the girls be able to spoil that little bambino?'' He gently patted her very rounded belly.

She shooed him away to finish the preparations. "Angel. Heather,'' she called. "Are you ready to learn how to make tortillas?''

The two let out whoops of affirmation as they dashed from their spots on the sagging sofa. Tom wandered over to the television where the video, *Chitty Chitty Bang Bang*—another ''loaner'' from Abby—was playing. He pushed the off button and eyed the room critically. Tiny flip-flops poked out from between the faded burgundy cushions of the sofa. On the end table a mound of books—a combination of schoolbooks, paperbacks and prereaders—clustered around the base of the lamp like a carelessly laid bonfire. Pretty-pink doll paraphernalia, the origin and purpose of which he had not a clue, lay strung out from one end of the coffee table to the other. The room had never looked more lived in, or alive.

Maybe everything in life is a trade-off, he thought. His well-structured life was history, but he had board games and Barbie dolls to replace it. His friends were moving on, but that was life.

"Daddy," a sweet voice chirped, making his heart catch in his chest. "Come try my tortilla. I made it just for you."

A tear started to form but he blinked it away. This was a celebration.

Later, as Tom leaned back in his chair, stuffed to the gills, Maria said, "You know, Tom, this new job won't start until August, but we could move in with my cousin if you and the girls want to move into your house."

Before Tom could reply, Angel said, "We're building a new bedroom and bathroom and we get to decorate it ourselves, don't we, Dad?"

She didn't wait for his answer, but told Maria, "In our old house, my mom had some lady come in and do the decorating. She picked out everything. Bedspreads, curtains, paint. It was okay and all, but this will be more like our own."

Tom noticed the enthusiasm in her voice. He hadn't realized how important this was to her, and he vowed to make sure the new rooms turned out right. "Go get the sketches, honey, and show them to Maria while Miguel and I clean up.''

After washing the few pots and pans and bowls, Tom and Miguel slipped outside. They wandered toward the horse corral that would soon have to be moved. For five years Tom had slept with the sounds of young mares snuffling about outside his window. It had meant more dust and flies than he liked, but the gentle night noises were a comfort, too.

The lack of a moon made the night inky black. The barn's bluish-green vapor light and the yellowish glow of the bug zapper near Ed's patio shone like ancient beacons. After the warmth of the dishwater, the air temperature seemed a shade too cool. Tom rolled down the sleeves of his shirt. It wouldn't be long before summer set in for good. Another change.

''Lots of changes,'' Miguel said as if reading Tom's mind.

''Too many for an old coot like me.''

Miguel made a motion toward Tom's haircut. ''You started from the top down, I see.''

Tom had fielded his share of razzing the past two days. Johnny Dee nearly swallowed his chaw when he bumped into Tom at the feed store. Maria faked a swoon when she first saw it. Miguel, as usual, had kept his opinions to himself.

''Gotta start someplace, I guess.''

With small, economical motions, Miguel rolled a cigarette and lit it. He inhaled deeply, savoring his vice, which he'd promised to give up by the time the baby arrived. ''Sometimes I think I'm going to miss this more than…the other. How did you do it?''

Tom didn't answer. His thoughts were elsewhere. *I wonder what Abby is doing.* Maria said she'd invited her to join them tonight, but she was busy. Busy with work? Or busy socially? A woman as attractive as Abby would surely have a long list of suitors.

Miguel punched him on the arm. "How did you do it?" he repeated.

"I...I never smoked."

Miguel's eyebrows rose together. "Not the smoking, the sex. How did you manage when your wife said you had to wait until after the baby is born?"

Tom bit back a smile. Lesley had wanted a massage every night, and Tom was happy to be of service because he loved the feel of her soft, supple skin stretched taut over the new life she carried. He found it extremely erotic, but she didn't. "Thanks," she'd say then roll over and go to sleep, leaving Tom to deal with his problem any way he chose. "Leather helped."

Choking, Miguel nearly swallowed his cigarette.

Tom patted his back with gusto. "Tooling leather. Saddles, bridles, belts. It kept my mind off other things. I made three saddlebags, sixteen belts and a purse for my mother. I've got the tools in the barn if you want them."

Exchanging ribald jests about who was the better leather tooler, the men returned to the porch where Maria was waiting. She scolded Miguel gently in Spanish then leaned over to give Tom a peck on the cheek. "I'm sorry Abby couldn't make it. You need some female companionship."

"I have two female companions who keep me very busy, thank you."

She made a face. "You know what I mean. Abby is the best person I know, next to you, maybe."

Miguel made a huffing sound and she cupped her

husband's face lovingly. "Other people, *mio*. No one compares to you. You know that."

Tom's heart felt heavy as he watched them drive away. It was difficult not to envy them their closeness, their love. He missed that part the most, he thought, even more than sex. He missed having another person with whom to share his innermost thoughts.

Maybe someday. Blending a family wasn't easy under any circumstances, but given his daughters' traumatic experience, it would take a truly special woman to handle this challenge.

ABBY HAD NEVER REGARDED herself as a clock-watcher, but this had to be the slowest Thursday on record. Granted, this was the first day of the Butler girls' foray into the Rainbows program, but since that didn't directly involve Abby, she saw no reason why it should keep popping up in her mind.

"Melina," she called out as familiar footsteps trotted past her doorway, "where's the Yang file?"

"In your Out basket, of course. Where is your head today?"

The exasperation in her friend's tone made Abby groan. "In my Out basket, obscuring the Yang file."

As she reached for the file, the phone rang.

"Abby Davis."

"Abby. I'm in trouble."

The breathless voice was Tom's. Her heart punched toward her throat. "Are you okay? Are the girls—"

He cut her off. "Nothing like that. I just ran in from the barn. One of my mares is foaling and there's a problem. The vet's on the way, but I can't leave and the girls are supposed to be in Fresno in an hour, and I kinda hoped you..."

With her heartbeat back to normal, Abby could respond. "I'll drive them."

"Are you sure? I know you're busy, but Maria's in Modesto and—"

"Tom, get off the phone so I can leave." She started to hang up, but his silence made her hesitate.

"I really do appreciate this," he said.

Abby's heart started jumping around again. That voice. That honest, heartfelt, tender appreciation did things to her she couldn't explain.

"Good luck with your mare. I'll be there in fifteen minutes."

She slipped the receiver back in place while shoveling two hours' worth of paperwork into her briefcase. She was halfway out the door when another body tried squeezing past her. "Daniel," Abby exclaimed, drawing her briefcase between them defensively. "Is it important? I have to run. The Butler children need..."

His cologne, probably more expensive than her mother's perfume, filled her nostrils, making her lose her train of thought.

"You mean that cowboy's kids?"

Something about his tone made Abby's hackles rise, but she nodded, not wanting to get into it.

"Abby, I've come to the decision you're too busy for your own good. Every time I call over here you're in family court or at a deposition or in the law library or with clients or meeting with contractors and draftsmen. You need a little downtime."

His concern seemed genuine, but since he was mostly to blame for her frenetic schedule she didn't answer.

"Have dinner with me Friday."

"Tomorrow?" Abby asked, her voice was a squeak.

"Yes. We'll drive up to Bass Lake. Have you ever eaten at Ducie's? It overlooks the lake. Very peaceful."

She'd been there with Landon. The setting was peaceful…and romantic.

"I'll pick you up early so we can take our time driving up. Say, five-thirty? Will that give you enough time to get home and change?"

As he well knew—since he approved her schedule— Abby ate lunch at her desk all week to be able to leave early on Fridays. "I always leave at four on Fridays."

"Great. See you then." He left with a casual touch on her shoulder.

Her equilibrium reeled—whether from the cologne or the railroading, she wasn't sure.

"Not a good idea, kiddo," Melina said, poking her head out of the adjoining office.

"It sure as hell wasn't mine."

Abby didn't wait to hear more. She had something to do. Something important. She and Donna had researched the Tomorrow's Rainbows program when it started up. They both recognized the validity of peer counseling—the kind of empathy adults couldn't give.

She got in her car. As she turned the key, an errant thought crossed her mind. Does Tom wear cologne? The only scents she could associate with him were fresh air, old leather and something utterly masculine she was sure couldn't be found in a bottle. She liked it a great deal more than Daniel's expensive cologne.

"THAT'S BOGUS and you know it," Angel ranted, anger making her voice crack.

Her father hung up the phone and looked at her, obviously trying to be patient. Angel didn't care. She had no intention of putting herself on the line with a bunch of strangers. It was bad enough having to be all perfect and chipper for Dr. Donna, who had an uncanny way of seeing through her mask to make Angel own up to feelings she'd have preferred to ignore.

"You like Abby," her father said. "She gave you that TV and VCR."

"Big whoop," Angel said, kicking off her scruffy mules and drawing her knees to her chest. She hadn't bothered changing out of her sweat pants and nightshirt because she saw how preoccupied her dad was with his horse and she was sure he'd forget about that stupid Rainbows thing.

"I don't want to go without you, either, Daddy," Heather said, showing surprising fortitude in the midst of the shouting match. Usually, the little dork would hide out in the bedroom whenever Angel and their dad got into it.

Angel reached for her soda can, but the couch cushions sank in the middle, throwing off her balance. The can wobbled, spilling soda on her wrist and fingers. "Damn ugly couch," she cursed. "Cheap piece of crap. Everything sucks in this house."

She regretted the words as soon as they left her mouth. Heather's mouth opened and closed like a guppy.

Her dad heaved a sigh, making Angel feel even more guilty—and mad. It wasn't her fault this stupid house was too small and had old furniture and crappy television reception. She didn't want to be here. She didn't want to be in the big house in Riverside with Val, either, but that wasn't the issue at the moment.

"C'mere, punkin," her father said, scooping up Heather in his arms as he headed for the door. "Angel, put down that book and follow me."

Oh, fuck. What now? she thought, laying her vampire novel on the floor so it wouldn't soak up any soda, and sticking her feet back into her slippers.

"I don't have a choice in this matter," he said, hurrying toward the barn. "But you do. Abby is on her way. She'll drive you to the meeting, wait for you and drive you home. I want to take you, but I can't. I have to help Blaze through this birth. I can't make you go, but I want you to."

"Mom wouldn't have made us go to another city with a stranger," Angel said, knowing her words were blatant manipulation, but if it worked…

"Dr. Jessup told you this peer-counseling thing is something that might help you years from now and can really help when you go to school and people ask you questions about what happened to your mom. I know how important this is and I know I should be the one to take you…"

He's gonna cave. Angel couldn't keep a triumphant smirk from her lips.

Her dad chose that minute to look back at her. She immediately wiped the smile off her face but it was too late. She could tell by the narrowing of his eyes. He speeded up, making her have to trot to keep up—not an easy thing to do in bedroom slippers. Little pebbles kept getting caught under her arches, making her cry out. Her dad ignored her plight.

When they reached the stall in the barn, he sat Heather atop a stack of bales not far from the spot where her stupid kittens lived. He pointed at a second bale and gave Angel a squinty-eyed look that made her stomach tighten nervously. He was really upset. The last time he was this upset with her was the summer before last when she and one of the migrant kids dumped half a bag of concrete in a mud puddle to make adobe bricks. The lye flew up in the kid's eyes and he pitched such a fit you'd have thought he was gonna die. Her dad made her clean it all up wearing big rubber gloves. The worst part was that by then the damn stuff was hard as bricks and twice as heavy.

"Sit," he ordered.

In one neat leap, he cleared the stall gate and resumed his examination of the horse. She was breathing hard and looked really tired. Angel liked horses and felt sorry for the struggling animal, but she wasn't above using the situation to keep from going to Fresno.

"She looks bad," Angel said, choosing an empty bucket, which she turned upside down, for her stool.

"Abby will be here in ten minutes," he said. "Blaze may die in that time, but you two are going to sit still and listen to me."

Angel crossed one knee over the other and drew a few strands of hair between her lips. She knew it bugged him, but that was fine with her. The last thing she wanted was to listen to some stupid story of his.

Normally, she loved his stories—he used to tell her a story every night before bed when she came to stay with him in the summer, but lately his stories all sounded more like lectures. Everything had turned so damn serious since her mother died. Nobody laughed anymore—except Abby. She was almost too damn bubbly. Angel wasn't sure if she liked Abby or not, but she knew she didn't want to ride all the way to Fresno with her. Maybe to go to the mall or something, but not to some disgusting group piss 'n moan session.

"When I was thirteen," her father said, still examining the mare, "I decided I was going to be the next world-champion roper. I had a pair of boots, some old gloves my dad threw out and a rope I found in the garbage dump. My friend, Marty Smith, lived down the road and his dad had a bunch of horses. He let us ride a couple.''

He looked over his shoulder. Angel checked her hair for split ends. Her mother always trimmed her hair. Who's going to trim my hair? she wondered, feeling the beginnings of a stomachache. She'd had a lot of those lately.

Her dad went on with his story. ''One old chestnut gelding knew a lot more about roping than I did and I worked with him every day after school. I got to be pretty good, and Marty wasn't half-bad, either.

''We entered the junior roping event in Chowchilla. Marty's dad hauled the horses into town. My mom sewed me a fancy shirt with mother-of-pearl snaps. I felt like I could rope anything that moved—my dog, Homer, was afraid to come out from under the porch 'cause I'd rope him.''

Heather giggled; Angel hid her smile behind her hair.

''When we got signed up, I discovered Marty was roping off my horse, which wasn't mine at all, of course. I was madder than hops, but what could I do? They called my name, and I hopped up on the strange horse. When they let go of the calf, I kicked that horse and flew out the gate and proceeded to rope myself right out of the saddle. I fell in a heap right in front of the grandstand.''

Angel had been to enough ropings to picture it. She couldn't keep from laughing. The mare made a noise that sounded like a person in pain. Her dad massaged the horse's bulging belly with slow, circular motions.

''Poor Daddy. You lost,'' Heather said sympathetically.

Angel flashed her a look of contempt. Talk about stating the obvious. "That sucks, Dad. I would have died of embarrassment," Angel admitted.

Her dad gave her a look that said she would have won the prize if there was one. The tightness around her heart lifted some. She really liked it when he looked at her like that.

"I hid out till Monday, then my mom made me go to school. I had to face Marty, who won my trophy on my horse, and all my friends who saw me eat dirt."

Angel wanted to ask but locked her lips together until Heather asked, "What happened?"

"We had a test in English. I got a B, I think."

"With your friends," Angel exclaimed. God, he could be so dense sometimes. "Did they laugh at you?"

He stopped rubbing the mare and looked at her. "Nope. Marty even came up to me and apologized. Said the trophy should have been mine."

The barn grew silent except for the mare's labored breathing.

Finally, giving in to curiosity, Angel asked, "What's that got to do with us going to this Rainbows thing?"

"I think you're afraid to face these other kids. I was afraid, too, but I found out my fears were a lot worse than reality.

"And, believe it or not, that was the day your mama moved to town. She was just a little bitty thing, three grades younger than me, but she was so pretty all the boys were talking about her. And she smiled at me. Not Marty. Me."

In the distance, the dogs began to bark. Angel's heart jumped. Don't let it be Abby. Not yet. I know I should go, but...

"Doc's here, girl, hang on," Tom whispered to the horse.

He stepped to the gate and looked at first Heather, then her. "Much as I want to, I can't take you girls to Fresno. Abby'll be here any minute. Whether you go with her or not is up to you. I can't make that decision for you, but I hope you'll go."

Angel scowled, not saying a word. She hated it when parents did this—made something her decision, as if he knew all along she'd do the right thing. Heather popped up to her knees and said, "Mommy showed me your picture with all your trophies and your pretty horse. I guess you got better, huh?"

Tom winked at her. "Yep, I did."

"I'm getting better, too, aren't I, Daddy? I didn't wet the bed last night." She looked at Angel, as if waiting for some signal, then she jumped to the ground. "I'll go with Abby, Daddy. Dr. Donna says we'll play games and sing songs like at my old preschool. She'd be sad if I didn't go, even sadder than you. Bye, Daddy. Hope your horsey feels better."

Angel watched her skip off.

"Dork," she muttered under her breath. She looked through the sheet of hair hanging in her eyes. Just as she expected, her dad was giving her that look of expectation, as if he'd be real let down if she didn't do the right thing.

"All right," she growled, scrambling to her feet. "I'll go, but if it sucks as bad as I think it's gonna suck— I'm outta there, even if I have to walk back." She stalked off without waiting for his reply. If she was gonna hang out with a bunch of kids, even loser freaks whose families were more screwed up than hers, she had to look good.

No TEAR TRACKS, but no smiles, either, Abby thought, watching her young charges exit the door of the hospital meeting room.

"Hey, girls," Abby said, rising stiffly. She'd paced for a while but then managed to immerse herself in work until her butt conformed to the molded-plastic chair.

Angel took Heather's hand and tugged her toward Abby. The twelve-year-old moved dully, with none of her usual verve.

"Ice cream," Abby said decisively. "Grammy always said ice cream was the best thing for a girl's troubles. I think she meant boy troubles, but it'll work for this, too. Let's go. I know just the place."

Abby cut across the still-familiar streets of her old hometown and pulled into a busy parking lot. A pink-and-white storefront spilled a welcoming glow into the dim twilight.

After placing their order, Abby led them to an outside table, sheltered from the cool breeze and noisy traffic by five-foot-tall panels of clear Plexiglas. Fresh air. No hospital smell. She passed out plastic spoons and napkins. "Are you sure one banana split is enough for all three of us?"

Angel smiled for the first time. "I'm not too hungry."

"Okay. Hot-fudge sundaes next time." *If there is a next time. If I don't blow it.* Abby felt way out of her league. This was Donna's job. Abby was a rookie.

A tinny voice crackled her name over a loudspeaker, and Abby jumped. *Ice cream! What was I thinking? I should have driven them straight home. They need their dad. So do I.*

Later, as three spoons dipped into the small, plastic boat of whipped cream, nuts and chocolate-swirl ice cream, Abby asked, "Do you miss the city?"

"Well, duh," Angel said with typical adolescent authority. "Who wouldn't? There's all this cool stuff to do and places to go. Like the mall. And all these cool guys."

"Like Jeremy Shmeramy," Heather teased in a sing-song manner.

Angel glared at her, but Heather appeared impervious, perhaps feeling safe in the company of strangers.

"I grew up in this city," Abby told them. "It wasn't quite so big then." She looked up, trying to spot a star through the umbrella of urban lights. "I don't think I could ever move back, even if my folks were still living here. The noise, the traffic." She sighed. "Actually, I envy you living in the country."

"My mom hated the ranch," Angel said. "She said the dust and the animals were much worse than smog."

"Real Daddy says my kitty gets to live in the house, but his brothers and sisters have to live in the barn and eat mice," Heather said, apropos of nothing.

Before Abby could comment on her odd name for Tom, Angel reached across the table and shoved her sister's shoulder, sending a glob of mushy ice cream to the floor. "I told you not to call him that anymore," she seethed. "We don't have two dads anymore. Only one. Can't you get that through your thick head?"

Big tears filled Heather's blue eyes and tumbled down her cheeks. In a small voice that broke Abby's heart, she said, "And no mommy, right?"

CHAPTER SIX

ONE LOOK was all Tom needed to send his heart plummeting.

"Bad, huh?" he asked, pulling Angel into a swallowing hug. That she went with no resistance spoke volumes.

She nodded, her long hair getting squeezed in the fold of his arms. "Ouch."

He loosened his hold and eased back, looking into her eyes. "Want to talk about it?"

She grimaced and shook her head. "I just wanna go to bed. Heather slept the whole way, but Mom always said the copilot's job is to keep the pilot awake." She looked over her shoulder at Abby. "I didn't mean that you'd fall asleep. I just..."

Abby brushed aside her apology with an understanding smile. "You're a terrific copilot. Now, go to bed. Sleep well. You deserve it."

Tom watched his daughter shuffle off like a beaten old woman. "Good grief," he whispered. "What did they do to my girls?"

"It's...everything...I guess...just...coming...together."

Tom spun toward her, expecting to find her in a heap on the floor, but she stood rigidly, as if any movement might be her undoing. Without thinking, he took her elbow and guided her to a chair at the kitchen table.

"Coffee. I'll heat up a cup right after I put Heather to bed. Sit. Stay." As soon as he was sure his instructions had penetrated the fog that enveloped her, he dashed to the Honda. Heather sat propped upright by the seat belt with Abby's sweater under her head. He eased open the door and unfastened the seat belt, then lifted his sleeping child.

Dead to the world, Heather didn't open an eye when he carried her into the bedroom and stripped off her stretchy pants and Tigger T-shirt. He left her in underpants and undershirt—knowing there'd be a change of sheets to worry about in the morning—and pulled up the spread, making sure her favorite stuffed rabbit was nearby. He kissed her cheek, noting the traces of dried tears.

An arrow of guilt twisted in his heart. "I love you both," he whispered, then withdrew, leaving the door ajar.

Abby apparently didn't know how to follow instructions. He found her standing in front of his new microwave, seemingly mesmerized by the slowly turning carousel inside the brightly lit box.

"New microwave?" she asked, her back to him.

"Maria threatened to cut off our tamale supply if I didn't buy one. And, I hate to admit it, but the darned thing is handy."

The bell's clang made her jump. He reached around her, being careful not to spook her. "Sit down. I'll carry these cups to the table. You look wiped out, too. What happened?"

He watched the effort it took for her to gather together her reserves. "I see victims at all stages of recovery. I deal with pain and heartbreak every day. I'm a professional," she said, emphasizing the word in a tone that made Tom's eyebrows rise. "I don't understand why this hit me so hard."

She pivoted on the heel of her crepe-soled loafers and walked to the table, but Tom sensed she was on the verge of walking out the door. He waited, hot cups steaming in each hand.

She plopped down in the chair like someone awaiting execution.

Tom set the coffee mug in front of her. "Cream? Sugar? Whiskey?"

A flickering smile almost caught on her lips but faded away.

He pulled out a chair and straddled it so he could look at her. Such a complicated lady. A stranger really, but a person he'd trusted with his most precious treasures, his daughters. What did that say about her? About him?

"I really let the girls down today," he said, taking a sip of the steaming, hours-old liquid. Its acidic bite felt good. "It was one of the hardest things I've ever done."

She looked up, immediately focusing on his pain, as he knew she would. "Being a single parent is the toughest job there is," she said with feeling.

"But what does it tell kids when their dad chooses a horse over them?" He'd wrestled with his guilt all afternoon and still didn't have an answer.

She took a sip of coffee after lightly blowing on it. Lesley always did that, too. "You'll talk about it tomorrow. They'll talk about it with Donna. They'll understand. If not right away, then someday...when they're parents."

He sighed, feeling years older than he had that morning. "Is it always gonna be this tough?"

A strangled sound, half laugh, half cry, slipped out

before she clapped her hand over her mouth. "You're asking the wrong person. I blew it and I'm the professional here."

"What do you mean you blew it?"

She took a deep breath and let it out slowly. "I could tell how frazzled the girls were after the session. It can get pretty intense right at first. Donna and I sat in on the inaugural session last year, and that first day I left feeling flogged—and I was just an observer. Everybody's in pain or denial or acting out—it's a little overwhelming, but in a good way because there's also a sense of relief knowing you can say anything and nobody will shut you down or try to minimize what you're feeling.

"Gradually, the individuals in the group begin to bond and form a cohesiveness, but right at first you're alone and people are asking you to put your fears and pain out there for everyone to see. Very scary stuff."

Tom watched, mesmerized, knowing she was revealing truths about herself she might not even realize.

"Would it have made a difference if I'd been there?"

"Yes." Bald, honest. Typical Abby. "Not in group, of course. They're on their own then. But afterward. You would have handled that better than me. I took them for ice cream." Her tone suggested she'd taken them to a porno flick.

"What's wrong with that? It sounds very nice. Thank you."

She shook her head sadly. "They were wiped out. They needed to be home with their dad. They didn't need some lame placebo. Shows you how much I know about mothering."

"Abby, what happened?"

She stared into her cup. "We were sharing a banana

split and talking about living in the city versus living in the country. They'd loosened up a little and even smiled once or twice. Then Heather said something Angel took exception to and...things went to hell in a handbasket, as my grammy used to say. Just like that they were both in tears and I...I was mopping up spilt ice cream, for heaven's sake. I didn't know what to say or how to help.

"Angel ran to the car, and I grabbed Heather and charged after her even though I knew she was embarrassed and wanted to be alone, but I couldn't let her be alone outside. Fresno's a big city and I know what happens to kids when..." She shuddered and looked away. "It was a disaster and it was all my fault. I knew they were emotionally spent and I should have driven them straight home and avoided the whole calamity. I'm sorry, Tom. You trusted me with your children and I blew it."

Tom's heart twisted precariously. He could fall for this woman who cared so deeply. He could fall hard.

"Come here," he said, standing up abruptly. "I want to show you something."

She followed without protest, even when he picked up a flashlight from beside the door and led her outside. She crossed her arms protectively against the mild evening chill. "Cold?" he asked.

She shook her head.

Liar. He took hold of her elbow—for safety's sake, he told himself—and guided her to the barn. She didn't speak, but Tom felt her tension.

"Life is funny," he said quietly, opening the door of the barn. The hinges groaned their usual protest, and nearby a dog gave a muffled bark. "Here I am kicking myself for being the world's worst dad..." He made a *tsk*ing sound when she started to protest. "And you're feeling bad because you couldn't stop two kids from having a spat.'' He couldn't help chuckling. ''We're a heck of a pair.''

She pulled away. Maybe she thought he was trivializing her dilemma.

He flicked off the flashlight; a heating lamp glowed softly within the cavern of one stall. He led her to the light.

''Oh,'' she cried softly. ''They both made it. Look at that beautiful baby. Oh, thank God.''

''And you.''

She shook her head firmly, sending tears tumbling.

''Abby,'' he said, wishing she'd look at him, but she kept her focus trained on the horses, ''if it hadn't been for you, I would have taken the girls—they are my top priority. I'd have left Blaze to fend for herself. Maybe Doc could have saved her alone, maybe not. It's a pretty safe bet the colt would have died. You gave me an option, which I took. Maybe it wasn't the right choice, but it's what I thought I had to do. The girls have to learn about life on a ranch. This is more than just our livelihood, it's our way of life. The animals are important, and an animal in pain hurts just as much as you or me.''

He watched her profile in the gentle glow. Her features were relaxed, softer somehow, as she watched the new mother standing guard over her tiny baby. He imagined what effect the light would have on her eyes. They'd probably reflect the golden light like a harvest moon in a bottomless pool. Tom's fingers itched to reach out, brush back the lock of red satin that framed her jaw, and make her look at him.

Get a hold, man. You're not a kid. You're an adult. He gripped the flashlight, willing himself not to draw her into his arms and kiss her. The night had held enough emotional turbulence for both of them.

He cleared his throat. "I did what I had to do. You went above and beyond the call of duty. What more can anybody ask?"

She didn't respond but Tom thought she seemed less distraught. "Besides," he said, smiling, "you mostly see the girls when they're on their best behavior. Those two fight all the time. They're sisters."

She rewarded him with a grateful smile. "Thank you. I probably overreacted. I've been a little stressed lately. Work, my boss..."

"No, thank *you*. For taking them, for caring, for everything." Despite his resolve, he gave her a hug. Knowing he had to cut his losses, he dropped his arms and turned away. "I'll walk you to your car." With that, they left the confines of the barn and moved toward her vehicle.

Tom aimed the beam of the flashlight on the door handle of the Honda, but she opened it before he could reach it. She slipped behind the steering wheel. Looking up at him, she said, "Talk to the girls. If I truly didn't blow this too badly, I'd be happy to drive to Rainbows anytime you need me." She smiled, an honest, Abby smile. "Believe it or not, Thursdays are my slow day, so I'm usually available. Just give me a call."

Her generosity and bravery touched him profoundly. After tonight's experience, Tom couldn't imagine any woman—except possibly Janey—who would have volunteered so freely. "I will."

When she started to close the door, he held it open. "I forgot to ask. What was the fight about?"

Turning away to reach for her keys, she mumbled, "I don't remember."

She tugged the door closed and gave him a quick wave.

"Liar," he said, when Rosie materialized at his knee. Reaching down to scratch the old dog behind the ear, he told her, "She'd be terrible at poker."

"WELL, HELLO THERE, my long-lost love goddess. Long time no see."

Abby grinned at Max Jessup's effusive greeting. She went into his burly open arms and returned his hug with true affection, giggling when he tried nuzzling his bushy salt-and-pepper beard in her neck. "Hi, Max. Good to see you."

"Are you two at it again?" a familiar voice asked from the entrance of the foyer. "Max, it's Sunday. Bring her inside before you scandalize the neighborhood."

Donna's teasing and her husband's warm greeting lifted a load from Abby's shoulders that had been weighing her down for the past two days. "God, it's nice to be here. Sanctuary. No phones. No people." She hurried to give her friend a hug of equal proportion.

"What are we, chopped liver?" Max asked, his latent New York accent filtering through the laid-back California humor.

"Friends. Much better than people."

"Hmm." He gave his wife an inscrutable look and told Abby, "I'll catch you at dinner, sugarplum. I've got a little project in the garage that needs my attention. You two lovelies will have to try to get along without me for a couple of hours."

His wife of twenty-some years snorted.

"What sort of project this time?" Abby asked. Max was a high-school teacher who always managed to find a kid in jeopardy and an old jalopy in need of repair and somehow fix them both in the restoration process.

"Fifty-six Ford," he said, grabbing a handful of chocolate-covered peanuts from a cut-glass candy dish sitting on an antique sewing-machine cabinet. Donna's house was filled to the brim with an eclectic jumble of antiques, collectibles and junk. Abby's mother called it Decorating's Black Hole, where all the lost and untreasured went to die.

"And a sixteen-year-old habitual truant," Donna added under her breath.

"He just needed the right teacher," her husband replied. "Why, he only missed three days of school this week, not counting Monday, which was an in-service day."

"Which means he was in school one day?" Abby asked, grinning.

"Yep."

Donna slapped his fingers when he tried for another handful of candy. "We're on a diet, remember? Go get greasy. I know you're never quite happy without grease under your fingernails."

"Diet, schmiet," he said, sneaking two little chunks. "You are perfect just as you are, my sweet. Isn't she perfect, Abby?"

He blew them both kisses then hurried down the hallway toward the garage.

Donna watched him; Abby watched her. What would it be like to be that comfortable with another person for so long? She'd give anything to know, and yet a part of her felt as though her chance of ever having that closeness was inching away each day. Or, in Daniel's case, inching too close every day.

"Let's get a beer and go outside," Donna suggested.

"Max said he'd grill the fish later, and I already made a salad, so we can just sit back and relax."

Abby smiled. "Just what the doctor ordered."

Donna poured two Coronas into chilled mugs and added a wedge of lime before handing one to Abby. "After your call Thursday night, I was afraid you might have committed hara-kiri before I got to see you."

Abby shrugged sheepishly. "Slight overreaction, I think. You said the girls were fine when you saw them on Friday, right?"

Donna pushed open the sliding glass doors and led the way to a shady spot beneath the veranda. A kidney-shaped pool and a molded fiberglass spa, housed in a redwood gazebo, competed for space in Donna's mini–rain forest backyard. With a big heart and too much work, she couldn't be bothered with pruning and trimming.

She dropped into a large, cushioned Adirondack chair and nodded for Abby to join her in its mate. "Heather and Angel looked great. Very rested and peppy. Their father, on the other hand, looked a lot like you. Gaunt. Bags under his eyes. Tense. Are you two trying to outdo eachother for guilt trip of the century?"

Abby sat down, drawing her bare legs under her. After her third sleepless night in a row, she'd tried to resume her usual Sunday-morning ritual: bagels and cappuccino then weeding and watering her garden. For some reason, the peace she usually found in the earthy flora of her small backyard escaped her.

"Angel called me Friday after work," she told Donna. "She apologized for screaming at her sister in public and making me feel bad. I asked her if her dad made her call me and she said, 'No, but he left your card by the phone when he and Heather went to town to buy groceries.' Wasn't that sweet?''

''She respects you for not telling Tom about the cause of the fight.''

''I couldn't do that, it would break his heart.''

Donna took a big gulp of beer then leaned back with a sigh. Abby did the same. She felt at peace, until Donna asked, ''You worry about the state of his heart, don't you?''

Abby groaned. ''Today's Sunday. No psychology allowed. I'm just here for food and booze.''

''Occupational hazard. Like you trying to help victims. In my case, it's easy to overlook my own psychological needs. In your case, you run the risk of becoming a victim of your own good nature.''

''I'm trying to keep my distance.''

Donna reached across the wide arms of the chair and squeezed her arm. ''I know you are, but there's a lot of need there right now. It's natural to want to help. I don't want you to get hurt.''

''Me, too.'' *Too late,* a small voice said inside her head.

Both women were silent for a few minutes, then Donna said, ''I fell for a client once.''

Nonplussed, Abby eyed her friend. ''You never told me this.''

''It was a long time ago. Right out of college. Before I met Max.''

''Who was he?''

''Just a man. A young man. A very attractive, very troubled young man. He had a sort of Joe Montana–Kevin Costner–esque quality about him.'' She grinned. ''And I was forty…all right, fifty, pounds lighter.

''He came to me because he was depressed. Couldn't

eat, couldn't sleep, couldn't achieve sexual gratification either alone or with someone.'' Donna smiled at Abby. "What really got to me was the way he improved when he was talking to me. His blue eyes would begin to sparkle and he'd grin. It was as if I had the power to bring him back to life. Heady stuff for one so young.''

"Did you actually…you know, have sex?''

"Clinically speaking? Yes.'' Donna, her plump cheeks a shade rosier than normal, grimaced. "I'm not proud of myself and I probably would have lost my license if a dear friend hadn't slapped me upside the head and told me I was crazy.''

"Clinically speaking?''

"And every other way. She was in the business, too. She suggested I start him on antidepressants and give him a referral.''

"Did it work?''

"Like a champ. And you know the kicker? Once he got better, I discovered he wasn't as attractive as I thought. What I was attracted to was the need, which, in turn, fed my ego. Sobering thought, huh? Want another beer?''

Abby finished the last of hers and rose. "Stay put. I'll get them.''

When she returned, she asked, "Why'd you tell me that story?''

Donna shrugged. "Guilt. I've been carrying around that awful truth for all these years and…''

"Bullshit.''

She chuckled. "You're human, Abby. Not superhuman. Just plain human. Just like me. Just like the rest of us. You beat yourself up over taking the Butler girls out for ice cream and for feeling attracted to their father when you know you shouldn't be, but the fact is, sometimes you don't have any control over these things.''

Abby studied her beer, not wanting to meet her friend's eyes.

"In my case," Donna continued, "I came to my senses in time to avoid any huge mess. My client got well and moved away. I switched to child psychology. A few years later, I got a notice from a psychologist in Houston requesting transcripts of my client's files. By then I was happily married, and I sent those puppies off with pure relief.''

"What about my case?" Abby asked, almost afraid to say the words out loud. "What about these feelings I have for Tom? Everything between us has been aboveboard, but there are these weird vibrations and I can't tell if I'm sending them or he is or what?''

"Vibrators? I leave you two alone for a minute and the next thing I know you're talking dirty," Max exclaimed from the kitchen. "Wait for me, damn it. I've got to finish hooking up the battery.''

Abby laughed. "God, I wish I'd found him first.''

Donna grinned. "Oh, pul...lease, as my teenage clients are wont to say, get real. You've already got three guys—make that two and a half, counting Landon—after you. What do you want with a hairy old fart like Max? By the way, what's the scoop on your big date?''

"Well—" Abby started, thinking back to the source of her second sleepless night.

"Wait," Donna interrupted. "Hold that thought. I want to hear all about it on an empty bladder. I'll be right back.''

Abby smiled as she watched her friend shuffle into the house, but the smile faded.

Friday night with Daniel, she thought, what can I say? In a way it was perfect, but—

"Have I told you how lovely you look tonight?" Daniel asked once the waitress delivered the bottle of '94 BV merlot. He raised his glass in toast. "To good times and good friends."

Abby lifted her glass to his. How could she not? He'd been the perfect gentleman from the moment he arrived at her house. He'd opened doors for her, chosen Vivaldi for the drive, and, best of all, kept the conversation in the car light and frivolous. Much to her surprise, she discovered they shared an interest in genealogy, although his family lineage was amazingly well documented, while hers was hit-and-miss. His story of his grandparents' and parents' internment in relocation camps in World War II truly touched her.

They'd arrived at Ducie's early enough to stroll around the grounds and watch families frolic in the waves created by speedboats zipping about in the narrow, man-made lake. The forested hillsides encircling the lake glowed in the early-evening twilight. Abby breathed the clean, crisp air and relaxed for the first time since lunch, when Melina had convinced her the evening was going to be a hot date—with Daniel bent on proving his male prowess to make up for his wife's rejection. So far, it was nothing of the kind. Abby tasted her wine. "This is lovely. Thank you."

"No. Thank you for coming. I really needed some friendly female company. No matter how civilized you think things are going to be, a divorce is never amiable. Suddenly that stupid clock somebody you can't even remember gave you for a wedding present becomes a prized possession. It's crazy."

Abby nodded sympathetically, but she had no personal experience with divorce. Billy died to get out of their relationship, and Landon moved in with another woman. The only household items she and Landon had owned jointly were the bar stools, which Abby liked, and a futon, which Abby hated. Since the futon cost twice as much as the stools, Landon was tickled to have it and leave the stools. Unfortunately, Abby thought as she sipped her wine, once Daniel opened the subject of his divorce, he couldn't get off the subject. She understood how important it was to him, and she tried to be consoling, but by the time she was finishing her salmon, she'd had her fill of the topic.

"What about dessert?" he asked, smiling warmly.

He truly was a handsome man. She liked him. But she knew now, better than before, that like was as much as there was to it. "I'm stuffed, thank you."

"I thought all women loved dessert. Marilyn would take home half her dinner just so she could have chocolate mousse."

Abby smiled mechanically. Maybe her lack of response finally connected in his brain because he dropped his head and sighed. "I've been a complete boor, haven't I?"

"Of course not."

"Yes, I have. I'm sorry. Can I make it up to you? Can I take you dancing?"

Melina's warning sounded in Abby's head. "Thank you, but I'm not all that energetic on Friday nights. I know that sounds like something my old-maid aunt would say, but it's been a long week at work."

He looked at her pointedly. "Is this about that cowboy and his kids?"

A funny buzz skipped through her chest. "I'm handling the Butler case, but it's just one of several. Roy was out two days with bronchitis, and Melina's got cruise fever, so things are hectic." He didn't say anything, but the inscrutable stare continued. "Why'd you ask about the Butlers?"

His finger tapped the leather folder containing their bill. "I don't know. I've had a sense that you're more...involved with this case than usual."

Abby's heartbeat sped up and her face felt warm. "Perhaps I am. Tom Butler's a friend of Maria Fuentes. Remember her from the Adelina Johnston case? I'm a sucker for kids in pain. What can I say?"

He looked up. "Does the same apply to men?"

Abby's pulse arched off the Richter scale. Did he mean Tom or himself? Fortunately, the waitress returned to pick up the check. While Daniel paid the bill, Abby excused herself to use the rest room.

They made small talk on the way home and he gave her a light peck on the cheek when he dropped her off at her front door.

"Well, girlfriend," Donna said, returning. "Tell me all about it."

Abby put the back of her hand to her forehead theatrically. "Oh, pul...lease, let's not go into that."

"I CALLED HER," Angel said, straddling the threshold of the doorway to her father's workroom.

He was seated on a metal stool at his workbench. She wasn't sure whether to go in or not. They hadn't really talked much since Thursday night. He'd offered, but she hadn't quite forgiven him for making her go to Rainbows, although in all honesty it hadn't been as bad as she'd thought it was going to be. In a way, she liked being able to talk to other kids who'd had some of the same kind of sad things in their lives. One boy, four years older than her, lost both his parents to a murder-suicide. He was living with his grandparents. Talk about sucky.

"Called who?" Tom asked, squinting against the bright sun behind her.

She rolled her eyes. "Abby. You're the one who left her card by the phone. Hint. Hint."

"Oh. That was nice of you. What'd she say?"

"That she was sorry if she contributed to our stress. Like it was her fault I yelled at Heather. Why'd she care?" Angel took a step into the room to escape the heat at her back. She'd forgotten how damn hot this valley got in summer. Val and her mom had talked about putting in a pool this year.

"Abby has a big heart, she cares a lot about everything. Remember what Maria told you about how Abby helped her cousin's family?"

Angel remembered. She'd listened avidly when Maria described her cousin's murder and the custody battle. She didn't know why, but lately she felt as if hearing about other people's problems would make her feel better. Donna told her it was a common reaction to traumatic events, but Angel didn't like the feeling. She planned on bringing it up at the next Rainbows meeting. It wouldn't bother her so much if other people felt the same way.

"Yeah, but I still don't get it. Most people are too busy worrying about their own lives to mess with anybody else's."

Her father looked at her sharply. "Are you suggesting Abby doesn't have a life of her own?"

"No," she said, surprised by his tone. "Abby has a life. She was getting ready for a date when I called."

"A date?"

Angel studied her father. He was trying to act indifferent, but Angel could tell he wasn't happy with her news. *Is he interested in Abby? She is pretty, but...* Angel let the thought go. She wasn't sure how she felt about the idea of her father dating. Even someone as nice as Abby. She'd have to think about it.

"Yeah, but she didn't sound too happy about it," Angel finally said. "When I asked her who the guy was, she said, 'An accident waiting to happen.'"

He shrugged his shoulders and made a grumbling sound. Definitely interested.

Angel stepped closer to see what he was doing. His big hands moved quickly, hammering tiny nails into a hunk of suede that was stretched on a wooden board. "Whatcha doing?"

"Stripping."

She giggled. The sound made her feel foolish, but his grin made her relax and smile back. "Eventually," he told her, "I'll braid the strips into reins, and after I tool a headstall and side pieces, I'll have a bridle. Miguel's daddy-to-be present. Do you want to learn how?"

Angel shrugged, determined not to look too interested. "I guess so. Might as well. Heather can't take her eyes off that damn colt and it's getting hot outside. Guess I got nothing better to do."

"Well, pull up a stool." He helped her uncover the only one in sight and draw it right up beside his. "I used to do this with my dad. I wish you could have known your Grandpa Walt. He died the Christmas before you were born. I always felt bad about that. He would have loved you something fierce."

Angel had to squeeze the hunk of leather he handed her real tight so she wouldn't cry. Fortunately, her dad changed the subject by the time he handed her a sharp little blade fitted into a wooden handle that was wrapped with a grubby, slightly sticky gauze. Without tears in her eyes, she'd be a lot less likely to make either of them bleed.

CHAPTER SEVEN

ABBY TURNED OFF the engine but didn't get out of the car right away. No dogs jumped up to scratch her door. The Butler homestead seemed oddly quiet considering she'd been invited specifically to help mitigate the first visit from Val, but it was a welcome sight to her eyes. The previous Thursday's Rainbows meeting after the long holiday weekend had been canceled, so Abby hadn't seen the Butler family in over a week.

Tom had called Abby the Monday after that disastrous first session and said both girls had pleaded with him to ask Abby to be their designated driver every Thursday. She wasn't sure she believed him, but Donna insisted it was natural for young girls to crave adult female companionship. With Maria preparing for both a baby and a move and Janey caught up in a health crisis, Abby was a likely candidate.

Abby had accidentally bumped into Janey the Friday before Memorial Day. She'd driven out to the ranch to drop off a bag of decorating magazines she kept forgetting to leave for the girls. When she parked in the semicircle in front of Tom's house, she saw Angel sitting on the stoop beside a gray-haired woman, their heads bent over a nest of brightly colored plastic lacing.

Abby didn't want to interrupt, but the older woman waved her over. "Hello there," she hailed warmly. Although the temperature was above ninety, the woman, who was about the same size and build as Angel, wore a two-piece jersey jogging suit that made Abby feel even hotter in her wilted linen suit. The outfit's heather-gray tone almost matched the woman's short-cropped, thinning curls. "You must be the wonderful Abby I've heard so much about."

Abby blushed, but the woman's words seemed sincere. "I can't imagine where you heard that."

"Little birds, I think," she said, making a fluttering motion with her thin, graceful hands. One hand stopped midflutter and thrust toward Abby. "I'm Janey Hastings."

Abby shifted the plastic bag to her other hand and reached out to shake hands. Janey Hastings's touch was cool but her grip forthright. "Abby Davis."

"I've been looking forward to meeting you, Abby Davis, ever since Maria suggested Thomas go see you. She can't say enough nice things about you. Took a judge to make Thomas go, though. For a smart man, he doesn't follow instructions too well, does he?" She looked at Angel for confirmation.

"Nope," Angel said, grinning.

"Most men are reluctant to ask for help," Abby said, rising to Tom's defense before she realized Janey was teasing. A warm blush claimed her cheeks when she noticed Janey eyeing her thoughtfully. "Um, what are you two doing?" Abby asked.

Angel held up a length of colorfully plaited plastic, the individual strands trailing behind like stiff ribbons. "Janey's teaching me how to make lanyards. For key rings and stuff."

The finely webbed lines around Janey's hazel eyes deepened with her smile. She possessed an ageless beauty that seemed only slightly muted by illness. Tom had mentioned Janey's battle with cancer when he explained about the ownership of the ranch. Abby was heartened to see the sparkle in the older woman's eyes at Angel's obvious enthusiasm for the project.

"I learned this back when I was younger than this girl," Janey said, looping a thin arm around Angel's shoulders. Angel's youth and vitality contrasted with a pallor and frailty that didn't come from age alone.

"Of course, back then the gimp was made out of leather," Janey said.

"Gimp?" Abby repeated, moving close enough to touch the thin, flat strands of purple and orange.

Angel ran her fingers through the rat's nest of plastic. "The string. Janey's friend gave her a bag of crafts to do at the hospital, and she brought some of them home to teach us."

Janey's mouth slanted in a wry grin. "My friend told me the reason I never used plastic when I was young was because it hadn't been invented yet. Some friend, huh?"

Abby laughed. "I have a friend like that, too."

Angel frowned, although Abby didn't understand why. Before she could ask, Angel said, "I'm making a necklace and ankle bracelet for Heather for her birthday in August." She consulted the sporty watch on her wrist then rose gracefully. "I'd better go hide this before Dad and Heather get back from checking the water gates. I'll bring it over to your house tomorrow, Janey, and we can work on it then, okay?"

"Not too early, please. I just can't seem to get going in the mornings anymore," Janey said, looking frustrated.

Abby hefted the bag in Angel's direction. "I've been carting these magazines around for a week. Melina's

aunts and cousins keep our waiting room stocked. There
are some fashion ones I thought you'd like and a couple
of things for Heather.''

Angel's smile was quick. ''Thanks,'' she said, clutch-
ing the bag to her chest. After giving Janey a quick hug,
she dashed off toward the barn.

''What a sweetheart! But she's hurting more than she
lets on,'' Janey said, rising a bit unsteadily. ''I wish I
could be around more to help them through this.''

''Are you okay?'' Abby asked.

Janey clasped the single upright post and shook her
head. ''As good as can be expected with all the poisons
they've poured into this old body. But if it kills the bad
cells then I guess I can put up with a little nausea and
dizziness.'' Her face took on a stern look. ''Doesn't
mean I plan to give up my way of life, though. Ed thinks
he can coddle me into staying home instead of helping
out with the roundup this weekend, but he's wrong.
Haven't missed one in forty-odd years. Don't plan to
start now.'' That was the first Abby heard of the annual
roundup that would take place in the foothills. The excitement in Janey's voice had made Abby long to be a
part of the festivities, but, naturally, she hadn't been
invited. Why would she be?

''Abby's here,'' a high-pitched voice sang out, jarring
Abby out of her reverie and back into the present.

Abby opened the car door and got out just in time
for a small, compact body to hurl itself into her arms.
Slightly overwhelmed by Heather's unexpected exuber-
ance, Abby hugged her tightly and planted a kiss on top
of her sweet-smelling curls.

''We been waiting. Did you bring the 'Tucky Fried?''

''Yep, and potato salad and coleslaw and biscuits. It's
all in a cooler in the trunk.''

"Come here." Heather tugged on Abby's hand, leading her to a frayed, nylon-webbed chaise longue plunked beneath the front yard's lone mulberry tree.

"We went to a roundup," Heather said, once the two were seated in the small, scratchy space. Her words were delivered with the solemnity of a sermon.

"Really?" Abby said, equally reverent.

"Yep, 'n me 'n Daddy slept right on the ground," Heather said, more animated than Abby had ever seen her. "Everybody else slept in tents, but me 'n Daddy were real cowboys. With stars and cows for company."

Abby pictured the scene. An ache behind her breastbone reminded her of the time her family went camping at Lake June and left her home with her grandmother. "You're too little, Abby. The mosquitoes will eat you alive," Abby's mother had explained. Grammy did her best to entertain Abby, but the sense of being left out had stuck with her a long time.

"Weren't you afraid of spiders and snakes and bugs?" Abby asked.

Heather's white-gold curls bounced back and forth. "Nope. Daddy put down a big blue tarp first. He said spiders and snakes were scared of plastic."

"Really?" Abby said. "I didn't know that."

The little girl nodded seriously, squeezing a bit more space out of the lawn chair they shared.

"Did you like sleeping under the stars?"

"Yes, but the frogs were noisy." She croaked theatrically.

Abby's heart swelled; she couldn't believe how good it felt to be snuggled next to this little munchkin. "Where'd Angel sleep?"

"In a tent." Heather wrinkled her nose disdainfully. "With the other girls."

"What other girls?"

"Anna and Rachel. Janey and Ed's granddaughters."

"Oh, right." Tom had mentioned Ed's son and his family were coming from Colorado to help with the roundup. "How old are they?"

"Old." Heather fingered a tiny embroidered rose on the lapel of Abby's sleeveless, denim blouse. "They go to college. But they were real nice. They want me 'n Angel to come visit them sometime. They live near some mountains and…"

Peripherally, Abby saw Tom round the corner of the house; he came to an abrupt halt when he spotted them. She didn't have a chance to read his look since Heather's reaction to seeing him was a high-pitched squeal of joy. "Daddy."

"There you are, my little baked clam," Tom growled in his best Big Bad Wolf imitation. "I've been looking for a sweet neck to nibble on." He charged forward, arms outstretched.

Heather clasped her arms around Abby's neck, nearly strangling her, but Heather's daddy was quicker. He scooped her up and tossed her in the air. "Gimme a bite," he cried, eliciting peals of laughter.

"No, Daddy, no. Let me down. I'm gonna wet my pants."

He set her down contritely. "Sorry, punkin."

She wiggled away, then stuck out her little pink tongue. "Just kidding. Ha. Ha. Fooled you." She dashed away toward the construction zone to the left of the house—the renovations were progressing well—ducking under the yellow Caution tape flapping in the midmorning breeze.

"Go clean out the litter box," he called after her.

Shaking his head in hopelessness, he dropped into the

second, ancient chaise longue. It creaked in protest. "Hi," he said, closing his eyes and heaving a big sigh. "I didn't hear you drive up. The dogs must have recognized your car."

Abby had a hard time forming a reply. He looked good—way too good. More relaxed than the last time she saw him, which had been when he'd shown her the new foal. Since then the sun had done nice things to his hair, which was growing out to a less military style, and the pale strip above his upper lip matched the rest of his face's healthy tan.

He'd swapped his usual cotton shirt for a black jersey T-shirt that sported an image of Garth Brooks on it. Evidence, no doubt, that Angel had carried through with her threat to perk up his wardrobe. Abby liked how it emphasized his muscular torso.

"I'm here." Well, duh, as Angel says.

He turned to face her and seemed mesmerized by something on her lips. She licked them to make sure her lipstick wasn't messed up from Heather's exuberant buss.

He sat up suddenly, swinging his legs over the side of the chaise to face her. "I really appreciate your coming. It's not a big deal, really—Val and I have always gotten along reasonably well, but it's his first time up here since—"

Abby understood, perhaps better than she should. She could almost feel his ambivalence about welcoming this man, this "other" daddy, into the world he was trying to create for his daughters.

"I wouldn't have bothered you if Ed and Janey were around, but Ed had to take Janey back to Stanford for another treatment."

No hat to shade his eyes. Abby couldn't help noticing

how the cloudless sky intensified the blue of his eyes. Way better than Paul Newman. She made herself look down. Sneakers instead of boots. Why does that make him more approachable?

"By the way, Janey said to tell you thanks for the flowers."

Abby shrugged, trying to keep her mind on the conversation. "My roses seem to thrive on neglect and cat poop." His chuckle twanged some errant chord inside her rib cage. "I really enjoyed meeting Janey. She reminds me of my grandmother. How's she doing?"

"Pretty good, but she tires easily and it really ticks her off. They had to come back early from the roundup, but Ed told Janey her body needed pampering, not sleeping in a camper." His rueful smile made certain body parts hum. "Lord, she hates it when Ed's right."

Abby looked away, blinking at the faintly visible outline of mountains. "Nice day, isn't it?" she asked inanely.

"We didn't pull you away from anything important, did we?" Tom asked, watching her face.

"No. Not really. I finally broke down and hired a gardener, so my weekends are a bit more relaxed."

A serious look pushed down on his flaxen eyebrows. "Can I ask you something personal?"

The gentleman, again. "Sure."

His Adam's apple rose and fell. "Are you seeing someone?" An endearing blush colored the hollows of his cheeks. "Angel told me that's the proper way to put it these days."

Am I? Do two dinner dates and one closed-mouth kiss qualify? Daniel had invited her to accompany him and his daughter and new son-in-law to Reno over the Memorial Day weekend, but she'd declined because of her traditional family get-together—one she'd have dumped in a heartbeat if someone had invited her to a roundup.

"You don't have to answer."

She brushed aside his disclaimer with a backhanded motion. "I'm still thinking. My boss is going through a divorce and he's asked me out a couple of times, but..."

Tom frowned. "People going through a divorce are dangerous," he said with feeling. "I know. I was hell on wheels."

Abby sat up, too. Their knees, hers bare, his in faded denim, almost touched. "You? You're too much of a gentleman."

"No such animal when your wife up and leaves you. I partied hardy for the better part of a year. Stomped on a couple of hearts along the way, too." He looked sad, and more than a little sheepish.

"I'm sure you didn't mean to hurt anyone."

"'Course not, but that doesn't help when it's your heart that's been stomped on."

Abby felt privileged to be the recipient of such heart-felt truths and replied in kind. "After Landon moved out, I went just the opposite way—I didn't even want to think about dating."

"He hurt you bad."

She looked at Tom's hands, loosely clasped between his knees. Powerful hands, toughened by life, yet gentle. "No. Landon's a great guy—fun-loving, gregarious, but after a while it was like being involved with the social director of a cruise ship. He'd come home at 3:00 a.m. singing Eagles songs, and I'd drag in at the same time after counseling a family whose child had been killed by a drunk driver. It just didn't work."

"What's the new guy like?"

"Daniel?" Abby thought a moment. "Suave, articulate, intense. He takes his job as seriously as I do mine, but I always feel as though he has another agenda. It's the politician in him.''

Tom's face soured. ''Never had much use for those types, 'specially after what happened with Heather.''

Abby knew all too well the frustration of plowing through the red tape of most criminal courts—a system even more convoluted when a child was involved.

Before she could stop herself, she reached out and clasped his forearm. His skin radiated warmth; bundled muscles bespoke strength and power. ''At least they're here now, and safe.''

''Dad,'' Angel called from inside the house, her tone oddly flat, ''Val just called on his cell phone. He's turning off 99. He says he'll be here in ten minutes.''

Abby jumped to her feet as if doused by a bucket of cold water. She moved back, giving Tom space to stand. He looked at her curiously before walking toward the house. Abby followed, wiping her sweaty palms on the backs of her khaki walking shorts.

''So,'' she said, bending down to pet Rosie before hurrying to catch up with Tom, ''you had a big roundup last weekend.''

They skirted the bright, unblemished concrete slab, which looked too small to possibly match the dimensions on the plan. She'd never ceased to marvel at this optical illusion.

Tom moved without haste, surveying the work. Tilting his head, he eyed it as if imagining the finished product…or, perhaps, picturing it through the eyes of the man who'd married his ex-wife.

''A few weeks behind schedule, but between Ed and Janey's troubles and mine…'' His broad shoulders rose and fell. ''It worked out.''

"What do you do at a roundup—other than the obvious, rounding up animals?" She sensed his tension and wished there were some way to soften the impact of this upcoming meeting.

"Brand, inoculate, castrate."

"Sounds charming."

"And tasty." He grinned at the face she made.

God, she liked his smile.

She made herself look away and saw Heather clamber to the top rail of the horse corral to scout for Val's vehicle. Abby returned the little girl's exuberant wave.

"Heather's sure excited," she said neutrally, knowing there was no easy way to get through this meeting. "The girls haven't seen their stepfather since the funeral, right?"

Tom squatted near a stand of copper pipes thrust through the concrete like amputated fingers. "He calls about once a week."

"Do you get the feeling Angel isn't quite as enthusiastic about this visit?"

Tom lifted one shoulder. "Sometimes I don't know what's going on in her head. She keeps everything inside. Has she said anything to Donna?"

Abby shook her head. "I don't know. The only thing she ever said to me was that her mother should never have left home that night in the first place." Abby sighed, remembering the months after Billy died. "It's natural to want someone to blame for what's happened. Maybe she blames Val."

He made a soft sound that made her ask, "Do you blame him?"

He looked away. When he answered, his voice was low and troubled. "No more than I blame myself."

She knew that feeling, and she also knew better than

to cover it up with empty platitudes. "Do you know anything more about the guy they arrested?"

Tom hunched over slightly, as if warding off a blow. "The girls are always around when Val calls, and I don't know how much to tell them. What do you think?"

She wasn't prepared for such a direct question. "Donna tells parents that as long as they're open, children will ask what they need to know when they need to know it."

"I just wish it was all behind us," he said tersely. Rising abruptly, he turned and walked away.

Abby didn't follow. She leaned against the wall of the house, letting the heat penetrate to the knot of tension between her shoulder blades. With her eyes closed she could almost picture the completed addition. The girls would begin painting and decorating, Tom would pretend to be overwhelmed. And where would Abby be? Back at college? Stuck in her same old rut at work? With Daniel? Alone?

"What about Val?"

Abby's eyes flew open; her heart jolted. Tom stood opposite her, barely a foot away, intently studying her face. She couldn't imagine how so large a man could move so quietly. "What?"

"What do we do about Val? Where does he fit in?"

Abby understood what he was asking. This wasn't about territory or custody. Tom would do what was best for his daughters even if it meant welcoming his ex-wife's second husband into his life. "I'd say play it by ear. Let the girls decide. Maybe he'll be a kind of uncle, an old friend of the family who made them happy once upon a time, a fatherlike figure they can rely on when their real father doesn't understand them." His frown segued into a scowl. "Believe me, Tom, no father understands his daughters all the time."

His scowl looked both fierce and endearing. She smiled to lighten the mood. "I speak from thirty years of experience, Tom." She pushed off from her resting place and paced, her leather sandals making sandpaper sounds on the smooth concrete. "My folks were at my brother's house for Memorial Day. Do you know what my dad said to me at the table in front of my teenage niece and nephew?"

Tom, who paced beside her, shook his head.

"He told me, 'You know, Abby, women over thirty have a better chance of getting hit by a car than getting married.' My poor sister-in-law nearly choked to death on a bite of blueberry pie."

She detected a smile trying to worm its way onto his lips. "He loves you."

"I know, but it was humiliating." She fought her own smile, but it overpowered her self-righteous indignation. Laughing together, Tom looped his arm, companionably, across her shoulders. Where that friendly gesture might have led, she'd never know, because at that moment the dogs began barking. Val had arrived.

ANGEL PLOPPED BACK DOWN on the lumpy sofa. She covered her face with a corduroy throw pillow that smelled faintly of her father, faintly of dust. Could a person smother oneself to death? she wondered. Probably not, some sort of self-protective system would kick in at the last minute, she decided. Too bad.

Her deep sigh warmed the space around her lips. She knew she couldn't stay hidden forever. She wasn't a silly kid like Heather who still couldn't play hide-and-seek worth beans. Heather always hid in the last place Angel did. Talk about unoriginal.

Unfortunately, there were no good hiding places on the ranch that her father couldn't find. Besides, Angel knew she was expected to help welcome Val to their home. Her dad had even invited Abby over to make it one big happy family.

Angel didn't understand that move. Not that she had anything against Abby. Abby was a nice person who tried very hard not to make waves, kinda like Heather. It had been Angel's idea to make Abby the driver to the Rainbows thing each week. It beat the hell out of listening to country music in her dad's crappy old truck. Abby let them choose the music, although last time she brought a cool book on tape, *Julie of the Wolves,* that really made the trip fly.

Nope. Angel didn't mind Abby's presence, even today when Val was coming. She figured her dad needed a little extra reinforcement in case something ugly happened, like if Angel found the keys to Ed's gun rack and shot Val.

"Damn," Angel swore, scrunching her face to keep the tears back. She liked Val, maybe even loved him once, but if he hadn't had a fight with her mother that night, Lesley would still be alive.

"SINCE WHEN does Santa Claus drive a sport utility vehicle?" Tom muttered, reaching into the cavernous opening for yet another box. Abby, who seemed to have affixed herself to his side since Val's arrival, let out a small laugh.

"He is sort of a one-man Toys for Tots," she said, her voice low, even though Val and Heather were thoroughly occupied on the lawn unpacking yet another crateful of goodies. Angel sat in a lawn chair, a small box of personal trinkets between her knees. She'd been unusually subdued today, and Tom was worried about her.

He was worried about a lot of things. "Where am I going to put all this cra…stuff?"

Dropping the box in place, Tom reversed positions and plopped his butt down on the threshold, inhaling a whiff of "new car" smell. Thirty grand. Minimum. Where did Val…? He put the thought aside, catching the speculative look on Abby's face.

She saw too much, and cared too much, and, damn, he liked her.

"The barn?" she suggested, tacking on a smile that made him tuck his hands under his butt. "It's the size of a small castle."

Using the respite to stretch muscles taxed by all the lifting and carrying, she arched her back, massaging her neck with one hand. Nothing about her conservative shorts and neatly pressed blouse cried "sexy," but the whole package—tousled hair, sun-kissed cheeks and radiant glow from pitching in where needed—made him ache to touch her.

The moment he'd seen her sitting with Heather, Tom realized how much he'd missed her—not that it came as any big surprise. Despite his best efforts to the contrary, he'd found himself thinking about her throughout the holiday weekend, alternately kicking himself for lacking the guts to invite her and congratulating himself on dodging a bullet.

He knew any kind of emotional involvement was out of the question at this point in his life, but the temptation to see her had overridden common sense when he asked her to join them for Val's visit.

A cursed weakness, his father would have called it. "We Butlers are accursed with two weaknesses, son," his father once told him. "Pride and fancy. We pride ourselves on always fancying the wrong women." Tom hadn't believed him, even after Lesley, but now he was beginning to wonder.

"Lose the scowl," she advised, turning back to the yawning mouth of the shiny black vehicle. "Here they come."

"I'm not scowling."

She peeked at him. "No, actually, that's more of a 'Meet me outside with your six-shooter' look, isn't it?" Her grin was too infectious to resist.

"What's so funny?" Angel asked, squeezing between them.

"Your dad's concerned about space since the addition won't be done for a few more weeks. I volunteered to store the video games and computer at my house."

"No way!" Angel started to pout until she caught Abby's wink. "If anything, you can store Heather's Barbies. She's got like six million."

Heather, hand firmly tucked in her stepfather's, was close enough to hear that comment and let out a cry. "That's not fair."

Tom rolled his eyes. "Time out. Abby was kidding. Since Val was nice enough to bring all this stuff, we'll find a place for it. But, some of it will have to stay in boxes until the addition is finished. Otherwise, there won't be room for us. So, pick out a few things that can fit in your room and we'll put the rest in a safe place in the barn, temporarily." He stressed the last word to short-circuit any tantrums.

To his surprise, both girls looked at Abby, then meekly sighed, "Okay."

After the last box was unloaded, Tom offered Val a beer.

"Great," Val said. "How 'bout you, Abby? Will you join us?"

Kneeling in the midst of what looked like a giant yard sale, she looked up, a fistful of Barbie-doll clothes in one hand, three of the long-tressed dolls in the other. So far, Heather hadn't been able to narrow down her selection to less than ten dolls. "Sure. Thanks. It's getting pretty warm," she said with a smile.

Always the ladies' man, Tom thought petulantly, before turning toward the house for the beers. *What is it about that guy that pisses me off?*

His designer clothes, for one thing, Tom thought. Angel, who seemed to be having a hard time giving her stepfather the time of day, practically gushed about Val's navy knee-length shorts and yellow, white and navy blue polo shirt. Tom didn't get it, but that didn't surprise him. What did surprise him was his reaction to the abundance of boxes Val had brought. Tom knew ahead of time Val planned to bring the remainder of the girls' clothes and possessions, but it shook him to the core to realize how much stuff his daughters owned—more than he'd ever thought of possessing. The rift between their two worlds seemed wider than the Grand Canyon. *How can I possibly make this work?*

Tom took three beers and two sodas from the refrigerator shelf and headed back outside, letting the screen door bounce closed behind him. Val sat at the weathered redwood picnic table, his back to Tom. His arms moved expressively, highlighting some story to Abby, who watched, rapt, directly across from him. Tom couldn't quite stifle a surge of jealousy.

He handed each girl a soda then plunked two cans on

the table before his guests. Abby eyed him, puzzled. He took a long swig of beer before sitting down beside Val—not his first choice, but the smart one.

"I was just telling Abby about the drive up. A maniac in a little red RX7 zipped in and out of traffic about ninety miles an hour. An accident waiting to happen. I expected to see it upside in the ditch, but a few miles down the road, the car was pulled over with two highway patrol units behind it and they had the driver in handcuffs." He paused dramatically. "It was a kid. He couldn't have been much older than Angel, sixteen max. Scary, isn't it?"

"What scares me is the fact that the kid's parents probably bought him that car," Abby said, popping open the tab on her beer can. "A lot of parents think they can buy a kid's love with things. But all the stuff in the world can't replace a parent's attention and discipline and love."

Val sat back as though she'd hit him, and Abby suddenly looked stricken, apparently realizing how her words might be taken in light of all the toys and gifts strewn across the lawn.

"I...I didn't mean you, Val. This is entirely different. These girls have been through something extraordinary, and what you've done is very generous and kind. I meant parents who abdicate the role of parenting and try to make up for it with..."

He waved off her explanation. "I know what you're saying and I agree. I know a lot of people like that. Lesley used to give me a hard time about my gift giving, but the truth is I'm just a compulsive shopper." He shrugged. "When I see something I think the girls would like, I buy it for them. I did the same with Lesley.

"After she passed away, I ran across three or four

things I'd bought for her but hadn't had a chance to give her. A sapphire ring in a platinum setting. She would have loved it.'' His dark eyes misted and he looked away.

In the beginning, Tom had been prepared to hate the man Lesley married, but he could never quite manage it in light of Val's earnest need to please. The man positively bent over backward to be nice to Tom.

''How have you been getting along?'' Tom asked, surprised to find he actually cared. ''Business okay?''

Val shrugged. Physically, he was Tom's match, but something about Val's weight-lifter build seemed contrived, as if the muscles were for show only. He wore his thinning black hair slicked back from his high forehead and gathered in a ponytail at the nape of his neck. For the first time, Tom noticed a few strands of silver threading through it.

''It was touch-and-go for a while,'' Val said soberly. ''I honestly didn't know if I'd be able to swing it. Les ran the daily show while I focused on marketing and promotions. She handled the books, contracts, employees, all that.

''Fortunately, Les's assistant, Bridget, kept a lid on things until I could take over. I just promoted her to assistant manager.'' Tom couldn't interpret his smile, but something made him wonder if Val had a personal interest in the woman. It wouldn't surprise him. Val didn't strike Tom as the kind of man who could stand to be alone for long.

Abby leaned forward, resting her elbows on the table. A modest pose, but from Tom's angle a gap between buttons exposed a tantalizing wisp of lace. The view, combined with an occasional hint of floral perfume, made him miss her question.

"What did you say?" he asked.

Her well-defined eyebrows arched.

"She asked the name of my business," Val answered, oblivious to Tom's muddle. "Fitness West, One and Two. We carved a pretty nice little niche for ourselves, but I have to admit, most of it was Lesley. She had this ability to read what people wanted before they knew what they wanted." He beamed with pride. "She introduced step aerobics before anyone else—even designed and marketed her own steps."

Tom frowned. It always surprised him, and hurt a little, to find out things about Lesley he wouldn't have dreamed possible. When she was his wife, she barely managed to balance the checkbook. How could he have been so blind to her capabilities and needs? No wonder he lost her.

"Dad?" Angel called from beneath the tree. "Can we keep the boom box?"

"It's yours from last Christmas, remember?" Val answered before Tom could say anything.

A spear of pain twisted in Tom's gut. He tried to keep it from showing, but the look of sympathy in Abby's eyes told him he wasn't successful.

"Oops," Val said. "Sorry. Old habit, I guess."

Tom shrugged. "No problem."

He twisted on the redwood bench seat to see what Angel was talking about. The molded plastic box in her hands looked ominous, like something gang members would hoist around in the mall. "We'll give it a try. But let's put a limit on the number of records you bring in."

"Records?" she exclaimed. "Nobody listens to records anymore."

"Tapes, then."

She rolled her eyes dramatically.

Tom looked to Abby for help.

"CDs," she mouthed softly.

"Ten CDs apiece. And nothing with bad language." He made his voice as stern as possible. He couldn't save much face, but he'd try for a little.

With the girls bickering over CD titles, Tom asked Val, "Any news about the suspect in Lesley's murder? What's the district attorney doing?"

Val's features hardened. "That bozo. I talked to my lawyer on Friday to see if we could sue for incompetence."

Abby sat forward. "It's a long frustrating process, Val, but it has to be done right or the defendant could walk."

Tom wondered if her defense came from feelings for her boss.

"Well, believe me, if the slimeball walks, he won't get far," Val said, tersely.

Abby reached out with both hands and covered Val's clenched fists. "Val, a terrible person took someone very special from you, but don't give him anything else. If you let your need for revenge consume you, he'll have taken your life, too."

All of a sudden Val's composure crumpled, tears welled up in his eyes and he dropped his head in his hands. "It's my fault. He killed her but it's my fault she was out there in the first place." Tom looked toward his daughters. Heather had disappeared but Angel sat frozen, staring at her stepfather, a look of anguish on her face.

"Val—" Tom started, but Abby shook her head.

"It's natural for survivors to blame themselves," she said softly.

"No," the anguished man cried. "You don't understand. We had a fight. Les thought I was having an affair. She took the girls and left because she was too upset to be around me. She said she couldn't bear to look at me.''

Tom felt his gut twist. A part of him wanted to grab Val on Lesley's behalf and shake the truth out of him. A more rational part understood all too well the daily makeup of a marriage, its highs and lows. He and Lesley had had their share of fights.

''Val, I won't ask you if you deserved it,'' Tom said, but before he could finish, Angel sprang at her stepfather, hitting him with her fists.

''Well, I will. Did you do it, Dad? Did you? Were you sleeping around? Is that why my mom is dead?'' she cried, pounding her fists against his hunched shoulders.

Tom caught her hands in his and pulled Angel to him, soothing her struggles just as he did Heather's troubled nightmares. ''Calm down, Angel-babe, it's okay. Let it go.''

Val turned to them, one hand hovering inches from Angel's shuddering back. ''No, Ang, I didn't do it, but I was thinking about it, and that makes me sick to my stomach.'' His face twisted. ''There was a girl at the club, a new member. I—your mom knew me like a book, and she knew I was looking and she wasn't about to let me get away with it.''

He gave a rough, hurtful laugh. ''At first, I was mad at your mom, but as soon as she left, I realized what a fool I was. I was married to the greatest woman in the world. I had the perfect family and I put it all in jeopardy because of a cute body.'' Tom glanced at Abby; her eyes were filled with sadness.

''I was writing out my apology—you know how much your mom loved seeing things in writing—'' a ghost of a smile touched his lips ''—when the police knocked on the door.''

Tom felt Angel's breath catch and hold. He loosened his grip. She wiped her tear-soaked face with her hands—a little-girl gesture that made his heart twist. ''Can I see it?''

Val looked at his hands. ''I burnt it. Along with my hair cream and—some other things. I was stupid, Angel. I don't deserve your forgiveness because I'll never forgive myself, but I hope you won't hate me forever.''

Angel looked at Tom with a softening he remembered seeing in her mother's eyes. Lesley's nature thrived on drama—they'd had their shouting matches, too, but the making up was always worth it because Lesley had too big a heart to hold a grudge for long.

Then Angel looked at Abby. ''They told me at Rainbows that blame kills people from the inside out,'' she said.

Abby smiled softly and nodded encouragingly. ''When there's no changing something, you have to let go so it doesn't eat you up.''

Angel put her hand on Val's shoulder. ''One guy in the group is only seventeen but he's got an ulcer. His brother died in a car wreck. They'd been drinking and smoking pot. The other brother was driving, but my friend still blames himself for not dying, instead.'' She shook her head, the long tresses dancing like a sheet of fine silk. ''Mom wouldn't want you to blame yourself forever.'' Her lips turned up a fraction. ''Maybe a couple of years, but not forever.''

Val blinked back tears and pulled her into a hug.

For once, Tom felt no competition, no angst. Angel had enough love to share with both her fathers. He should have known that all along.

CHAPTER EIGHT

"Wal-Mart."

"Toys 'R' Us."

Why did I think I could handle this? Abby silently groaned, listening to the argument between Heather and Angela escalate. Taking the girls shopping for a baby gift had been her bright idea, but suddenly Abby felt way out of her league.

"The mall," Abby stated assertively. "Most of the stores there are in Modesto, too, and Maria can exchange anything she doesn't need."

Angel huffed moodily. "Wal-Mart's cheaper."

"Toys 'R' Us has more stuff," Heather grumbled.

"But I'm driving, and you're giving me a headache."

That quieted them down. For their ages, both Butler girls showed remarkable empathy. Abby attributed that to their dad. She'd never met a man as sensitive to her thought patterns and emotions. When she'd called to invite the girls shopping, he suggested they wait until she'd had time to recuperate from Friday's court date. That he even recalled her casual mention of the victim statement she was scheduled to deliver for a non-English-speaking family blew her away.

"Sorry, Abby," Angel said sheepishly. "Are you all right?"

Abby waved off her concern. "Fine. Just a little tired. It was a crazy week at work."

Friction at work—an undercurrent generated by Daniel's attention—added to her tension, but Abby was honest enough to admit that the birth of Maria and Miguel's new son, Aurelio Miguel, on Wednesday, had triggered old angst, and a new, disturbing reaction—envy. Dueling conflicts battled in her mind. "Why not me?" one side cried. "You had your chance and blew it," the other side taunted.

"So," Abby said, hoping to rekindle some spark of enthusiasm in her young charges, "did you talk to Maria? Is he the most beautiful baby ever born?"

"We saw him," Heather said from the back seat. "Daddy took us to the hosp'tal. He's red and really ugly, but Maria likes him."

Abby glanced in the rearview mirror. Heather's outfit consisted of an eye-straining combination of hot-pink shorts with a violet-and-orange-striped tank top. At least she'll be easy to spot in a crowd, Abby thought.

Summer vacations traditionally meant swimming parties, slumber parties, family vacations. What would it mean to Tom and his daughters? she wondered, recalling the way Angela had showed off her independent study report card as if it were a "get-out-of-jail-free" card. Abby had recognized Tom's look of worry, too.

"Any ideas for a gift?" Abby asked, cracking open her window. A succession of big rigs roared past, but the midmorning air felt invigorating.

Both girls simultaneously shouted suggestions above the highway din.

"Wait." Abby hastily rolled up her window. "We need a list. I'm not too experienced in these matters. My mom and sister-in-law picked out a crib and layette for my new niece. All I had to do was write a check. I don't even know what kinds of things a baby needs."

When both girls started speaking, Abby held up a hand. "One at a time. Angela first."

Angel, in frayed cutoff shorts and a belly-exposing top right out of the sixties, twisted to face her. "Well, I know Maria's mom and sisters gave her a shower and she got tons of practical stuff—two or three baby monitors, a stroller, a backpack, a bunch of diapers and a couple of diaper bags. And Miguel's brother gave them a crib and all that stuff."

"Zikes. We're in trouble."

Heather piped up. "Babies like toys."

"You like toys," her sister growled. "Babies can't even see toys right away. Their eyes aren't focused all the way."

Abby recognized the tone of authority. "How do you know so much about babies, Angel?"

"I used to help out on Saturday mornings at my mom's step aerobics class. I worked in the child-care room. She'd pay me, plus I got tips. Two of the moms traded off, too, and I listened to them talk." She settled back in the seat and her voice became more wistful. "Afterward, Mom would take me out to lunch and sometimes we'd go shopping. Mom was a great shopper."

It was the first time Abby had heard Angel open up about her mother. "Well, I'm a terrible shopper and we could use all the help we can get, so...how 'bout we take your mom along with us today?"

"What?" Angel gawked as if Abby had lost her mind. "She's dead."

Abby nodded, tightening her grip on the steering wheel. This was more Donna's department, but she plunged ahead, anyway. "True, but your memories of her are very much alive, so we can use those to help us pick out the right gift. In a way, she'll be guiding us.''

Abby let the idea sink in a minute then asked, ''What kinds of things would your mom be looking for if she were shopping for a baby gift?''

''Toys,'' Heather piped up.

Angel shot her a quelling look. ''Shut up, dufus. This is serious. Mom took shopping seriously but she had a good time doing it. Sometimes, she bought silly stuff. Things that made you laugh but made you feel special, too.''

''Like what?'' Abby prompted.

''Well…at Christmas, Mom bought Val a juggling set.'' She grinned at her sister. ''Remember? One of the balls broke the lamp and she wanted to get mad at him but couldn't and we all laughed.''

Abby relaxed a little. ''Let's start with that. Item number one—something silly. What else?''

Heather leaned as far forward as her seat belt allowed. ''She picked out nice stuff, too. Like Angel's doctor boots.''

Angel, who'd exchanged her standard black combat boots for a pair of sandals, explained. ''Doc Martens. Mom said where shoes were concerned you should buy quality over quantity.''

Abby wiggled her toes against the cork sole of her Birkenstocks. ''I agree. Let's make that number two—something nice.''

She caught Heather's beaming smile in the mirror.

''Mom had a way of always finding something special,'' Angel said softly. ''Like this necklace she gave me for my birthday.'' She fingered the fine filigreed chain at her neck. A small pendant encircled a golden-hued stone. ''It's my birthstone. I told her I liked opals better, but she said this was her favorite because it stood for the day I was born, which was one of the two best days of her life.''

Tears clustered behind Abby's eyelids. She brushed aside the moisture beneath her sunglasses. ''Your mom would want us to make this a happy day because babies are happy things, right?''

Angel shifted, visibly shaking off the sad memories. ''Right.''

''Three gifts—silly, nice and special. Three of us—four, counting your mom. How hard can it be?'' she asked, pulling into the parking lot. ''Let's go.''

AN HOUR and forty-five minutes later, Abby's feet hurt and her shoulder ached from carrying her purse. They found the first two items on their list easily—perhaps nudged with a little heavenly help—but the third eluded them, and all three earthly shoppers were getting cranky.

''This is heavy,'' Heather complained, toting a Goofy gift bag sprouting yellow and blue tissue paper. Inside nested a ridiculously overpriced two-piece outfit that would be outgrown in six months tops, but its giraffes playing catch were too cute to pass up.

''Shut up,'' Angel grumbled. ''That's nothing compared to this.'' In her arms rested a two-foot by three-foot gaily wrapped box containing a little red wagon—every boy's first wheels. Heather spotted it right off the bat and couldn't be dissuaded, even though baby Aurelio wouldn't be able to use it for a couple of years.

''I'll pull him in it when he gets older,'' she vowed.

Abby and Angel had acquiesced, deeming it a truly silly gift for a baby.

Abby looked at her watch. She'd told Tom they'd meet him at Miguel and Maria's at one o'clock. ''Let's get a frozen yogurt," she suggested. "I always knew shopping was hard work. Maybe that's why I don't do it."

"How do you buy things? Presents and stuff?" Heather asked, holding the bag in one hand, Abby's hand in the other.

Abby squeezed it lightly. She couldn't believe how warm and anchoring that little hand felt. "Catalogs. I order books and CDs off the Internet. At Christmas, I give my niece and nephew savings bonds. Not glamorous, but they get so much stuff from their parents and grandparents, it's almost obscene."

"You can never be too obscene at Christmas," Angel quipped.

Abby smiled. To her surprise, she'd enjoyed the morning. Both girls were bright and intelligent and fun. They helped ward off a peculiar emptiness she'd felt growing in recent weeks. Melina, naturally, attributed Abby's mood to Daniel's low-key but persistent pursuit.

"Tell him the truth, Abby," Melina suggested at dinner the previous night—Abby's excuse for avoiding Daniel's invitation to a gala fund-raiser. "Tell him you could never fall for a guy who doesn't wear cowboy boots."

Abby didn't bother protesting. As Melina put it, if Tom and Daniel were Web sites, Tom's "hits" would have outnumbered Daniel's five to one. Unfortunately, Abby couldn't dabble with that site without doing real damage to her entire operating system.

"Oh, look," Angel said breathlessly, bringing Abby back to the present.

Abby followed the girl's outstretched finger to a kiosk in the center of the mall's rotunda. Against a lattice background hung a small, perfectly executed quilt. Its puffy sky of pale blue material with fuzzy white clouds hosted a heavenly collection of ruddy-faced cherubs.

"It's b*eeuu*tiful," Heather gushed, letting go of Abby's hand to rush forward.

Abby agreed. The craftsperson had bestowed upon each angel a different personality: peaceful, mischievous, serene and joyous.

Abby dug in her purse for her credit card.

"Don't you want to know how much it is?" Angel eyed her questioningly.

"Nope. It's perfect. That angel up in the corner has eyes the color of your birthstone. And that little guy on the cloud has your hair, Heather. I'd say your mom is one terrific shopper, wouldn't you?"

Both girls looked at each other before nodding—at first tentatively, then with glee.

TOM LEANED his head back against the nappy fabric of the Fuenteses' couch and closed his eyes. The tiny child sleeping in the crook of his arm brought back memories that made tears form beneath his eyelids. He would never forget the joy and knee-bending fear that walloped him the instant he held Angel—a squalling bundle with black hair and red, furious cheeks—in his arms. A bolt of love, possessiveness, responsibility—he wasn't sure he could name it—hit him like a fist to the gut. He knew his life would never be the same.

"You're tired, Tom," a soft voice said. "Let me take him."

Tom opened one eye. Maria, looking both exhilarated and exhausted, stood before him in a shapeless dress, a diaper hooked over one shoulder. "Oh no you don't," he whispered back. "As long as I've got him, I can take a break."

In all honesty, this week had been hell. The backhoe driver installing underground power lines uprooted some mangled telephone cable. News from Stanford wasn't good: Janey's adverse reaction to some drug had scared the bejesus out of Ed. With Miguel freaking out over false labor, then the real thing, Tom found his workload doubled. Plus, he wasn't prepared for summer vacation, or, more to the point, his daughters' expectations of a fun-filled, action-packed summer.

If it hadn't been for Abby ferrying the girls to Fresno and taking them shopping this morning, he wouldn't have known a minute's peace, although, in a way, she compounded his problems, too.

Tom shifted against the cushions. There was no excuse for such juvenile dreams in a man his age. Just when Heather's bad dreams seemed to be slacking off so he could get a decent night's sleep, erotic images of Abby plagued his dreams, leaving him drained, edgy and damn horny.

''Daddy's got the baby!'' a voice exclaimed, jolting Tom back to reality.

The cushions to his right sank as Heather jumped to his side. ''Can I hold him?''

Angel sank down beside him on his left. ''Shh, he's sleeping,'' she whispered. ''Hey, he looks better, doesn't he? Abby, come see him.''

Tom's heart jumped skittishly, forcing a lump into his windpipe. Juggling her purse, car keys and the packages his daughters dumped in her arms, Abby looked harried but beautiful. He couldn't read the look in her eyes but sensed her hesitation.

''Come,'' he beckoned.

She set the gifts on the floor beside a spanking-new baby stroller and took two tentative steps toward the couch. Not fast enough to suit Heather, who bounced to her knees and stretched to grab Abby's hand. "He won't bite. He doesn't have any teeth yet."

Abby's smile made his pulse jerk.

She looped her hair behind her ears and leaned over. Her fair skin looked as soft and touchable as baby Rey's; Tom could have spent hours tracing the scattered freckles across her shoulders.

"He's beautiful," she said, blinking rapidly.

Tom detected her scent—a subtle, fresh floral, above the nose-prickling samples his daughters had obviously doused on every available spot. He started to offer her the baby, but she backed away, a blush claiming her cheeks.

"No, thanks. I'm not good with babies. But you look right at home."

Without thinking, he lifted Rey in his arms, kissing his petal-soft skin, inhaling that remarkable baby scent. "I love babies," he said. "Horse babies, pig babies, girl babies." He winked at Heather, making her giggle.

"Hi, Abby," Maria said, hurrying in through the doorway that led to the dining room and kitchen. "Thanks so much for coming. And for the flowers. They're so pretty."

Tom watched with interest the way Abby deflected any praise that came her way. When Miguel joined them to open the gifts, Tom noticed she stayed out of the hoopla, letting the girls bask in the praise. While she seemed pleased by Maria and Miguel's exclamations of pleasure over the presents, she remained detached, as if visiting with clients, not involved with friends.

"You must stay for dinner," Miguel told her, giving Abby a friendly squeeze around the shoulders. "We have enough food to feed an army. Tell her, Tom, she has to stay.''

Tom grinned. ''Maria's mother would be insulted if you didn't. And, believe me, you don't want to insult Señora Garza. She may be tiny, but she's powerful. Miguel calls her Mighty Mouse.''

''Shh….'' Miguel put a finger to his lips, mischievously.

Abby smiled back. ''Okay. I'll stay. Thank you.''

''No. Thank you for all these great gifts. This wagon is terrific.'' He snatched up the box. ''I'm going to the barn. Coming, Tom?''

''No way, amigo. You've worked me hard enough this week.''

Once Miguel left the room, Abby shifted on the straight-back chair nestled in the small bay window. The afternoon sunlight, spilling in through the windows, imbued an aura of gold around her shoulders and head. She crossed one long, sleek leg over her knee, unconsciously displaying her nervousness.

''I must owe you a small fortune,'' Tom said.

She brushed back a lock of hair. ''Forget it. The money you sent with Angel was fine. Everything was on sale, except for the quilt, and that was my gift.''

He watched her inspect the house, not surprised by the small knot in the pit of his stomach. Despite Maria's cheerful wallpaper and lace curtains, there was no disguising the basic simplicity of the house. To the left of the front door was the living room, to the right a nook Tom had intended to use as an office. Maria's sewing machine and various baby paraphernalia made it look cluttered.

A sudden cry from the bundle in his arms brought three females out of the woodwork. Abby, he noticed, instinctively started forward but stopped herself.

"He's probably hungry," Maria said, plucking him from Tom's arms. "I'll go feed him. Do you girls want to come?"

Tom started to intervene, remembering how Lesley liked to nurse Angel in private—he didn't know if she'd nursed Heather—but Maria and his daughters were up the stairs and out of sight before Tom could open his mouth.

"You're good with babies," Abby said.

Tom heard a stiltedness in her tone he didn't understand.

He reached for his long-ignored beer and took a drink. "Ugh," he said, making a face. "Warm. I know where Miguel keeps his stash. Wanna come?"

She didn't answer but followed him through the sunny, south-facing kitchen to the back porch where a red plastic ice chest sat beside a wooden swing suspended from the rafters. When Tom bought the place, the ratty appendage had housed two broken washing machines and a dysfunctional freezer. He'd immediately replaced the screens and installed the swing, picturing a romantic spot where he and Lesley could smooch and grow old.

He plucked two dripping cans from the icy water and sat down on the swing, leaving plenty of room for Abby to join him. The heat of the previous week had eased off when a Delta breeze swept southward, bringing blue skies and moderate temperatures. The view was as picturesque as a postcard.

"How charming! I love porches. This is a great place," she said, sitting stiffly against the upright back.

Her praise relaxed a knot in his stomach and opened

a door to feelings he'd been trying valiantly to ignore. "Thanks. It was a labor of love."

At her puzzled look, he said, "Didn't you know? This house is mine. I bought it ten—no, eleven, years ago. It was pretty run-down and I fixed it up."

A dark look crossed her face and he saw her fingers tighten around the can. He didn't understand her reaction.

"Is there something wrong with that?"

"No," she said firmly.

"You seem upset."

"Just surprised." She took a small sip of beer. "You never mentioned it before. It's a wonderful house. You could have moved in here and saved the headache of building the addition."

"And kick these guys out? Not my style."

Her gaze dropped to her hands as if embarrassed. "Of course not."

Tom fought the urge to lift her chin and kiss her.

After choking down a big gulp of beer, he pointed toward the fenced pasture spread out behind the small barn and detached garage. Half a dozen horses grazed on the irrigated land. "The house came with fifteen acres. I could have put in almonds or pistachios, but Miguel and I decided to go together on a little breeding operation. Quarter horses."

"Really? Land baron and breeder?" She shook her head, obviously bemused by something. "You play your cards pretty tight to the vest, as they say."

Puzzled by her tone, Tom cocked his head and waited for an explanation.

"My grandfather died before I was born. Everyone says he was kind and generous to a fault..." Like his granddaughter, Tom would have added, if she hadn't plowed ahead. "But he never discussed finances with his wife and, when he died, he left my grandmother penniless. Worse, actually, since he was hospitalized for several months with no insurance. Grammy had to move in with my folks and basically start from scratch."

"Are you saying I'm like your grandfather because I didn't tell you about this house?"

She held up a hand. "It's your business, and I know you're not comfortable talking about finances."

He bit down on a smile. She was so damn pretty, especially when she got a burr under her saddle.

"I admit I'm a little closemouthed about money— mainly 'cause I don't have much, but we can talk about it if you want." A sudden thought struck him, something his father used to tell him: "Marry a woman you like to talk to. When you get older you'll be doing a lot of it."

She shrugged one shoulder regally. "The point is…"

Tom decided to cut to the chase. "The point is, something's going on between us that's got you nervous, so it's easier to make up reasons not to like me."

A flash of color swept across her features; her eyes changed to a stormy gold-green that would haunt his dreams tonight.

"I…I like you." Chin up, defiant, her protest lost impact when her gaze slipped to his chin. "You're a very nice man. A gentleman." She almost didn't get out the last word because Tom leaned over and pressed his lips to hers. Still moving, butterfly-like beneath his own, their sweetness, even flavored with beer, sent a shaft of desire burning through him.

Undoubtedly startled, she put up a hand to push him back, but as he deepened the kiss, tasting her, she left the hand resting against his shirtfront. Her response pushed him further than he meant to go.

When he looped his arm around her shoulders, she jumped back as though electrocuted.

"This is terribly unprofessional and I apologize," she said, rising and moving away a step on what looked like wobbly legs.

Tom wasn't too steady himself. "I kiss you, and you apologize? How come?"

She peeked through the square of glass in the kitchen door before turning back to face him. The glow in her cheeks made him long to pull her into his arms and finish what he'd started—it would be sweet and hot and…. He shook his head, making himself focus on her words, not her lips.

"…your daughters' advocate. I have a job to do and it's unprofessional to—you know what I mean, Tom. This is the real world."

He didn't like her cool, professional tone. Or the truth behind her words.

"Angel and Heather are the only ones that matter here," she said.

He couldn't fault her commitment to his children, but he sensed something else in her reaction and the way she couldn't quite bring herself to meet his gaze. He'd never met anyone like her, so complex, so caring and so damn sexy in the most understated way.

She sighed. She eyed the seat beside him but opted to sit on the cooler instead. "Tom, we haven't spoken about this, but I'm thinking of quitting my job either this fall or next spring so I can go back to school."

One part of him yipped in glee—if she wasn't his daughters' advocate, she could be his…something else. Another part realized she was talking about leaving.

"Why?"

She tucked a swath of hair behind her ear. He hadn't paid close attention to her ears before, but they were perfect. Not pierced, he noticed.

She cleared her throat, drawing his attention back to her eyes. A man could never grow tired of looking at those eyes. "A lot of reasons. All personal."

Her tone slammed the door on his speculation and fantasy.

"This shouldn't have happened, but since it did we need to put it behind us for your daughters' sake. They've made a lot of headway, but they're not through the woods yet. There are four seasons of grief. And they're just starting summer."

Her words were more effective than his midnight cold shower.

"You're right. The girls need you, and I don't want to do anything that messes that up." He hunched forward, careful not to touch her. "I like you, Abby. A lot. And we both put something in that kiss, but...I know my duty. It won't happen again."

"HIS DUTY," Abby muttered, snatching a container of Ben and Jerry's out of Donna's freezer.

Abby slammed the door of the bottom freezer compartment, kicking it for good measure.

"Why am I letting this get to me?" she asked, ignoring Donna's bemused look. "It was just a little kiss, and he backed off when I told him to."

Donna's sandy eyebrows shot up. "Because you're disappointed? You didn't really want him to stop."

"No. Yes. Was that a question?" Abby shoveled a spoon into the frozen block of calories. "You know I wouldn't get involved with a client. We've already had this talk.''

Donna fenced her spoon against Abby's. "Talk is cheap. Unless you're on the phone with a lawyer. Speaking of lawyers, I saw Daniel at the arts council fund-raiser last night. The man looks fabulous in a tux.''

Abby shrugged. "I don't want to talk about Daniel. I've got to have a talk with him—he's just not my cup of tea, although I promise to be more diplomatic than that.'' She swallowed a bite of frozen nectar. "Did I tell you I think I made a real breakthrough with the girls?''

"And their father.''

Abby stuck out her tongue. "It was so neat this morning. They opened up to me about their mom. They might be moving into another stage of grief.''

"What stage is Tom in?''

Abby looked for cynicism in her friend's tone but couldn't find it. "I don't know. You know it must have been very hard for him not to share in Heather's birth. He loves babies. You should have seen him holding baby Rey. His hands are so big, you'd think he'd be clumsy, but he was gentle as a surgeon. I've never seen a man as comfortable with a baby.''

Abby read Donna's speculative look. "What?''

"You're in love with the man.''

Abby's mouth dropped open but the words of denial wouldn't come. She couldn't move past the image of Tom, after dinner, tenderly rocking the restless baby until Rey's whimpers diminished. Watching the scene, an old pain surfaced, reminding her of a heartache she'd buried years before. A yearning so poignant and sharp, all breath left her lungs, making her turn away before she humiliated herself by falling to her knees crying.

"I don't want to talk about it," she said wistfully.

"Yes, you do. But I'm not the person you need to talk to."

Abby looked away from the truth in her friend's eyes. "What's wrong with me, Donna? I thought all this was behind me."

Donna squeezed her arm supportively. "Old wounds that aren't quite healed can lie dormant for years, slowly festering. It only takes a pinprick to make them open up, gushing all that toxic waste."

Abby groaned. "What a disgusting metaphor!"

"It's late. Come back tomorrow and I'll have a better one, but I'll have to charge you full price." She eyed Abby with a look Abby knew all too well. "Why are you so sure Tom would be scandalized by something that happened almost ten years ago? Something you had no control over?"

Abby swallowed. "Tom epitomizes old-world sensibilities, Donna. He wouldn't condemn me, but he wouldn't understand. Women in his world don't have abortions." She said the words in a rush, inwardly sickened by the memories they provoked. "He'd be kind and sympathetic but secretly horrified."

Donna shook her head. "We could go into the history of this if you need to, but I'm more curious why you're so convinced Tom's response would be negative. Maybe you're more afraid he would understand. What would you do then?"

The truth of her friend's words brought already raw emotions even closer to the surface.

Donna walked to Abby's side and looped her arm around Abby's shoulders. "I don't know Tom well enough to say what he'd think, but, honey, if you can't be open with him, you can't go forward in the relationship. And if you can't go forward, you can't get involved. He's not another Landon.''

Abby almost smiled at the ludicrous comparison. ''I know that.''

In a tone Abby remembered from her time as a patient, Donna told her, ''Then you need to begin distancing yourself from that family, Abby. For all of your sakes.''

Abby closed her eyes. ''I know.''

CHAPTER NINE

MUD MADE gulping sounds around his boots as Tom finished unearthing the recently soaked dirt covering the lid of the new septic tank. Once the plumbing was hooked up, this larger tank would serve the bunkhouse and addition as well as a new shower and toilet added to the barn. Late Friday afternoon the construction crew backfilled the gaping hole to avoid any accidents, and thoughtfully soaked the dirt to assure compacting.

Unfortunately, someone forgot to cover the open flange, a three-inch-wide black plastic hole in the floor of what would soon be Heather and Angel's new bathroom. How—*why* a kitten would crawl into such a small, uninviting opening was beyond him, but Heather's kitten somehow managed to do just that and now it was his job to rescue the little thing.

"Gad, it's hotter than Hades and not even noon," Tom said, swiping at a grimy rivulet coursing down his cheek.

He dropped to his knees in the mud, leaning forward to gain purchase for his lever. A muscle in his lower back sputtered, warning him not to go there.

They'd already spent a futile hour at the other end of the pipe, dangling bits of salami on a string like a fishing lure, listening to mournful meows.

"I can hear her, Daddy," Heather said, one ear flat to the ground. "She knows you're coming."

And she's probably backing up even farther in the pipe, he groused silently, trying to figure out how he was going to coax the frightened creature into the tank.

"You've gotta save her, Daddy," Heather pleaded, dirt highlighting streaks of tears. "It's dark in there, and she's scared. I know she is. Oh, please, Daddy, please get her out."

Heather's wail multiplied Tom's frustration factor. The kitten wasn't the only one fearing the outcome of this rescue—Tom didn't know how he'd live with himself if he failed to save his little girl's pet.

Using the flattened end of a crowbar, he pried open the lid. Grimacing, he upended the heavy cover, letting it topple to the mound of odoriferous, baking mud. He stretched out perpendicular to the inky crater, pebbles and twigs poking his chest.

Craning into the pit, he eyeballed the black hole at the top of the concrete tank.

"Here, kitty, kitty," he called.

The hollow chamber echoed like a tomb.

"Do you see her, Daddy?" Heather asked, flopping down beside him. "Is she okay? Is she safe? Why doesn't she come out, Daddy? What if she's stuck?"

An image of his little girl crashing headfirst into the empty cavern made him elbow her back. Rising to his knees, he drew Heather to her feet and gave her a gentle shake to stop the panic he could feel building inside her. "Run get Angel, honey. She's helping Janey with paperwork. I'll have to drop this ladder in here. She can fit down there easier than me." He maneuvered the fiberglass ladder into the hole, propping its protruding rungs against the far side of the opening.

"Abby's coming, Daddy," Heather said, watching him. "She could do it."

"Abby? Who called her?" He regretted his angry tone and flinched at Heather's puzzled look, but the last thing he needed today was Abby. She seldom left his thoughts as it was, but, at least, he'd managed to avoid any face-to-face meetings throughout the past two weeks.

"I did, Daddy. She helped me name Esmy, remember? She has to be here." Esmeralda the kitten was named for a character in *The Hunchback of Notre Dame* video—Abby's halfway-through-Rainbows gift to the girls. Despite the awkwardness stemming from Tom's impromptu kiss, Abby continued to work on his daughters' behalf, as well as running interference on the remodeling job by keeping tempers cool and optimism high. He'd have had an ulcer by now if it weren't for Abby, but that didn't mean he was ready to see her.

"I know, honey, but you shouldn't have bothered her. Saturday is her day off."

Heather tilted her head, eyeing him as if he were suddenly spouting Greek. "Daddy, we're not her work. We're her family."

Something hot and painful burned in his throat, and Tom had to look away. Fortunately, the dogs alerted him to Abby's approach and he had several seconds to get control of his emotions before a cloud of dust preceded a screeching Honda into the yard.

Abby flew out of the car and raced to the mud pit.

Tom squinted against the white glare of the noon sun reflecting off gravel, trying to see more than a willowy shadow. When she squatted to hug Heather, his mouth turned to sandpaper; his knees would have buckled if he hadn't been flat on his belly. Tank top, no bra and skimpy shorts that barely covered her fanny. Even his fantasies hadn't come up with that one.

"Hi," she said breathlessly. "I came as fast as I could. Is Esmy okay?"

"Still meowing," he replied, when he found his voice. "Heather, go get your sister."

"Okay, Daddy."

In the yawning silence Tom swore he could hear his sweat forming. A rivulet inched past his ear. His T-shirt felt like a soggy body cast and smelled like ripe horse manure.

Something white dangled in front of his salt-blurred vision. He blinked. A pristine tissue extended from Abby's long, graceful fingers—half moons of dirt beneath each nail. "You're going to evaporate in this sun," she said. "Isn't there some other way of getting the kitten out?"

Her concern didn't lessen his frustration. "We're going to try Angel in here on the ladder."

"I could—"

"No," he snapped. He already owed her too much without adding to the debt. He grabbed the first thought that came into his head. "Liability. Couldn't risk it."

The tissue slipped from her grasp, fluttering like a dead dove to the bottom of the tank.

A clatter of metal and a chorus of voices interceded on his behalf. He twisted around to see Ed and Angel lugging a white net bag between them. Janey and Heather brought up the rear, moving at a slower pace. Janey, at home for a two-week hiatus between cancer protocols, looked wan but determined to get on with her project of researching her family tree. She'd proven a real lifesaver by hiring his bored and belligerent elder daughter as a secretary and assistant.

"We brought a sunshade," Angel said, helping Ed

to dump the various aluminum tubes and canvas awning on the ground. "Hi, Abby."

"Hello, Abby. Why didn't you call us sooner, Tom?" Ed asked, surveying the situation with a grin. Not waiting for an answer or a greeting, he said, "'Course, that's not the way to handle a cat stuck in a sewer pipe, you know."

Tom climbed to his feet, brushing off globs of mud. "Really?"

"Yep, just leave it be…"

"Now, Ed, just hold your mouth," Janey scolded. "'Morning, Abby, you look nice and cool, despite the heat."

Abby looked down as if just then realizing what she was wearing. Her face flushed red. "I was gardening when Heather called," she said, plucking at the fabric that clung so provocatively to her breasts. "I didn't stop to change, just jumped in the car." As if to divert attention from herself, she asked, "Should you be out in the sun? It's hotter than blazes."

"Damn right," Ed said, scowling, "but the darn woman won't take it easy. Tom, give me a hand here."

The last thing Tom needed was an audience.

"I'll do that," Abby said. "My brother's got a sunshade just like this."

A glimpse of white bottom beneath a fringe of shorts when she bent over to pick up the aluminum poles made Tom's knees buckle. "We don't have to turn this into a sideshow," he muttered. "Angel, shimmy down the ladder and call the cat. When she pokes her head out, grab her," Tom said, pointing to the hole.

Angel looked at him as though he'd just sprouted a second head. "Me? No way. Uh-uh. I'm not going down some smelly hole.'' She backed away from him, eyes flashing.

Normally, Tom might have paid more attention to Angel's pallor and odd reaction. After all, she'd always been part tomboy ready to jump into any kind of foolish danger. But today, heat and hormones blurred his observation skills. ''It's not smelly. It's brand-new. Besides, you're not going all the way in it. Just a few steps down the ladder.''

She eyed the muddy, boxlike gap like a young colt ready to bolt. ''No. I won't do it. You can't make me.'' Her tone was shrill with a tremor of hysteria.

Abby, who was anchoring one slim post upright while Heather and Janey held two other corner posts, abandoned her post and rushed to Angel's side. ''It's okay, sweetheart,'' she said, stepping between Angel and the hole. ''Lot's of people are afraid of small spaces. It's called claustrophobia.''

Angel's back stiffened. ''I'm not afraid of anything, but I'm not going down that hole.'' Her bottom lip trembled.

Abby looked at Tom. ''Let me do it.''

Tom's frustration level rose a notch. Not only should Abby not be here, she had no business interfering with him and his daughters. ''No. Angel can do it. It's not dangerous.''

Abby put her hands on her hips and gave him an exasperated look. ''Tom, you're being unreasonable.''

Janey suddenly appeared at Tom's elbow. ''This sun is getting to be too much for me, after all, Thomas. Heather, dear, let's go inside and try to sweet-talk your kitty out on that end. She's a girl, right?'' Heather, who hovered near Janey's leg, showing her usual signs of unease when tempers started to flare, nodded vigorously.

"Well, sometimes girls need a little wooing. Let's go try."

Tom wondered if that last hint was for his benefit. An image of Lesley flashed into his head. "You can be so damn stubborn, Tom Butler," Lesley used to say. "When you get something stuck in your head, I need dynamite to change your mind."

"All right, be my guest," he said to Abby. "But if you fall—"

Abby gave Angel a quick squeeze then moved to his side. Together they walked to the edge of the hole. Tom looked at Abby and realized in a flash of insight she was as terrified of the prospect of going into that small, dark space as Angel was. She squared her shoulders and flashed him a brave smile. "Okay then. Let's do it."

Tom's heart melted, and he knew in that instant he loved her. He opened his mouth to speak, but a sudden shout stopped him. "Daddy. Daddy," Heather's high-pitched voice called. Tom looked over his shoulder and saw her running toward them, a tiny glob of fur squeezed against her chest. "She came right out of the toilet, Daddy. Esmy's safe."

Tom's head pounded and his heart hurt. It could have been heatstroke, but he was afraid it was more permanent than that. He turned to Ed, who was leaning against the half-assembled sunshade. The older man seemed highly amused about something.

"I think you're right about checking on the herd, Ed. I'll take off as soon as we have this situation under control," he said. Ed's suggestion last night to take a couple of days in the mountains had fallen on deaf ears, but that had been then. Now he needed some time alone to get his thoughts together. "I hate to ask, but could you and Janey watch the girls overnight?"

''They could come home with me,'' Abby said before Ed could answer. ''Donna's visiting her son and Melina's on a cruise. I don't have any plans and I'd love the company. Really.''

Tom hesitated—not on behalf of his children.

''I have to stop by and feed Donna's cat, but she has a pool. Do you guys swim?'' she asked the girls.

Their whoops of joy made Tom flinch.

''And we could pick up pizza and some movies,'' Abby went on. ''It'll be kind of like a slumber party.''

''Sounds cool. Can we, Dad?'' Angel asked, not quite meeting Tom's gaze.

Tom knew she was embarrassed about her earlier scene. He pulled her into his arms and gave her a hug.

''Looks like you're outvoted, boy,'' Ed said, guffawing. ''As we say in the fishing business, it's time to cut bait 'n go home.''

Tom recognized the truth in the older man's words. Unfortunately, this time he was the fish, and he was hooked good.

BY SATURDAY EVENING Abby's family-room carpet resembled a war zone between the Popcorn Fanatics and the Jelly-Belly Coalition. The glass-and-cherrywood coffee table had been pushed aside to accommodate two young bodies and Abby's cat, Tubby, wooed against his better judgment by bits of lime candy and eager affection.

''I like the Mulan bedspread best,'' Heather said, using elbow jabs to secure a better position over the pile of magazine clippings.

A manila envelope filled with decorating ideas gleaned from glossy magazines and a scaled-down floor plan of the girls' new room had arrived in the mail while Abby was at the ranch.

"Too red," Angel argued, nudging Heather's paper bed out of the way. "I like this one—pink and green. Pretty, without being geeky. What do you think, Abby?"

From her perch on the couch, Abby eyed the arrangement. "Very feminine. You have a good eye for color, Angel. The Mulan print is pretty, too, Heather, but it'll be out of style as soon as the next Disney movie comes out. I doubt if your dad will want to fork out the cost for a new one every year. And, remember, girls, my mother never sent a price list with these cutouts. Knowing her, I bet they were clipped from the ritziest magazines on the market."

Angel sighed. "You sound just like my dad."

"Do I?" The comparison made Abby smile. Abby regretted the awkward stiffness between her and Tom that hadn't been there before their fateful kiss, but she could hardly blame him, since she'd gone out of her way to maintain a professional detachment. Then, something had happened during their tussle over who was going into the septic tank. His attitude changed. He seemed resigned about something. What it was, she hadn't a clue.

Abby glanced at her watch. "Six bells. I'd better start the pizza. You guys ready for our appetizers?"

Too absorbed in their planning to answer, both girls nodded.

Abby headed for the kitchen. Not unscathed in the youthful occupation, the usually pristine countertops displayed a collection of juice bottles, popcorn bowls, an unopened box of sugarcoated cereal that made Abby's teeth ache just looking at it, and three plastic video boxes. So far, they'd only watched one movie about twins who try to get their divorced parents back together. Heather liked the funny parts; Angel seemed intrigued by the romance between the father and mother.

Abby and Angel had carried on a rather in-depth discussion about divorce while sharing a bowl of popcorn. "People who have children shouldn't get divorced," Angel maintained. Heather and the cat were stretched out a few feet away on the floor in front of the entertainment center.

"I'm sure they all wish things had worked out differently," Abby said. "A big part of my job is counseling victims of domestic abuse. I tell them no one should stay in a relationship where one person bullies the other, children or no children."

"That didn't happen with my mom and dad."

"No, of course not. Your dad is kind and gentle and very big-hearted. Whatever happened between him and your mom stemmed from something else that made them unhappy. Believe me, there are as many reasons for divorce as there are people."

Angel fiddled with the remote and in a low voice said, "Maybe if they'd stayed together, she'd still be alive."

Impulsively, Abby put her arm around the young girl's shoulders and squeezed. "Hasn't Donna told you about the troublemaker words?"

Angel sniffed and shook her head.

"Woulda, coulda, shoulda and if. She has a story about each of them. Let's take 'if.' Haven't you heard the old saying 'If the dog hadn't stopped to pee, he'd have caught the rabbit'?"

"Yeah," Angel said, grinning. "Dad says it all the time."

"Well, if you're the dog, that's a bad thing—you go

hungry, but if you're the rabbit, you get home safely and everybody's happy. Either way, what happened happened and there's no going back, so *if* isn't a very useful word, is it?''

Angel smiled and nestled comfortably against Abby's shoulder until the movie ended, then she plopped belly-first on the floor to help her sister spread out the clippings. Abby didn't know if her words had helped in any way, but she felt a bond between them that hadn't been there before.

The phone rang as Abby pulled the take-'n-bake pizza out of the refrigerator. She set it on the counter, picked up the portable and walked back to the oven to adjust the setting. ''Abby Davis.''

''How spontaneous are you?''

Abby's heart plummeted. Tom was miles from a phone, but one part of her had hoped it might be him.

''Hi, Daniel. What's up?''

''You. Me. A little waterskiing?''

Abby glanced out the window. Long shadows were creeping across the lawn. Sunset may have been a couple of hours off, but the nearest lake was forty minutes away.

''Tonight?''

''Not exactly. I thought we'd drive to my cabin at Big Bear, spend the night, then go skiing right after breakfast...unless something better comes up.'' The message couldn't have been clearer.

''I have houseguests this weekend, Daniel. Angela and Heather Butler.''

''That cowboy's kids?'' His tone sounded petulant, little-boyish.

''Yes. We're having a slumber party.''

He grumbled something about ''juvenile escapism''

before hanging up. I've got to clear the air about this next week, Abby told herself. How could she date Daniel when his kisses left her cold, while Tom's one kiss haunted her dreams and played havoc with her mind?

Abby replaced the phone and popped the pizza—half plain cheese and half mushroom, red peppers, olives and salami, into the oven. When she turned around, Angel was standing in the doorway.

"I DIDN'T MEAN to eavesdrop, but…did you just blow off a date because of us?" Angel asked. So far, she'd had a pretty decent time at Abby's, and she sensed Abby liked having them there, but she'd understand if Abby wanted to dump them off on Janey and Ed so she could be with her boyfriend.

Abby poured cranberry-kiwi juice into one wineglass and white wine into another and motioned to a stool. Angel slipped into it and reached for the juice.

"The man who called is my boss, and, although we've gone out to dinner a couple of times, I don't think it's a good idea to date someone you work with. I plan to make that clear to him on Monday."

Angel took a sip of juice, then asked, "Would that let my dad out?"

The three plates in Abby's hand clattered against the tile countertop. "I beg your pardon?"

"You and Dad don't exactly work together but you kinda got together because of your work and I just wondered if you'd go out with him…if he asked you." Before Abby could answer, Angel went on, "I think he's lonely. He says he's too busy to be lonely and we're all the company he needs, but Janey says men need women more than women need men."

"She does?" Abby transferred her chopping board

and a bunch of parsley to the island, keeping her focus on Angel. It was one of the things Angel liked best about Abby—she paid attention. Adults rarely did.

"Dad told you Janey hired me to help research her family tree, right?"

Abby nodded. "Tom said you were helping out, but he didn't say how," she said, taking a sip of wine. "That's awesome. Can I hire you next? My family tree's a mess. There's this whole limb that's lost somewhere in Romania."

Angel smiled. One thing she knew about Abby was she didn't say things she didn't mean. "Beats doing nothing," Angel said.

"What about friends? Surely there are kids your age around?"

"I hang out with a couple of girls at Rainbows, but that's…different." Angel didn't try to explain, but she could tell by Abby's nod that she understood.

"Two summers ago, I met some girls at Bible camp, and Dad's been bugging me to call them, but…" Angel couldn't explain why she didn't want to renew her old friendships. Maybe she was too weird to fit in now. After all, she didn't have a mother.

Abby seemed to hear what wasn't said. "I know what you mean. It's hard to pick up relationships after a period of time has passed. It'll be even more awkward for your friends, too, because people are always afraid of saying something wrong. But it sure beats being bored to tears." She took a sip of wine. "I used to live for summer vacation, then when it got here, I'd drive my grandmother up the wall moaning and groaning about not having anything to do." Abby smiled and seemed to drift back in time a minute. "Do you know what she did one day? She carted me off to the library and told me, 'Read all these books. That'll give you plenty to do.'"

Angel made a face. "Don't tell that one to my dad. He already nags me about watching too much boob tube."

"I won't. I promise."

Angel took a drink of juice. Lately, it felt as though she couldn't do anything to please her dad. He praised her for working with Janey but seemed disappointed when he came home and found the house a mess. He never complained, but Angel could tell he was disappointed.

Janey said Tom was just overly tired from handling so much responsibility, but Angel thought it was something else. In the six months she'd been living at the ranch, he'd gone from his laid-back self to a grumpy old father. If her theory was right, Abby might be the one to help get her dad back to normal, and maybe even help salvage Angel's summer vacation.

"Janey said men aren't emotionally equipped to raise a family alone." Angel didn't know if she believed that, but it got her thinking about how her dad felt about being stuck with her and Heather. Maybe he'd get desperate and marry the first woman who came along. Would she and Heather have any say in the matter?

Abby handed Angel a paring knife and two lemons. "Would you please cut them into wedges for our shrimp?" She nibbled on a piece of parsley, then said thoughtfully, "I'm not sure I agree with Janey. I think that some people just make better parents. Period. Your dad is miles beyond me in that respect."

Angel heard something sad in her tone. "How do you know? You don't have any kids."

Abby's face changed. Angel swore she could see a sad, haunted look in her eyes, like how her dad looked when he talked about her mother. The look disappeared in a flash and Abby said brightly, "I've observed a lot of families over the years, and as far as I can see, your dad's doing a great job of parenting."

"I know," Angel said grudgingly. She cut into the first lemon, breathing deeply of the clean citrus smell. She liked the smell of Abby's house, in general. Little bowls of potpourri and scented candles added a feminine touch missing from her dad's house. It made Angel homesick in a way she couldn't explain, because Val had allergies so her mother had never bought fragrant things. But there were still the smells of the cleaning person and her mother's perfume and something intangible Angel couldn't name but missed just the same. "I'm not complaining. But I know Dad had to change his whole life because of us. I don't know how much he dated before, but having two kids can't make it any easier getting a date."

Abby laughed in that way that always made Angel want to laugh, too. "Are you kidding? Two kids as neat as you and your sister are pure gravy. He'll be beating women off with a stick once he's ready to start dating."

Angel lined up the lemon halves and cleanly quartered them. She glanced up to find Abby looking at her. Abby was beautiful, not like a model but in a real way. She was a good person and she seemed to like them. Angel had been thinking about it for a couple of weeks, and she'd decided if her dad had to have a woman in his life, he could do worse than Abby. Then, this septic-tank thing today clinched it. Angel almost cried with gratitude when Abby took her side. It was almost as if Abby knew that looking at that black hole made Angel think of her mother's grave.

"You never answered my question. Would you date Dad if he asked?"

Abby's cheeks colored and she stuttered, "I...um, it would be very unprofessional of me to...that is..."

The oven timer clanged, making Abby knock a pile of minced parsley to the floor. "The pizza's half done," she said, rushing to the pantry for a broom. "We need to serve our shrimp appetizers. Why don't you call Heather to wash up?"

Angel knew avoidance when she saw it. Adults were masters of it. She shrugged. "Okay."

EVEN THOUGH he knew he was late, Tom took his time driving to Abby's house. He followed the directions she'd given him, studying the neighborhood. Abby's house, situated at an angle on a corner lot, appeared older than its neighbors—stucco siding, shake roof, forest-green shutters and mature trees lent a charm the newer, bigger houses lacked.

He left his hat on the seat and ran his fingers through his unruly locks, wishing he'd had time for more than a quick dip in the chilly lake with a bar of soap.

"Hi, Daddy," Heather called from the doorway. "We stayed up till midnight 'n watched three movies and I slept with Tabby—he really likes me, but Abby calls him Tubby 'cause he's kinda fat." Heather whispered the last word before sprinting barefoot across the hot sidewalk and launching herself into Tom's open arms.

She wore a bright orange, two-piece swimsuit he hadn't seen before. He squeezed her until she protested. "Not so tight, Daddy. Tubby doesn't like it when I squeeze him either. See?" She thrust out her hand. A Day-Glo orange adhesive strip bisected her hand. "Abby wanted to call the doctor 'cause it bleeded, but Angel told her it was nothing. We went to the store and I got to pick out the ban'age. It matches my new swimming suit."

"New…?"

She backhanded him, muffling his words. "Kiss it to make it feel better. Mommy always did."

He obliged with a gallant flourish. "Does it still hurt?"

"No, silly. It was just a scratch. Angel says Abby worries too much. She worried about you, too."

"Why me?"

"You said noon and it's nearly four," Abby said softly from the shadow of the doorway. The arched portal lent a European flavor to the entry; a twiggy wreath thick with dried flowers hung on the planked door.

"Sorry about that. I got a late start. Couldn't find a couple of cows." He wished he hadn't accidentally sat on his sunglasses; they'd have given him something to hide behind. Although he'd spent the better part of two days trying to talk some sense into himself, the truth couldn't be denied: he was in love with Abby Davis.

"Were they okay?" Abby asked, holding open the door to admit him. Her khaki shorts were fashionably sloppy; the rust-colored top was cropped, exposing bare midriff. A plastic clip of some kind held her hair back, but errant strands framed her face. Tom's fingers itched to brush them back behind her ears.

He interpreted her tone as polite and caring, but still cool, as it had been since their kiss. Obviously, this gut-wrenching desire was all one-sided.

"Yep. One had a new calf."

He ducked going through the doorway and shifted Heather to his left hip. The tiled foyer was cool and welcoming. "Sounds like you guys had a good time."

Abby closed the door and smiled at Heather, who planted a big, sloppy kiss on Tom's cheek. The worried look left Abby's eyes and he heard her soft, wistful sigh. "We had fun, didn't we, Heather?"

Heather's bright curls danced across his line of vision and she used her small hands to turn his face to look into her eyes. "We ate pizza 'n nachos 'n jelly beans 'n popcorn…"

"Don't give away all our secrets," Abby scolded teasingly. "He'll never let you come back."

To Tom, she said, "We pigged out on junk food yesterday, but we ate real food today. There's pasta and shrimp salad left, if you want some."

He started to decline, planning to pick up a fast-food sandwich on the way home, but Heather wiggled free and pulled his hand, leading the way through the hallway toward the back of the house. "Come on, Daddy. Try it. Abby's a good cook. Real good."

Tom would have liked more than a quick glimpse of the dozen or so family photos grouped together on the wall, but Abby ushered him into a light-filled kitchen with a counter bar. An adjoining dining room seemed to share duty as a greenhouse, by the look of the lush, ceiling-high tropical plants.

Sitting on a soft stool, elbow up to the bar in the snug, aromatic kitchen with three females to wait on him, almost made up for his lonely night, Tom decided. The mountains had offered quiet, but the peace he craved eluded him. Too many thoughts raced through his head, and heart. They followed him down the hill, but he put them aside to watch in fascination the interplay between Abby and his daughters.

"Didn't you say your dad would like that new salad dressing?" Abby asked Heather, who was hanging on the open refrigerator door.

"The Parmesan cheese is on the counter, Angel," she said, giving the girl room to toss, quite messily, the reheated fettuccine. "You added just the right amount at lunch."

Angel served him a heaping mound of noodles adorned with pretty touches of red and green. "Wow," he said after the first bite, his taste buds exploding. "This is great. What is it?"

Abby's cheeks colored like a schoolgirl's. "Just pasta with sun-dried tomatoes, fresh parsley and roasted garlic. Your daughters helped every step of the process."

Heather climbed into the chair beside him. "We picked the green stuff from Abby's garden. You can eat it if you have bad breath." In a lower voice, she added, "But it doesn't taste as good as gum."

Abby's eyes twinkled as she looked up from putting a plate in the dishwasher. He'd have given anything to be able to take her in his arms and kiss her. Fortunately, he had his daughters close by to keep him sane.

When Abby and Heather disappeared into what Tom guessed to be the living room, he asked Angel, "Did you guys get along okay? Heather didn't have a nightmare? Or wet the bed?"

She reached across the counter to put a hand on his arm in such an adult gesture of reassurance it almost took his breath away. My little Angel-babe is growing up. "No more wet beds, Dad. Wait till you see the great underpants Abby bought for Heather. They work like nighttime diapers only they look like real pants. Abby's sister-in-law told her about them."

"Great. I'll buy a box. What about the nightmares?"

Angel shrugged. "She didn't wake up once."

"Really? Wow."

"I think we wore poor Heather out, didn't we, Angel?" Abby said, walking in during Tom's exclamation. "We went swimming at Donna's, grocery shopping, watched two and a half movies and ate nonstop." She puffed out her cheeks.

If she'd put on an extra ounce of weight it sure didn't

show, Tom thought. He noted a bit of color on her legs and arms, though. "Did you put sunscreen on Heather? She swims like a fish but burns easily."

Abby poked her upper arm and frowned. "I kept Heather lathered up but forgot about myself. I'd have fried if Angel hadn't warned me."

Tom scowled. He didn't like the idea of Abby neglecting her own safety.

"Dad," Angel said, distracting him, "we need a couple of minutes to get ready." She leaned into him and whispered, "Keep Abby busy, okay? We're making her something, and it's not quite done."

He nodded just before she disappeared.

"What was that all about?" Abby asked, refilling his glass of water.

He pushed back his plate and rose, stretching to relieve the cranky muscles that hadn't been in a saddle for several weeks. "They need a couple of minutes to get their things together."

"I'll help…" She started to turn toward the doorway, but Tom caught her arm, stopping her in her tracks. She looked at him, her eyes big and surprisingly brown today.

"They need privacy. Something for you, I believe."

Her lips formed an O but no sound came out.

Tom knew the smart thing would be to let go of her, but his fingers thought otherwise. They tightened, just enough to absorb the energy and warmth from her rosy skin. "I thought about you," he admitted, immediately wishing he could take back the words.

"You shouldn't."

"Lots of things I should and shouldn't do, but some things I don't seem to have control over. You're one of 'em. I head out to my special place where the wild grass stays green all summer and the frogs sing and the crick-

ets talk and I lie down at night and look at the billion
or so stars and I tell myself, 'Don't think about her.'
But wham. There you are.''

Instead of pulling back as he expected, she stepped
closer to him. Close enough to smell. ''What kind of
perfume is that?''

Her forehead knit. ''I'm not wearing perfume.''

He closed his eyes and breathed deeply. ''I like it.''

His free hand went to the base of her spine and reeled
her in. His fingertips connected with bare skin, warm
and velvety. Her hips met his at a good spot. Her breasts
touched his chest.

''Are you dancing, Daddy?'' Heather asked, poking
her head through the doorway. ''Where's the music?''

Abby jumped back guiltily. ''Good point. I'll go put
some on.''

''Coward,'' he softly murmured, then looked at his
daughter, who was far too young to have such a mischievous look on her angelic face.

The soft strains of something classical filtered into the
room.

''So,'' Abby said, joining Tom and the girls a moment later. This time she left an arm's length between
them. ''What's up?''

Angel surreptitiously handed her sister a piece of paper the size of a greeting card. Heather stepped forward
and handed it to Abby. ''We made this last night while
you were in the shower.''

Abby accepted it with great formality and held it out
so Tom could see it, too. The cover displayed brightly
colored explosions above a patch of green. The red,
white and blue flags scattered around made Tom's stomach tighten.

''It's beautiful,'' Abby said. ''I'm so glad we ran
across that old box of color crayons.''

''Open it up,'' Angel said, a look of mischief on her face.

Abby opened the folded piece of paper. ''Please join us for our Fourth of July party,'' she read aloud.

Tom's stomach turned all the way over. He had no trouble picturing Abby with his friends and family, but what would she think of a small-town festival complete with rinky-dink parade, barbecue and dance? Would a city girl have fun or be bored to tears?

Abby glanced at him, as if waiting for some encouragement. ''I'd love to come, but maybe you should work this out with your dad first. He may have already invited other people.''

Angel snorted. ''Yeah, his friends and their stupid kids. But there won't be anybody I know there except you and Ed and Janey. Please say you'll come.''

Tom wondered if this had something to do with Angel's moodiness. Was she afraid to meet other kids? Maybe having Abby around would make it easier for her, another safety net or something.

''Yeah, Abby. I need you there, too,'' Heather said. ''What if I have to go potty and can't find Angel? Daddy can't take me 'cause he's a boy, 'n I don't wanna go alone. Mommy always told me I had to take a buddy with me. She was my buddy before but now she's not.'' Her bottom lip popped out.

Abby sank to one knee and opened her arms. ''Okay, sweetie. I'll go. You can be my buddy and I'll be yours.'' Heather surged into her arms and hugged her fiercely. Abby looked up as if begging for approval.

Tom smiled. It was either that, or cry.

CHAPTER TEN

ANGEL CHOSE one of the few remaining picnic tables in the park and heaved the wicker hamper onto the graffiti-grooved planks. She hopped up beside it to wait for the others.

What a geek fest, she thought, eyeing the small community park. People were already starting to stake out spots on the curb for the Fourth of July parade. Big whoop. The high-school band, some National Guard guys with flags, a few fat men on horses and politicians in convertibles. Big deal. When Heather first brought it up at Abby's house, Angel saw this as a way to get Abby and her dad together, but now she didn't care. She wasn't speaking to him anymore.

Mom would have understood, Angel thought, drawing a strand of hair between her lips. At least she wouldn't have had a cow if I asked to go home for a week.

A week in Riverside. See Caitlin and everybody. Shop in some real stores. Hang out. Big deal.

But when she asked her dad, he went all closed up and squinty-eyed.

"Did you talk to Val about this?" he demanded.

"No. I'd rather stay with Caitlin. Paige—Caitlin's mother—said I was welcome anytime."

He never really answered her, but Angel knew he didn't want her to go. Janey said he was just being over-protective and told her to be patient. Donna wouldn't back her up, either. "It's a bigger step than you think," Donna told Angel. "Maybe your father is wise to want to hold off."

Sweeping her hair over one shoulder, Angel saw her father wrestle a cooler out of the back of the truck. Even being mad at him, she couldn't help being proud of how he looked.

He exchanged greetings with a dozen different people—while organizing their picnic supplies. Angel's heart flip-flopped in her chest. He worked so hard, doing all the things it took to run a ranch, plus caring for them, but there were things he just didn't understand.

Peeking through a curtain of hair, Angel scanned the park. Old people and families. Her dad had invited some of his friends, who had kids her age, but the last thing Angel needed was to be foisted on some poor kid who had enough friends of her own.

"Hey, aren't you Angel Butler?" a voice asked.

Angel spun around, drawing up her knees so her feet were flat on the table.

She recognized the chubby blonde who rushed up to greet her but before Angel could answer, the girl asked, "Remember me? I'm Trudy Gills." She pushed her palms against her cheeks and opened and closed her lips, fishlike.

"Yeah, sure, I remember."

The girl hopped up on the table beside her. The legs of her madras-plaid shorts rode up, pinching her plump thighs, and her white eyelet blouse tied just below fledgling bosoms exposed folded layers of baby fat. Suddenly, Angel didn't feel so bad about her choice of outfit: black denim shorts and rust-red tank top with spaghetti straps.

"I'm going to 4-H horse camp this year," Trudy told her. "Second week of August. They still got openings if you wanna come."

"I might be going back ho...down to Riverside to see friends."

Trudy lowered her voice. "All of the J-hotties are going to be there."

"Really. What's a J-hotty?"

"Jared Thomas. Jorges de Mano. Joey Dimenico."

"Oh." Boys.

"Move your butt, Angel, this is heavy," her father said, lugging the oversize cooler toward the table.

She and Trudy scrambled down. Suddenly unsure of herself, she stood mute, feeling stupid.

"Hi, Mr. Butler. Remember me?"

After dumping his load, Tom plopped down on the seat so he was eye level with the smiling girl. "Larry Gills's daughter, right? Tanya?"

Her bubbly laugh eased something tight in Angel's chest. "Trudy," both girls said at once.

"Oh, right. Sorry."

"That's okay. I kinda like Tanya better." She turned to Angel. "Wanna go get a snow cone? The line gets like a mile long after the parade."

Angel looked at her father. They hadn't spoken since last night when she'd stormed off to the barn, cussing as loudly and colorfully as possible.

His eyes were shaded by his cowboy hat, but his lips curled up at the corners. He fished a couple of bucks out of his pocket. "Have fun. Come back when you're hungry. Bring anybody you can round up. Between Abby and Maria, we've got enough food to feed an army."

Angel took a step, but for some reason turned back

and hugged her dad. Tears threatened to ruin the makeup she'd put on just to spite him, but she forced them back. Fortunately, Trudy was busy tying the laces of her thick-soled patent-leather sneakers.

"Nice shoes."

"Thanks. You can borrow them sometime."

"Cool."

"Did you ever meet Jenna Macabbee? Her brother's band's playing this afternoon. He's the coolest. Wait till you see his tattoo."

TOM WATCHED Angel and her friend walk away. His heart hurt. If his arm were tingling, he'd have thought he was having a heart attack. Did this kind of thing happen to dads who grew up with their kids instead of jumping into their lives midstream?

"She's made a friend. How wonderful!" a familiar voice said behind him.

"They knew each other from when Angel was here before." He couldn't turn around until he was sure there weren't any tears in his eyes. "I've been trying to get Angel to call Trudy, but Angel wasn't interested."

"The timing wasn't right. She wasn't ready and now she is. I think it's great."

Tom glanced behind him. Abby's arms were heaped to eye level. A bag of marshmallows teetered on top. He spun around in time to field the puffy bag.

"My mother would have called that a lazy man's load," he said, his voice too stern. He relieved her of three quilts and a rattan mat, revealing the top half of her sleeveless, V-neck denim sundress. Pebble-sized red, white and blue beads nestled against her lightly tanned throat.

She cocked her head at him and smiled, her glossy

honey-colored lipstick inviting a kiss. "Tell that to your other daughter. She's the one who loaded me up."

She turned away to spread out the remaining quilt. Despite her effort to bend demurely, her dress, a loosely tailored affair with buttons from top to bottom, rose above midthigh, giving Tom a great view of her legs and a glimpse of red lace.

Suddenly sweating, Tom opened the second button of his shirt and rolled up his sleeves one more turn. He made himself turn away. "Where's Heather?"

"Helping Janey and Ed. I hope Ed remembered his dolly." After spreading out the other blankets, she straightened up and wiped a bead of sweat from her upper lip. "Is it too early for a beer?"

Tom laughed. For the first time in weeks he felt relaxed. He couldn't explain it. Last night's confrontation with Angel, a week of dreading how he'd handle his attraction toward Abby in public all just sloughed off like old skin.

THREE HOURS LATER, amidst a triangle of aluminum tables, portable grills and folding lawn chairs, Tom stretched out on a musty-smelling sleeping bag and cocked his hat over his face to block the sun filtering through the canopy of trees. The noisy horde of friends and family had disappeared, spreading out in all directions. Closing his eyes, Tom listened to the hum of voices and laughter.

What a great day! They'd lucked out, weatherwise. Unseasonably mild with rare high clouds leading the way for some misguided Pacific front, the valley sky was true blue, the temperature well below ninety.

"Looky there," Janey exclaimed, her voice laced

with humor. "Just proves my mama was right. There's no fool like an old fool."

Tom rose up on one elbow. Regally sitting in a rattan peacock chair, her baldness disguised by a Middle Eastern print turban, Janey looked exotic, not recuperative. Tom followed her outstretched finger.

Ed—dead center in a cluster of men, each pushing seventy—elbowed his way to the throw line of the horseshoe pit, posturing for the sake of the decades-younger women at the opposing pit.

"When you got it, flaunt it," Tom said dryly.

"He can tell that to his chiropractor tomorrow."

Tom chuckled and eased back down.

"How come you're not over there with them?" She made a snuffling noise. "Oh, I know. You're above all that foolishness. You don't need a woman in your life."

Tom readjusted his hat. He heard a lecture in the offing.

Janey threw something that managed to knock his hat askew.

Groaning, he sat up, crossing his legs. "Okay. Let's hear it."

"You're wound tighter than a pig's tail in January. It's plain as day you care about Abby and, for a smart woman, she's positively goofy when you're anywhere in sight. Why don't you do something about it?"

"Not that simple."

"Hmmph," she snorted. "Truth is, dear heart, you're wrong. Nothing like a brush with death to get your priorities straight.

"Did Ed tell you Peter and Maureen are flying out next week? They're thinking about selling their empty nest and moving out here to be closer to us. I begged Pete to do that years ago—before you came to live here—but he had to do his own thing. One thing cancer's shown me is life doesn't wait for us to make time for it.''

Tom traced the groove of his inseam with this thumbnail. ''I know what you mean, but there's not just me to consider. I don't want to upset the girls.''

''Pooh.'' She fanned the air with a folded fan Heather had made for her. ''You don't think the girls were upset all week watching you mope around? They love you, Tom. They want to see you happy.''

''I am happy. Most of the time. The girls have only been here six months. It's not like I was a big dater before they came. I can get by. Besides, a ready-made family with two kids in therapy isn't exactly the kind of thing you spring on somebody.''

''Don't blow that smoke around me, Tom Butler. We're not talking about somebody. We're talking about Abby. Cancer gives a person twenty-twenty where bullshit is concerned. You love that gal.''

He reached for his hat, any kind of protection from this blunt honesty.

''You're afraid, aren't you? You think Abby might do the same thing Lesley did—love you and leave you.''

He crammed the hat down tight. ''It's crossed my mind.''

''Lesley Pimental was looking for a ticket outta this one-horse town and you were it. Her mama was the same way. Ruby thought a man was the answer to her problems. Five husbands later and she still hasn't got a clue.'' She shook her head in disgust. ''I learned a long time ago that answers come from inside, not outside. Abby already knows that. She has the answer, she just hasn't asked the right question yet. But she will.''

Janey reached out and took his hand. He thumbed the

yellowish bruise left by the IV needle. "I went to a counseling group at the hospital, Tom. Know what one gal with colon cancer told me? She said, 'When I was first diagnosed, I was afraid of dying. Now, I'm only afraid of not truly living.'"

Tom thought about her words a moment then squeezed her hand. "You're one smart lady, Janey Hastings. I don't know what I'd do without you."

She squeezed back. "Well, I'm licking this damn disease, so you're not going to have to worry about that for a long, long time. Now go find your girls. All three of 'em."

"BETH, LET ME GET a picture of you and Johnny Dee," Abby said, motioning the Moores together in front of the bandstand. The music, such as it was, had attracted a large group of young people, including Angel and Trudy and a substantial following of teenage boys and girls. Johnny seemed convinced something sexual would take place if he wasn't on patrol. Beth ribbed him about old guilt coming back to haunt him. Nearby, Heather stood with a group of youngsters watching a clown juggle bright scarves.

Abby focused the wide-angle lens. A nice couple. Fourteen years of marriage, Beth told her. Thirteen good, this past one not so hot. But they were working at it.

"Smile."

As soon as the shutter snapped, Johnny swooped Beth into a backward dip and lip lock.

Grinning, Abby turned away, casually scanning the crowd. She was enjoying the day, after all. Her week-long trepidation about meeting Tom's friends had eased once Maria and Miguel arrived with baby Rey. The

Fuenteses and the Hastingses went out of their way to make Abby feel welcome. Chad "Chubs" Raines and his wife, Annette, had eyed her curiously but were distracted by the arrival of the Moores, who'd brought their two kids plus a niece and nephew the same age.

After a huge lunch of hot dogs and barbecued steaks and more side dishes than she could count, Abby found herself chatting with the other women about children, families and the economy. Every once in a while she'd feel Tom's gaze on her, but she was too replete to worry about it.

Johnny broke her mellow reverie when he stepped toward her, hand out. "Your turn. Let me get one of you and Tom."

Abby's heart lurched. "Tom?" She looked toward the blankets where she'd left him napping. From nowhere, a lanky form in faded denims, crisp white shirt with sleeves rolled back to the elbows and gray leather "pointy-toe spider killers," as Ed described Tom's dress boots, materialized at her side. She took a step back.

Johnny snatched the camera from her numb fingers and shoved her to the right. "Closer, not farther apart."

Tom's solid shoulder kept her from stumbling. Abby glanced at Beth, who grinned knowingly. "Smile, Abby."

Lowering the camera, Johnny made a face. "Take off the damn hat, Tom. Why don't you learn to wear a ball cap like everybody else?"

Abby felt him shrug. To her extrasensitive skin, even that slight motion felt full of portent. It set other feelings in motion, making her jiggly inside. "Just take the darned picture, Dee," Tom told him.

"Put your arm around her."

"Take the darned picture," Tom and Abby said together.

Fighting a grin, she looked at him; his lips turned upward, too. Even shaded by the brim of his hat, his eyes reflected the cloudless blue of the sky. Damn, she missed being able to look into his eyes.

"Now, that was more like it," Johnny said, walking up to them. He passed the camera to Abby, who accepted it, unable to make herself break the connection with Tom. "Listen, buddy, we have to do something before it's too late."

"About what?" Tom's eyes held a question that didn't seem to have anything to do with Johnny Dee.

"Them."

Tom also seemed reluctant to move away from Abby, but Johnny stiff-armed him, sending him back a step. "Boys. Walking, talking pillars of raging hormones."

While the two men discussed youthful lust, Beth drew Abby's attention to a group of women Beth called the "town scions, such as they are." Abby only partially listened.

"If that was my guy, I'd have my claws out about now," Beth said in a low voice.

Confused, Abby looked around, finally spotting Tom and Johnny a few feet away. Tom seemed to have acquired a new appendage—a twenty-something redhead in extremely short shorts and halter top plastered to his front, her belly button pressed tight to the big silver buckle at his waist.

A rush of adrenaline fueled by jealously surged through Abby's system before she could stop it. Fighting a slight wave of nausea, she asked in a stiff voice, "Who is she?"

"Laurie Pimental. His ex-wife's ex-sister-in-law."

"I beg your pardon?"

"Laurie used to be married to Lesley's brother, Raymond. He's in jail, she probably ought to be."

Abby looked away, hating the way the young woman's fawning made her gut churn. "Tom can handle it, if he wants to. Some men like that."

Beth shot her a look. "Not Tom Butler. You're obviously the person he's interested in, and Tom wouldn't dream of two-timing somebody. He's the most honorable man I have ever met."

Beth took Abby's arm and led her a few steps away. "Let me tell you about Tom. Johnny and I started dating in eighth grade. We broke up once right before senior prom, and I sort of threw myself at Tom. He was so kind and sweet I ended up crying my eyes out and telling him my whole life story. There was a lot of alcohol abuse in my family, and Johnny was partying pretty heavy back then. The idea of reliving my mom's life terrified me. Tom is the one who made Johnny go to counseling with me."

Beth stepped closer and lowered her voice. "You probably don't know this, but Johnny and I are the reason Tom wasn't home when the cops first called about Lesley. We were fighting, and I'd packed up the kids and moved to my folks' place in Fresno. Johnny and Chubs went out drinking and bumped into Tom. He'd been up in the mountains for a week. He's not much of a drinker, and he hadn't eaten all day. Anyway, the booze did a real number on him. Johnny hid his keys and left him sleeping it off in his truck. That's where the highway patrol found him the next morning."

She frowned. "He blamed himself, not Johnny or me."

Abby could picture it. Honorable. Noble. She knew

that about him, respected him for it, possibly even loved him for it, but that didn't change things between them.

To keep from looking at Tom and the human leach, Abby scanned the crowd for Heather, who had been ten feet away not three minutes earlier. Squinting, she pivoted in each direction. No mop of white-blond curls in sight.

"Heather," Abby called, instinctively heading in the direction where she'd last seen her. "Beth, do you see Heather anywhere?"

"She was here a second ago."

Abby's heart sped up. She spotted Angel and waved her over. "Have you seen Heather?"

Angel shook her head, as did her pudgy shadow.

"Run to the picnic spot, see if she's with Janey."

Obviously alert to the fear in Abby's voice, Angel didn't hesitate.

Abby sent Beth back to enlist Tom and Johnny in the search while she headed toward the 4-H and FFA exhibits. Heather loved animals.

Fighting back all the dire images of faces on milk cartons, Abby picked her way through the crowd, trying to look in all directions at once. A throng of people blocked her way. As she eased around them, she realized she'd reached the line for the portable bathrooms, which were at the outskirts of the festivities.

She turned back, recalling a wire-fenced enclosure beneath a stay of elms. The 4-H petting zoo. As she neared a fence of straw bales, a flash of white caught her eye. In the far corner of the pen sat Heather, a huge duck on her lap.

Abby flew past the startled young attendant. "Heather," she cried breathlessly, tears brimming. She dropped to her knees, the scratchy straw poking her bare skin. "Why didn't you tell me where you were going? I thought I lost you."

Clearly puzzled by Abby's tone, Heather shook her head. "I only just walked here. This is Ferdinand. Like in the movie."

Abby shooed the duck away then pulled Heather into her arms. Rocking back and forth, she squeezed her tight. Relief opened the floodgate. She closed her eyes but couldn't stop the tears. "Oh, baby, don't ever scare me like that again."

When she opened her eyes, she found Tom watching from just outside the fence. His smile thanked her for finding his daughter; the look in his eyes made her heart dance.

ABBY CLOSED HER EYES and inhaled. No smell on earth could be sweeter than a man's scent mingled with spray starch. Tom's shoulder beneath his neatly pressed shirt made the kind of pillow she could lean her head against for the rest of her life, if she let herself—which, of course, she couldn't. But, Abby told herself, one night can't hurt.

With tiny, white lights twinkling in the trees surrounding the grass dance floor, Abby felt like Cinderella at the ball. The magic would disappear at midnight and she would go back to being responsible, but for the moment she was free to drink it all in, every splendid moment.

The band, a fifty-something ensemble complete with an accordion player, set the mood with old standards like "Stardust" and "Fly Me to the Moon." Tom danced with simple grace. He held her close but with respect and dignity. His strong arms made her feel safe. His heart seemed to beat in time with hers.

"Look," he said, directing Abby's attention to the row of kids perched on the split-rail fence that flanked the band shell. Angel, laughing and pointing with the others, looked happy—quite a change from the petulant youngster Abby had escorted to Fresno on Thursday. "They think because we're old we can't have fun. I'm having fun. What about you?"

"I don't think *fun* quite covers it," she said, looking into his eyes, wishing she could memorize the twinkling humor she saw reflected. So often lately, he'd been as serious and somber as his elder daughter, but tonight both seemed transformed. Angel because she'd reconnected with her friends; Tom because...Abby wasn't brave enough to explore that one.

His oh-so-masculine lips narrowed slightly and his forehead creased. "No?"

"No. A *fun* day earns a paragraph or two in my journal. This one's more like four or five pages," she told him honestly. He rewarded her candor with a sweet kiss at each corner of her lips. It would have been so easy to turn her head to meet his lips, but a swell in the level of heckling made her bury her face against his shoulder.

"My brother always said I'd pay for sneaking up on him when he was making out with his girlfriend," she muttered.

Tom's chuckle rumbled through his chest.

"Daddy," Heather cried, wedging between their legs. "It's time for the fireworks. Look, Abby, look."

Tom hoisted Heather to one hip and took Abby's hand, leading the way to the curb, where the rest of their group had gathered. Abby glanced over her shoulder and saw Angel and her friends racing to find a good vantage point. A sudden sense of fullness, of perfection within a moment, brought tears to her eyes. She squeezed Tom's hand. Her handsome prince with two wonderful daughters. Cinderella never had it so good.

CHAPTER ELEVEN

TOM HUNG UP the receiver of the phone with exquisite care to keep from hurling it across the room.

"Something wrong?" Ed asked, poking his head in the doorway of the box-filled room that would soon be the ranch's new office. Janey had commandeered the old office for her genealogy research, telling Ed, "Thirty-five years of having an office in my house is long enough."

Ed used the move as an excuse to buy a new computer, which he planned to coerce Tom into using. First, Tom had to find time to get it out of its box.

Tom sighed and ran a hand through his hair. "I think it's called the brush-off, but it's been so long since I've dated, I'm not real sure," he said honestly.

On the Fourth of July, Tom was certain things were heating up between him and Abby. They'd danced, laughed, even squeezed in a furtive kiss before Angel and her friends found them. By the time he fell asleep that night, he could picture their wedding and the birth of their child. But that was Sunday. Now it was Friday afternoon and he had yet to talk to Abby, let alone do anything that could result in propagation.

She'd even bailed on driving the girls to Rainbows yesterday, telling Angel her boss had scheduled a meeting, which she couldn't avoid. When Tom tried calling her at home after their return at ten, there'd been no answer. He figured this was the same boss who was trying to date her.

Tom rolled his shoulders trying to ease some of the tension. "I finally made a decision about allowing Angel to go to Riverside and wanted to run it past Abby," he told Ed. Tom trusted Abby's judgment; he needed her input. He missed her, damn it.

"Did you try her office?" Ed asked, lowering his body to the used but serviceable leather couch.

Tom nodded. "I just talked to her friend, Melina. She sounded apologetic as hell, but she said Abby has been in meetings all week—something about their boss finding some money to hire two new employees, and Abby handling all the interviews."

"She's a busy lady."

Tom sighed. "I know. But—"

"You thought things had changed between you."

Tom eyed his friend, the man who in many ways knew him better than his father. "Yep."

Ed steepled his callused fingers. "Could be Abby's just plain busy. Could be she's developed a case of what's commonly called cold feet. You've seen it happen when you're breaking a colt," Ed told him. "You get 'em to a spot you think they're comfortable with you, then—*wham*—somethin' spooks 'em. Just takes time and patience."

Tom sighed. "A part of me knows that. The girls need time. I need time. Abby needs time." He looked at the freshly painted walls of what had once been the tack room. "But then there's the seventeen-year-old inside me who wants it all right now."

Ed hooted. "At least you're honest." He rose, using the arm of the sofa for leverage. "Son," he said, "do yourself a favor. Go drown that kid in a cold shower, then load up your girls and take 'em down south. Janey don't have to go back till Thursday so I can keep an eye on things. Angel needs to make peace with her old life, and I'm thinkin' it might not hurt to put a little space between you and Abby for a time. Might be her feet'll warm up by the time you get back.''

ABBY COULDN'T CONTAIN the excitement bubbling in her chest as she pulled into the Hastingses' driveway. She hadn't seen Tom in a week. Last Sunday, the Fourth of July, something had changed between them, something that both thrilled and terrified Abby. She hadn't been deliberately avoiding Tom all week—well, maybe she had, a little, but work had provided the perfect excuse not to see him until she could get things straightened out in her own mind.

As Melina told Tom, Daniel had appointed Abby moderator of the hiring committee. Her days were packed with résumés and interviews; her nights were filled with dreams of dancing in Tom's arms.

She could have called or made a better effort to return his calls, but she didn't want to do that until she knew what she was going to say. Indecisiveness was not a trait she liked in herself or others, but Abby found herself flip-flopping on this issue like a politician before election day.

And my decision is? she thought, slowly extricating herself from the car. She looked toward the newly painted addition visible through the leafy walnuts. *To go for it, of course.*

Janey's invitation to Sunday dinner gave Abby a much-welcomed chance to see the family she missed. With any luck she and Tom could slip away to discuss the possibility of seeing each other socially. It was a big step, one that meant she would have to reassign his case to another advocate, but she thought he'd agree.

"Hi, Abby," Ed said, opening the door for her. "Come in. We're tickled pink you could come."

Abby walked into the flagstone foyer. Straight ahead, in the step-down living room, a wall of glass provided a panoramic view of fields and orchards beyond the knoll. "What a view!" Abby exclaimed, handing Ed the bottle of wine in her hands.

He ushered her into the room. "We like it. Makes me feel like a king some days."

Janey, entering through a swinging door to the right, hurried to Abby's side and took her hands in a warm greeting. "Hello, dear," she said, smiling. "We're so glad you could come. I'd hoped Tom and the girls would be here, but they won't be back from down south until Wednesday. Heather absolutely refused to miss the Rainbows picnic."

Abby knew all about the picnic. She couldn't go because of Daniel's first-ever VOCAP four-day staff retreat that she was coordinating. Melina said it was retribution for dumping him. Abby argued the dumping was mutual, since Daniel was the one who'd called her into his office two weeks earlier and demanded to know whether they had a relationship or not. Abby couldn't lie. She felt bad for letting him think he'd ever had a chance to win her heart. Her only solace was that rumor had it Daniel was already involved with a woman from the mayor's office.

Abby's disappointment must have shown, although she did her best to hide it. Ed handed her a glass of wine. "Here. This'll help."

"I didn't know he'd made up his mind to let Angel go," Abby said, sipping the red wine.

Janey glanced at her husband. "I think Ed helped point Tom in that direction. Ed told him Angel needed to put a few ghosts to rest. I sure hope it was the right decision."

Ed shrugged his burly shoulders. "You can't go forward with your life if you're always looking back," he said sagely. "Now that Angel's got some friends around here, she's got something to compare to her old life. She has a good head on her shoulders and she's always liked the ranch. I think it'll work out the way it should."

Abby hoped he was right. She hadn't had a chance to talk to Angel about her new friends, but Heather told Donna that Tom was thinking about getting Call Waiting because Angel was constantly on the phone.

During dinner Janey explained about Tom's compromise: he agreed to drive Angel back to Riverside if she agreed to four days, not a week. That way he could take Heather to a few amusement parks, and even visit a guy who was interested in purchasing one of Tom's colts.

Abby was impressed, but not surprised. Tom's flexibility was one of the things she admired most about him. She only hoped that it extended to his social life, because as much as she wanted to be included in that life, she knew she wasn't going to be able to give him what he'd want—marriage, babies, the whole nine yards. She hoped he'd settle for a love affair.

"THANK YOU, dear," Grace Davis said, practically patting Abby on the head like a child. "Come back for me around four."

"Come back?" Abby exclaimed. "Mother, you can't be serious. You can't just...I need...the girls don't even..."

Abby knew Heather and Angel were staring at her as

if she'd lost her mind. Maybe she had. Her mother, the woman who'd unloaded her infant daughter on her mother-in-law to raise, had just volunteered to hang wallpaper with two children—children she'd never even met until ten minutes earlier. Granted, Grace had talked with them on the phone before deciding on which decorating scheme to follow, but still.

"You...you want me to leave?"

"Yes, dear," Grace said, relieving Abby of the two oversize shopping bags she'd just hauled in from the car.

"But I can help." Abby detested the pleading sound in her voice.

Grace looked at Abby through the fashionable, gold-rimmed reading glasses perched on the end of her nose. "Don't you remember what happened when we tried wallpapering your guest room?"

Abby shuddered. A near brush with matricide. If Melina hadn't intervened, Abby would have dumped a pan of wallpaper paste over her mother's head.

While Abby watched, Grace rolled back the sleeves of her paint-splattered smock and handed a wide roll of wallpaper to Angel and two smaller rolls—the border—to Heather. "Clear off the kitchen table, girls. We need room to spread out." She looked toward the dining nook. "My, what a nice fifties dinette!"

Grace briefly surveyed the room before turning her attention back to the collection of shopping bags at her feet. She tapped a tastefully lacquered nail against her still-smooth cheek and hummed, thinking.

She never really ages, Abby thought, admiring her mother's punkish haircut, an avant-garde blend of silver and red. Grace would be seventy next year, but she still worked four days a week and played golf the other three. Abby both envied her and resented her.

"I believe I have everything I need, dear," she said, smiling warmly. "This will give you a couple of free hours to yourself. You work much too hard."

That theme had been discussed at length last night; Abby wasn't about to get into it again. "But, Mom, I want to help."

Grace's lips pursed—a look Abby remembered well from childhood. It meant her mind was made up. "You and I don't work well together, dear. We're too much alike, I guess."

Abby blanched at the thought.

"But the girls—"

"Look eager and intelligent," she said, cutting Abby off. Grace beamed at her two helpers as if genuinely pleased to spend time with them. "And we've already determined they have exquisite taste. Don't worry, dear, we'll get along fine."

Heather and Angel, avidly watching the interplay, smiled back. *But I want to spend time with them.* She'd missed them, having barely managed twenty minutes with them in the past three weeks, thanks to Daniel. He'd scheduled an employee orientation meeting so Abby wasn't able to drive the girls to their final Rainbows meeting. She'd shared the pain but been cheated out of the triumph.

"Come see our room," Heather said, taking Grace's hand. Abby's heart constricted jealously.

"Oh, Abby," Grace said. "Let's not forget a before-and-after picture. Where's my camera? I know your father packed it somewhere." Abby's father had remained in Palm Desert.

Abby fished a small silver Nikon out of Grace's tote

bag and followed them to the addition. She hadn't seen it since the carpet went in.

"Light and airy," Grace said. "Very good choice of carpet, Abby."

It wasn't much, but compliments from Grace Davis were rare. "Thanks."

After a dozen shots, Grace hustled Abby off.

"Wait," Heather said, dashing to Abby's side. With a conciliatory smile, she deposited a marble-size piece of blue bubble gum in Abby's hand.

Abby popped the rock-hard treat in her mouth and left with a smile on her face. Masticating with conviction, she plopped down on the front step. Heat, that ghastly, pizza-oven heat of summer, immediately tried to melt her. A sprinkler methodically arched back and forth over the ragged little patch of lawn, dousing Heather's bike with staccato bursts. "Now what?" Abby asked Rosie, who hogged the only available patch of shade. The old dog thumped her thick tail twice— whether in greeting or to annoy the flies, Abby wasn't sure.

She held her hand to her forehead and squinted through desertlike heat waves toward the ranch house. Abby knew Janey and Ed were back in Stanford for Janey's final series of treatments.

Abby had meant to call to wish them good luck, but the time flew by in a haze of tension generated by the new staff and Daniel's autocratic attitude. Abby would have postponed her mother's visit except she didn't want to disappoint the girls, who couldn't wait to add the finishing touches to their new bedroom. Last night, after her mother went to bed, Abby worked up the nerve to call Tom, but Angel, who, along with Trudy Gills, was baby-sitting Heather, told her Tom was at a fish fry at the Elks Club with Johnny. It seemed everyone had a life but her.

"So," Abby said, stroking Rosie's sun-heated coat, "do I drive all the way home and come back in two hours or what?"

Rosie's ears perked up. Abby tilted her head and strained to listen, too. A clanking sound echoed from the direction of the new horse corral. Curious, she rose and headed in that direction.

If a picture was worth a thousand words, the image of Tom, shirtless, sweating, looking like a model for some sexy calendar, was worth a million. Abby's fingers tingled as if she'd just touched metal after walking over carpet. A smile sprang to her lips even when she tried to banish it. This feast for the eyes nourished something puny and starved in her soul. Suddenly, whatever was lacking in her life—that essence that made daylight brighter, jokes funnier and oranges sweeter—hit her full force. A little dizzy, she grabbed for the closest fence post.

With legs spread a shoulder-width apart on either side of the steel fence post he was in the process of driving into the ground, Tom lifted a heavy-looking tool in place above the post and slammed it down with brute force. His gloved hands curled tighter on the handles of the pounding tool. He raised it a few inches and repeated the process. With each upward stroke, his shoulder muscles bunched from the strain, giving Abby a heart-stopping display of muscle power. His pectorals were molded like a young Arnold Schwarzenegger's. Although she'd long admired Tom's solid build, Abby hadn't realized the strength that went along with those muscles.

Each clanging sound made Abby's blood pulse in her ears.

A miniature dust devil sent the powdery soil at his feet billowing upward. Coughing, he reached for a water bottle sitting in the skinny strip of shade at the base of a previously positioned post. Without a belt, his jeans rode low, giving Abby a glimpse of shorts and white skin. The upper three inches of denim around his waist was dark with sweat.

His thumb popped the cap. He took a gulp then tilted his head back, squirting water across his face. Under his frayed, misshapen straw cowboy hat, a blue bandanna was knotted to absorb moisture. His skin looked flushed from the heat and sun. Grimy rivulets of perspiration and water coursed down his neck, leaving trails meandering over dust-coated muscles, fanning out in the diamond-shaped patch of chest hair.

He swished a mouthful of water from cheek to cheek then turned and spat. The stream landed two feet in front of her. A few drops sprinkled her bare toes, making her jump.

His eyes narrowed. "Sorry. Didn't see you there."

"Hi," she said, her gum getting tangled with her tongue. Blushing, she moved the nasty wad to one side.

He lifted one hand to push back his hat a notch. A lukewarm greeting, at best.

Suddenly, a bolt of lust swept through her. Why in the hell was she being so damn noble? She had needs, too. She was trying to be adult about this, trying to be circumspect, to do the right thing for his sake and the sake of his children. Did he appreciate her restraint? Apparently not. He was looking at her as if he thought she'd been avoiding him on purpose, as if she didn't

want him. What woman in her right mind wouldn't want
him?

The force of the blood moving through her veins
made her chest ache. Her palms were sweaty while her
feet felt cold. Wavy lines across her vision made her
blink. This is either lust or heatstroke. Either way, there
was only one cure.

TOM'S HEART SLAMMED against his chest.

"Hello, Abby." He kept his tone neutral, studying
her face and eyes with a trainer's intuitiveness. What
had Ed said about giving her time to recognize her feelings? Was that desire he saw? Wasn't this too soon to
try again?

One part of his brain shouted out the obvious: cutoff
shorts and flip-flops. Too much leg and ten toes with
lilac polish. Little blue tank top and white lace under-
things. Shit. She didn't play fair.

He dropped the sport bottle, giving it a kick for good
measure. When he reached for the heavy-gauge steel
post driver, the top-heavy post wobbled drunkenly. He'd
have kicked it, too, but probably would have broken a
toe.

He looked again. The raw desire in her eyes nearly
sent him over the edge. Where the hell were her sunglasses when he needed them?

Goddamn it, how much am I expected to take? Tear-
ing his gaze from her, he stalked to the newly installed
water trough. Yanking off his gloves, he let them drop
then pitched his hat toward the barn and plunged his
upper torso into the tepid water. Blindly, he reached for
the shirt that should have been hanging on the post.

"Here," she said.

Squeezing out his soaked bandanna, he used it to

wipe his eyes. She stood an arm's-length away, offering him the shirt like an invitation—one she knew damn well that he couldn't resist.

With a groan, he pulled her against his bare, dripping chest and crushed her lips beneath his. Her arms flew around his neck. He felt his shirt drop from her grasp and slide down his bare back. She pressed her body against him as if trying to crawl under his skin.

Her tongue met his with a passion he didn't expect. Part defense, part offense. He couldn't really tell where one started and the other left off. She tasted of bubble gum; the silliness of it made a laugh catch in his throat.

Choking, he pulled back. "Why are you here?" he asked with his first good breath.

"You know I can't stay away."

She reached up and pulled his head down to finish what he'd started. Her fingers moved in his wet hair. Her scent, as fresh and intoxicating as a field of wildflowers filled his nostrils. He followed the flowery trail lower, spreading kisses along her jaw, stopping to nuzzle the tender depression at the top of her breastbone.

Her sweet moan tantalized him, spurring him lower. He placed his hand over her breast, and felt her tremble. Her nipple solidified through both shirt and bra. He pulled the shirt free from the waistband of her shorts and worked his hand upward, lifting the jersey material over her quivering ribs. His focus centered on the rounded white breast and rose-tipped nipple straining against translucent material.

Forcing his impatient brain to slow down, he dipped a finger beneath the lace.

"Small..." she started to say.

He stopped her words with a kiss. Kneading the breast that fit his hand perfectly, he deepened the kiss.

A groan deep in her throat almost sent him over the edge. Whatever illusion of control he thought he possessed disappeared like a sinner's good intentions.

Her hips wiggled provocatively against his. His body ached to do what it was designed to do. Tom reached behind her with both hands cupping her buttocks and lifted her that inch or so to fit against him.

She moaned against his lips. "Tom, I've missed you. I need you."

His heart quickened its already frantic beat. His chest sizzled from the sensation of her rigid nipples pressing against him. In his mind, he could almost taste her. Honey. She'd taste like honey. His mouth watered, but when he tried to swallow, nothing happened.

Like a freight train braking at full speed, it took a minute for the message to reach all the way down the line.

With a groan of pure agony, he pulled back. "No."

Her hand slid around from his buttocks to the hard length between them. She cupped him; her thumb flicked across the straining zipper. "Your body says yes."

Her simmering, husky tone beckoned like a siren in a Greek tragedy. Months of longing pushed toward the point of no return. Do it. This is what he wanted. Why wait? Take what she's offering. Where? The barn. He knew where to find an old sleeping bag. Or they could use the couch in his office. No lock, but...

The images imploded.

"No." He shook his head, trying to move the blood back from his extremities. "Not here. Not like this."

He put both hands on her shoulders and moved her back a step. "My body says, 'Yes, please, God, yes.' My heart says, 'Yes.' But my head says, 'Get a grip, man. We're not seventeen and Abby deserves better than a roll in the hay.'"

The glimmer of passion, which had turned her eyes copper, was extinguished like a flame in a storm. She dropped her chin. Tom pulled her back into his arms. The heat still surged between them, but he could control it now. He had to. This was too important.

"We need to talk."

She wouldn't meet his eyes but nodded. "I know."

"Wait here." He glanced around for a spot of shade, but the glare of direct sunlight had turned the whole south side of the barn into a convection oven. Funny, he thought, I didn't notice that a minute ago. "No. It's hotter than hell here. Come to my office."

He stooped to pick up his shirt then took her hand, which felt as small and compliant as Heather's, and led her into the barn. The interior passage was shadowy, but Tom could have found his way blindfolded.

He opened the door, letting her go in first. The small room was crowded to the point of claustrophobia. Two five-foot file cabinets in one corner, a fax machine under the window, his grandfather's old oak desk heaped with papers, and in the far corner a stack of unopened boxes—his new computer.

"This used to be the tack room." Tom sniffed. "Still smells like one, but what do you expect? This is a ranch."

She stood unmoving. His heart sped up. This wasn't going to be easy. He tried to inject a bit of levity. "Maybe I could hire your mother to decorate it."

He gave her credit for trying, but the wished-for smile dissolved before it registered on her lips.

"Is it cool enough in here?" he asked, slipping his arms into his shirt. A tiny air conditioner hummed in the lower half of the window. "Why don't you turn it up?"

Robotlike, she took a step in that direction, but stopped in front of the fax machine.

"You got a fax," she said, not turning around. "It's from Daniel. I recognize the letterhead."

He walked to his desk and eyed the sheet of paper. "What's it about?" he asked before he picked it up.

"A formality. Informing you that you've been assigned a new caseworker."

He snatched it out of the tray. "Why? What's wrong with my old one?"

She turned to face him. "She's either promoted or fired. She's not sure which, and frankly, she doesn't care."

Tom hated this lethargy. It was such a far cry from the passion he'd witnessed just minutes before. He reached out and took her hand. "Come and sit down. Do you want a soda or anything?"

She shook her head.

They sat side-by-side, hunched forward, hands resting on their knees.

Tom wasn't sure how to begin.

"I'm sorry," Abby started.

He put a finger to her lips and shook his head. Water drops sprinkled his arm. He finger-combed his wet hair with an impatient swipe.

"Abby, what happened outside was…great. Incredible." He grimaced, wishing he were a cowboy poet instead of just a cowboy. "I'm pretty sure it would have been the best sex of my life. But I want more than that."

She looked sideways. Finally, a spark of curiosity kindled in her eyes.

"Abby, I love you."

Her eyes opened wider.

He didn't wait to see if she'd tell him she loved him back. He knew she cared; he was pretty sure she loved him, or at least loved his daughters and liked him a lot. He could work with that, but first they had to get past the obstacles she kept erecting to keep him at a distance.

"Abby, I need to know why you always kiss and run."

Her mouth opened and closed like a guppy.

"Whenever something starts happening between us, you head for the hills. I don't know what the problem is, but I know it's not because of your job."

"True." She took a deep breath then went on in a rush, "I knew about Daniel's decision before I came out here today, but it wouldn't have mattered. I'd already made up my mind that you and I...that we...it was going to happen." She made a futile attempt at a smile. "I just didn't think it would happen like that." Her cheeks blossomed with color.

He loved her blush and had to make a fist to keep from touching her.

"I feel like I got sideswiped by a truck." She pretended to peek over her shoulder. "Are there skid marks?"

He waited, letting her lead the way. After yesterday's session, Tom asked Donna about his daughters' progress and asked whether or not it would be wise to date Abby. Donna, in her mystic, patient-client tone, told him, "Abby has ghosts. We all do. You show her yours, and maybe she'll show you hers."

Not totally convinced psychology wasn't just a bunch of hooey, he was willing to give it a try. "Is it because of the girls and Lesley? That 'year-of-grieving' thing you told me about?"

Her left eyebrow rose. "The four seasons of grief?"

"Right. I asked Donna about that, and she said the girls will always miss Les and in some ways they'll always grieve for her, but they've come a long way toward getting past the worst of it. Heather only has nightmares once or twice a week now. But if you think they need a year, then we'll wait. I don't need a year, Abby. I did my grieving a long time ago." His jaw tightened, and he made himself flex his fingers to relax. He didn't like talking about that time in his life. "I took it pretty hard when Lesley left me. Drank too much. It was ugly." He shook his head. "Got even worse when I found out she was pregnant with Heather. I parked my truck with a camper shell on the back in front of her apartment building. Les told the manager I was a stalker. He called the police.

"I came home to lick my wounds, but I still thought—hoped—she'd come back to me. I don't suppose I really gave up hoping till she married Val. But that was four years ago."

He looked at her. Sympathy and understanding showed in her expressive eyes. She always had empathy for others but so little for herself.

"Tell me about Billy," he said gently

She sat back as though he'd slapped her. "Did Donna tell you…?"

"No. She said that's up to you."

BILLY.

Abby took a deep breath. "I fell in love with him when I was seventeen—without really knowing him. I loved an image, a product of his mother's hopes and my imagination."

Abby told him about the report she did for school,

the story of a heroic soldier who lost his leg in the war. She told him about meeting Billy years later at his mother's funeral, his tragic aura, a lost soul in need of succor. "I thought I could heal him. I thought my love could make him whole."

Tom settled back, positioning himself with enough room to watch her face. She couldn't bring herself to meet his eyes. Her humiliation over throwing herself at him was bad enough, but dredging up these old memories was worse.

"I more or less threw myself at him, but Billy was looking for something, too. Maybe he thought I was the answer. He invited me to move in with him but refused to make love with me until he was tested for AIDS because he'd been with a lot of women in Hawaii." Abby sighed. "I found that incredibly noble." Saying the words made her throat constrict. She'd kept these memories locked away for a reason—they hurt.

"When my folks found out about us, there was a big uproar because of the difference in our ages, but I ignored it." Abby had expected her parents to be upset, but it crushed her that her brothers couldn't support her choice. The worst part was learning they were right.

"Billy tried. It wasn't all his fault, but I built that pedestal awfully high. Gradually he fell back into his old habits, blocking his pain with drugs and alcohol."

Tom took her hand. The room was far from chilly, but her extremities were frigid.

"I switched my major from prelaw to psychology. I thought I could cure him. Unfortunately, I couldn't even help myself or..." She pinched off the thought. She couldn't open that door. Not yet.

"Donna and I've talked a lot about this. She thinks Billy was suffering from clinical depression, but it could have been manic depression because sometimes he'd stay up for four or five days at a time.'' Abby sighed. ''Of course, that could have been from the drugs. I was so damn naive, but I learned a lot in a hurry. One thing I learned is, you can't save someone who doesn't want to be saved.''

She rubbed her neck. Tom brushed her fingers away and gently prodded the tense muscle. She closed her eyes. ''One day I came home from school and found him passed out. The place was a mess. I hadn't been feeling too great myself, and I said some things I shouldn't have said.''

Her heart raced, remembering the look on Billy's face. '''So much for hero worship,' he said. Then he told me what really happened in Nam. How he lost his leg. Not because of bravery but because of a drunken mistake.

''I felt so sorry for him. But when I tried to comfort him, he freaked out. He—'' She flashed back to that moment when her world went haywire. Billy lashing out. Those powerful arms that could be so tender and loving, suddenly turning to weapons, squeezing her, punching her. Abby didn't know if it was memory or imagination, but she swore she could tell the exact blow that ended their child's life, even though she hadn't known she was pregnant at the time.

She didn't realize she was shaking until Tom put his arms around her.

''It's all in the past, Abby,'' he told her softly.

She relaxed her fingers and made herself breathe. ''I...I left and didn't come back for three days. Maybe he thought I wasn't coming back. I'll never know. He didn't leave a note.''

Tom made a harsh sound; Abby couldn't look at him.

"Death by hot tub," she said, trying to be flip. "The coroner ruled it an accidental overdose of drugs and alcohol combined with the hot water."

Tom squeezed her shoulders supportively.

"In his will, he left me the house. My dad and brothers cleaned it out, sold the hot tub and gave Billy's stuff to some veterans' group. They found me an apartment close to school and listed the house with a rental agency."

She smiled, picturing a happier memory. "Four years later, Donna and I went to the house together. It wasn't so bad. There were crayon marks on the wall. The ghosts were gone."

He stroked the side of her face with the back of his finger. "Are they?"

She nodded, wishing it were that simple.

"I love you, Abby. I know the timing stinks, but there's not much I can do about that. We have a shot at something good, if you're ready to try."

He waited, ever so patiently. Kindness and love warmed his blue eyes to the color of a robin's egg. His love was that fragile, too. She could hurt him. Badly.

"I love you, too. I think."

His forehead knotted, creating deep furrows. "You're not sure."

"I'm not exactly an expert. This isn't anything like what I felt for Billy."

"Thank God." He frowned. "And Landon?"

"That wasn't love. We were just good friends who slept together."

He made a primitive growling sound.

She grimaced. "I'm sorry. But it happened."

"I know. I had a couple of flings after Lesley." He moved closer. "I'm not an expert on love, Abby, but I know how I feel about you. I want to make love with you. I want to wake up in the morning and see your face on the pillow beside me. I want the rocker next to yours in the old folks' home.''

She closed her eyes, hating herself for what was coming, powerless to change it. Why do we have to make life so complicated? Why do we have to get hung up on lifelong commitments and families?

When she opened them, she found him sitting back, a wounded look on his face. "You're not going to marry me, are you?" he asked. "You'll have sex with me. You'd have done that in the hayloft if I'd pointed the way, but you won't marry me.''

His insight frightened her more than she wanted to admit. "I...I can't marry you.''

"Why not?''

Abby knew she'd had her chance to be a mother, and she'd failed to protect her child. How could she trust herself to be responsible for the lives of Heather and Angel—the only two children Tom would ever have if he married her since she was no longer able to conceive? "The girls.''

His mouth dropped open and his eyes filled with hurt and confusion. "You love the girls, and they love you.''

It took every ounce of strength she possessed to stand up. She put her hand on his shoulder—felt him flinch as though struck. "I know. That's why I can't marry you. Trust me, Tom. I'm not the person you want to be their mother. I wish I were, but I'm not.''

She was one heartbeat away from tears. "This isn't easy for me, Tom, and it may not make sense, but I know my limitations. I suck at relationships. I loved Billy, but, basically, when it comes right down to it, I killed him.''

"Abby," he cried, "that's not true."

She put her finger to his lips, touched by his impassioned support.

She moved away, putting some distance between them. "I thought I could do this, Tom—get involved with you without really getting involved, but I can't. It wouldn't be fair to you or the girls.

"It may look cowardly but I'm trying to do the brave thing. The right thing for you and your family. I never meant for it to come to this. I'm sorry."

"What did you think would happen between us, Abby?" His voice was keen with hurt and disappointment.

She closed her eyes. "Sex. Friendship. I don't know. Maybe if we could take it slow, I could—"

When she looked at him she saw the truth, a truth she'd always known. Tom was an all-or-nothing kind of guy. He loved with all his heart and expected the same from the person he loved. Abby wanted to be that person, but it wasn't possible. She wasn't whole; a part of her was missing.

"I'm sorry, Tom," she said, not daring to look at him one last time. She left the office and hurried through the barn.

THE SUN AND HEAT stopped her halfway to the house; a pain in her gut doubled her over. Deep breaths helped, just as Donna taught her so many years before. By the time she got to the porch, her hands had almost quit shaking. She knocked politely and called out in a voice that almost sounded normal.

"We're not done yet," Angel said, opening the door for her. "But it looks great. Come see."

Abby did her best to act enthused—the job was spectacular. The border—a looping trail of hyacinth and delicate ivy—encircled the room. The west wall and desk area was papered with a complementary print. Lacy curtains created a Victorian flavor. Her mother's expert touches were subtle but dramatic.

"Mom, I'm not feeling well," Abby said lamely. "The heat's done a number on me."

Her mother eyed her shrewdly. The girls looked at her with concern.

"You look pale. Why don't you go home, dear? Lie down. I'm sure Mr. Butler will give me a ride when I'm done here."

As much as she hated to burden Tom with her mother, Abby welcomed the chance to be alone to come to grips with her decision. Her loss. Even if it was the right thing to do, it hurt like hell.

"Bye, baby love," Abby said, giving Heather a squeeze. "Be good."

Heather's bottom lip popped out, perhaps she was sensing Abby's tribulation.

Angel followed Abby to the car. "What's going on? Did you and Dad have a fight?"

Her intuitiveness unnerved Abby. She went for a half-truth. "I got fired from your case today. Your dad has the fax in his office."

"So?" Angel asked, hands on hips. "You don't come here to be with us because it's your job. Do you?"

A quick hurt now would save a bigger hurt later, but Abby couldn't bring herself to lie. "Of course not, but it gave me a good excuse to be here. Now I won't have one because they gave your case to one of the new field officers, whom I will be training. Which is why I won't have a lot of time to socialize."

Angel frowned, a dark scowl Abby hadn't seen for a

while. "But I'll still take you guys shopping for school clothes if you want me to," she said, trying to sound upbeat. "Remember? The Modesto Mall. The Friday after horse camp."

"What about Dad?" Angel asked. "When we were driving back from Riverside, we talked about you and him maybe getting together."

"You did?"

"Yeah. He asked me how I'd feel about you two going out."

Abby's hand tightened on the Honda's door handle. The heat seared her palm, but it was so much less painful than the hurt in her chest, she ignored it. "What did you say?" Abby asked in a small voice.

Angel shrugged, her long air bouncing as a single sheath. "I told him to go for it." She gave Abby a serious look. "Mom always hoped he'd remarry. She said he was the kind of man who needed a family."

Abby flinched, holding back her tears by sheer willpower alone. "I agree. But—" She couldn't say more.

Angel's face screwed up in confusion. "You turned him down?"

Abby opened the car door, turning her back to Angel. "It's not the right time for either of us, Angel. Your dad's busy with the ranch and you guys, and I'm going back to college—"

"That's bogus," Angel interrupted. Her eyes got all squinty like Tom's. "Totally fucking bogus and you know it! Adults make me sick." She turned around and stalked to the house. The screen door slammed behind her. Its reverberation hummed in Abby's chest all the way home.

CHAPTER TWELVE

THE HUM OF ENERGY in the VOCAP office drowned out the therapeutic sound of Abby's tiny waterfall. Marta, the most recent hire, was a large, bilingual woman whose voice penetrated the walls like gamma rays. She'd spent twelve years in the Sacramento City Attorney's Office before going back to school to get her degree in counseling. What she lacked in experience, she made up for in opinions.

Abby told herself the new energy was a good thing, but one part of her longed for the low-key craziness of years past.

Kicking off her open-toe pumps, Abby pulled out her bottom drawer and withdrew a pair of sneakers. She'd arranged for Friday afternoon off so she could take Angel and Heather shopping. A staff meeting that morning with Daniel and the others had required her presence in business dress—silk, lime-colored walking shorts with tangerine shell and matching jacket that she hoped lent her an air of confidence, but she wasn't about to crucify her calves for fashion.

Melina sidled into the room like a spy. She closed the door. "Are you ever going to tell me what happened between you and that cowboy?"

"I already did."

"The whole story," Melina persisted.

I found him then I let him go. End of story.

After her steamy confrontation with Tom, Abby did something her grandmother called "mustering your chickens." She sealed up those painful aspects of her life and focused entirely on the one thing that had given her so much joy over the years—her work. She'd bustled into the office the following Monday morning with a box of jelly doughnuts and a big smile and set about mending fences and building new relationships with the crew that she'd pretty much overlooked for three weeks.

By the end of the day, Abby feared her effort was too little, too late. Melina, naturally, supported her without hesitation, but the other original advocates seemed dazzled by Daniel's promises to streamline operations. The new people were loyal to Daniel, whose restructuring plan seemed intent on downsizing Abby's role in VOCAP.

When she approached Daniel about her concerns, he'd ripped into her. "You used to be the best. Dedicated. Focused. But you lost it, Abby. I don't know if it had to do with that cowboy and his kids or if it's just plain burnout, but you're not the same person anymore, Abby. I don't know where that person is."

Abby had tried to muster a defense, but her heart wasn't in it. Maybe her heart had vacated the premises along with the person Daniel thought he knew.

"I'll get it out of you someday," Melina said, brushing back a lock of thick, ebony bangs. "Anyway, Tom Butler's the least of your problems. Daniel may have a new girlfriend, but his feelings were hurt when you brushed him off. Forget women scorned. He's as dangerous as a wounded moose."

Abby couldn't help but smile.

"This isn't funny," Melina scolded. "He can't take your head but he'd probably settle for your job."

After Melina left, Abby rocked back in the chair she'd occupied for almost seven years. Melina's perceptions were sound. Things were changing. Did she care? Not as much as she should, she thought with a sigh. Maybe it was burnout. Maybe it was something deeper, a dissatisfaction with her choices in general. She knew what Donna called it.

Abby's midweek inquiry about sleeping pills had prompted a three-hour session over pizza and beer. "You're losing it here, pal," Donna had said. "Zonk-city."

"Show me that term in a psychology textbook."

"That's my word. The preferred terminology is fucked-up. Now, stop playing the martyr and tell me what's going on."

Abby swallowed her pride and admitted her feelings for Tom. She even went into some detail about their encounter outside the barn. To her surprise, Donna grinned and said, "Max would be so jealous. He's always had this fantasy about doing it in a hayloft."

Abby slugged her. "We didn't do anything. Well, we kissed, and he told me he loved me, but that was it."

"That sounds like a pretty big it, girlfriend. I know people who lived together for several years and never used the L-word." Abby caught the reference to her relationship to Landon and stuck out her tongue. Donna laughed. "Abby, decide. Do you love him? Yes or no."

"It's not that simple."

"Why not?"

"The girls…"

"Crapola," Donna said with such force a piece of pepperoni flew off her pizza. "It's not about Heather and Angel. It's about you forgiving yourself. It's always been about that."

Abby recognized the truth in her friend's words, but knowing with your head and knowing with your gut were two different things.

"Angel came to session alone yesterday," Donna told her. "Heather had a sore throat, and—"

"Anything serious?" Abby interrupted.

"Not your concern. You opted out of that role, remember?"

A pain shot through Abby's chest. "Go on."

"She spent the whole time talking about you and her father. She said you called her the next day, after she cussed you out."

"She didn't cuss me out. She was upset. I didn't realize how upset until Tom called—"

Donna interrupted. "He called you? The woman who turned him down? Brave man."

"He is brave and kind and a wonderful caring father who has so much to share, and I'm a sniveling coward."

Donna nodded. "Agreed."

"I can't do it, Donna. I can't tell him what I did."

Donna sighed. She wiped her greasy fingers on a paper napkin then laid a plump hand on Abby's arm. "We talked this out years ago, Abby. You didn't have a choice."

"We always have choices, Donna. That's what life is—one big choice. I blew it, and I don't deserve anyone as wonderful as Tom."

Donna gave Abby a hug. "You're pretty wonderful yourself, my friend, and I think seven years with VOCAP constitutes penance. Why don't you give yourself time to let all this soak in then reevaluate? You've only known the man for four months. You can both use the time. If he asks my opinion I'll tell him not to give up, just give you time."

Abby glanced at the clock on her a desk: eleven-fifty. She didn't have time to stew about her problems today—she was going shopping for school clothes with her two favorite girls.

"WHAT ABOUT this sweater, Abby? Do you think it makes me look fat?"

Abby eyed the model—willowy as a young sapling with fledgling breasts giving definition to the hideous, olive-green turtleneck. They'd already filled a shopping bag with underclothes, including two new training bras. Abby hoped Tom didn't have a coronary when he saw them.

"I like the striped one better. That color clashes with the pants." The drab brown polyester hip huggers reminded Abby of a cross between something she would have worn as a teen and something the old men at the rest home wore. "What do you think, Heather?"

"It's ugly."

Angel stuck out her tongue. All three of her reflections in the mirror did the same, making Heather laugh.

"Maybe I'll try the orange top. Mom always said orange was my color."

Abby smiled. "Honey, with those cheekbones and skin tone, any color is your color."

She was rewarded by a happy smile. Their conversation on the way to Modesto seemed to have eased any remaining ambivalence Angel had about what had happened between Abby and her father. Abby had started by admitting she hadn't been honest with Angel. "I didn't treat you fairly, Angel. You're a very perceptive person, and I wasn't prepared to answer questions about my relationship with your father. I didn't mean to hurt your feelings."

"I'm not five, you know," she said softly, although Heather, in the back seat, seemed engrossed with a talking book Val had sent her. "I knew something was going on between you two."

"We have feelings for each other, but we're trying to do the right thing. The adult thing."

"Why can't you two just be together? I don't get it."

Abby struggled with her answer, finally telling her, "It's a matter of timing. Mine sucks."

Angel snickered at Abby's colloquialism.

"You and your sister are your dad's first priority. It has to be that way. It isn't fair to any of you to have me in the picture right now. I care about him, Angel. I care a great deal, and I think he feels the same about me, but our relationship is secondary to making sure you and Heather get back on track."

"If it weren't for us—"

Abby didn't let her finish the thought. "If it weren't for you, I'd never even have met your dad. Sweetie, think about it. Next week you start at a new school. That's a big deal. New teachers. New friends. You're going to need your dad's help, and he wants to be there for you. Being a single parent is a tough job. He'll need to stay focused. Doesn't that make sense?"

"I guess," she conceded. "But you could still date."

Abby's heart squeezed at the hopeful sound in her voice. "We'll still see each other because I'll still see you guys. It's just that relationships take time and energy. Didn't you tell me things had changed between you and your friend in Riverside when you went down to visit?"

"Yeah, Caitlin was totally weird. She acted like I'd been living on another planet."

"Well, this is the Valley," Abby said, drawing a

chuckle. "I don't know what will happen between your dad and me," she added honestly. "But I hope you and I can be friends, no matter what, okay?"

"Okay."

Now, waiting for Angel to change, Abby shifted the shopping bag to her left hand and reached out to stroke the satiny curls of the blond head at her side. "Do you like your new outfits, Heather?"

Heather nodded and yawned simultaneously. When they'd arrived at the mall, their first stop had been McDonald's for lunch then they'd headed right to the largest department store because its children's section carried variations of all elementary-school uniforms. Today's choices were less strict than Abby remembered from her parochial-school days. According to the list Heather's school had provided, children could choose from a mix-and-match selection of slacks and skirts in several colors.

"All these clothes aren't my birthday presents, are they?" she asked, apprehensively eyeing the bulging bag.

"Of course not. These are school things. What do you want for your birthday?" Abby knew Heather was turning six in eight days. She wondered if Tom had a birthday party planned.

"A pony. Like Blaze's baby. Only he's a boy, and Daddy says boy ponies aren't as nice as girl ponies. Like, duh."

Abby laughed. This vibrant little person had come a long way since that first day when Tom carried her into VOCAP. Grace was thoroughly charmed by Heather, and apparently the feeling was mutual since the first thing Heather asked when she saw Abby was, "Did you bring my fairy grandmother with you?"

''What else do you want?'' Abby asked.

''A potty Barbie.''

Abby's mouth dropped open. ''Excuse me?''

''She comes with a little toilet and real toilet paper.''

Abby couldn't believe such a thing existed, but Heather seemed certain of it. Abby's gift, a set of Kipling stories, included *Riki Tiki Tavi*—one of her favorites from childhood. Probably a geeky gift, Abby thought, but she could picture herself reading it to her. Then, like an arrow in the heart, reality struck.

Tom hadn't even stuck around to see her today. He'd left an envelope with twelve twenty-dollar bills on the table and a scribbled note that read, ''Abby, Thanks for doing this, Tom.'' How could she blame him for not wanting to see her? He'd offered her his love and she'd turned him down cold. She didn't deserve any better.

''This is way cooler, huh?'' Angel asked, spinning in a little circle. The bright color made her olive skin tone glow. Such a beauty on the verge of womanhood. Abby remembered what a painful, awkward time that was in her life without having a woman in whom she could confide. Could she help Angel through these years or had she blown that, too?

Abby blinked away unwanted tears. ''Very nice.''

''What about it, Squirt? Do you like it? Heather? Where's Heather?''

Abby glanced around. ''She was right here a second ago.'' Dropping to one knee, she peered under the clothing racks. ''Heather? Come out, come out, wherever you are.'' No small feet in brand-new burgundy Mary Janes.

Straightening up, she put her hands on her hips and let out a sigh of frustration. ''Not again,'' she said, remembering the petting-zoo incident. Fear and panic bubbled on a back burner, but she ignored them. "She can't have gone far."

Angel looked furious. "Why does she do this? Dad gave her a huge lecture about scaring you when she ran off at the picnic."

"Well, let's not panic. You change, and I'll start looking. You don't suppose they have any ducks around here, do they?"

Abby spotted her first, just moments later. A tiny towhead at the perfume counter is not easy to miss. Abby slowed her pace and walked toward Heather, framing in her mind the appropriate scolding. It wasn't easy disciplining someone who looked so adorable standing on her tiptoes looking at little winged sculptures masquerading as perfume bottles. Abby was no more than two steps away from Heather when Angel flew into her line of sight, a scowl the size of Milwaukee on her face.

Abby reached out for Heather the same instant Heather reached out to touch the fragile-looking bottle closest to her.

"You little twit," Angel barked. "It's my turn to try on clothes. You already had your turn."

Heather, who seemed almost transfixed by the perfume bottle, jumped, her hand accidentally knocking over one of the little glass vials. The fragile glass orb did a roly-poly dance then toppled over the edge of the table, shattering on the black-and-white marble floor.

Before anyone could react, Heather opened her mouth and let out a cry of such anguish Abby and Angel both froze in their tracks. Abby saw two attendants in pink smocks rushing toward them. Other shoppers turned in horror.

Abby dashed forward, dropping to one knee. "Heather, honey, are you cut?" she cried, pulling the shrieking child into her arms. "Heather, it's okay. I'm here. I've got you."

Heather didn't answer. The small container seemed to have disintegrated on impact, leaving behind only a cloying aroma and a hysterical child.

Abby rose. Heather's little legs automatically locked around Abby's waist. Using her free hand to dig in her purse, Abby tossed two twenties on the counter. "Sorry," she said to the clerks, then shouldered her way through the assembling crowd.

Lugging their many bags of clothing, Angel raced ahead to hold the door open.

Abby looked at her over the sobbing child's head. Angel's bottom lip quivered, too. "That was our mother's perfume. It was the only kind she wore."

TOM LEANED OVER and placed a gentle kiss on Heather's forehead. Asleep at last. He'd been sitting beside her for the past twenty minutes, holding her hand, waiting for the sedative Donna gave her to take effect.

"You'd better get to sleep, too, Angel-babe," he whispered toward the other twin bed where Angel was reading.

Angel snapped off her bedside lamp. The ever-present glow from the night-light in their adjoining bathroom cast a comforting glow in the room. Tom never ceased to marvel at how lovely their bedroom addition had turned out. The pale green bedspreads and subtle purple touches were both warm and whimsical.

"I love you, Dad. Tell Abby we're sorry."

She'd told him the whole story of their afternoon shopping adventure and Heather's calamity. Poor Abby. This experience would have been ten times worse than the one at the picnic.

Tom kissed Angel on the cheek. "I will. Sleep well."

He closed the bedroom door and walked down the hall, drawn to the low murmur of voices. The new hall runner, an "addition-warming" gift from Al Carroll, absorbed the sound of his boot steps.

Two women sat at the kitchen table. One he'd come to respect and admire; the other he loved more than he thought possible. Donna's back was to him. Abby was talking in low, hoarse tones. The telltale red around her nose and puffiness beneath her eyes told him how much she cared.

"Heather's asleep," he told them. "And Angel soon will be."

Donna turned in her seat to look at him. Abby dropped her head to her hands as if her neck was too weak to support the weight.

"I need a drink. How 'bout you two?"

"I'll pass," Donna said. "But make Abby's a double."

Abby shook her head. "I need to drive home."

Donna took her hand and said in a slow, deliberate cadence, as if giving instructions to a child, "No, you don't. You need to stay here in case Heather wakes up. She'll need to see you and be sure you're all right. That was an extremely turbulent event and you two need to comfort each other to get past it."

Tom poured two juice glasses a quarter full of brandy. Where the bottle came from he hadn't a clue.

"I could come back first thing..." Abby started.

Donna shook her head. "No. I've given Heather a light sedative to help calm her, but Angel was just as traumatized—she just hides it better. Like you."

Tom set the glass in front of Abby and took the chair to her right. "Drink. You need this."

She wouldn't look at him. He knew she blamed herself, even though Angel's version of the event proved no one was to blame. He breathed a little easier when she lifted the liquor to her lips and swallowed, grimacing at the harsh flavor.

Donna signaled him with her eyes. Tom looked toward the door. Abby's purse was on the floor, along with four department-store bags. Apparently they'd accomplished quite a bit of shopping before Heather's mishap. Tom rose and collected the whole assortment and carried it to the far corner of his bedroom. She couldn't leave without her keys and her keys were in her purse, he'd stake his life on it.

When he came out, Donna was talking in a low, serious voice. "I want you to stay here, Abby. I don't want you to be alone. Tom will make sure you're okay."

The look of anguish in her green eyes nearly broke his heart. "Don't make him do that, Donna. He must hate me."

Tom strode to her side in two giant steps. He squatted beside her and waited until she looked at him. "Don't ever say that again. No matter what happens between us, I know how much you love those kids, and I know you want what's best for them."

Donna gently scolded her friend. "You know how I feel about fault and blame, Abby. The bottom line is—both girls are safe.

"In a way, this might even have been the key we needed to reach deeper into Heather's subconscious. Abby said Heather cried herself to sleep in the car, sobbing for her mother," Donna told Tom. "Do you realize she hasn't once brought up the subject of her mother in session? The Rainbows counselors said the same thing.

Outwardly, she's adjusting well, but she ignores any effort to bring out her feelings about her mother's death.''

Tom pictured an incident that had confounded him last week, then said, ''I gave her a picture I had of Lesley. In a frame. Put it on her dresser. The next day it was gone. She'd put it in the drawer. When I asked her how come, she just shrugged and said, 'I don't know.'''

Abby withdrew a limp tissue from the pocket of her wrinkled silk jacket. ''Angel and I kept talking to her, trying to get through. Finally, she just played out. She fell asleep sobbing, 'Mommy, Mommy, Mommy.' It broke my heart. There wasn't anything I could do.''

Donna pushed the brandy closer and made her take another sip. ''You were with her—that's all anyone can do. This is something she needed to face.''

''What do you suppose set her off?'' Tom asked.

''The perfume,'' Donna and Abby said together.

''How? Why?''

''Angel said that brand is the kind their mother wore,'' Donna said. ''So Heather associates it with Lesley. Maybe the shattered bottle signifies death in a way a five-year-old can understand.'' She rose, and put a hand on Tom's shoulder. ''Call me if she wakes up before morning, but I think she'll make it through the night. I'd like to see them both tomorrow. Any time.''

''Tomorrow is Saturday.''

She shrugged. ''Healing happens when it happens— days, months, years later.'' The last she seemed to direct toward Abby, who looked away. ''I'd like to follow through while it's still fresh and a little scary.''

She pointed a finger at Abby. ''Stay here. This is where you belong. Okay?''

When Abby hesitated, Tom stepped in. ''She'll stay. I promise.''

After Donna was gone, Tom wedged an old Zane Grey novel, one of his father's favorite authors, under the door to keep it open and turned off the air conditioner. The little window unit did its best, but the two-week heat wave taxed it to the max. He walked to the window above the kitchen sink. "More brandy?" he asked, slamming the heels of both hands against the frame of the window above the kitchen sink. The sticky sash inched upward.

"No thanks. My stomach's on fire the way it is."

"Are you hungry? Maybe you should eat—"

"I couldn't. Thanks." She let out a little sigh. "You're being awfully nice about this."

He propped open the back door and turned off the porch light so the bugs wouldn't congregate. "Abby, this wasn't your fault," he said, walking toward the table.

She rose and stretched, one hand massaging her lower back. Tom remembered her saying she'd carried Heather all the way to the car. He sped up. "Let me."

She jumped, as if poked with a stick. "No. I'm fine."

"You're not fine. You just went through hell and back. Heck, shopping itself is my idea of hell. Notice I wasn't brave enough to go with you." His humor seemed to loosen her up a little. She let him guide her to the couch. "Sit sideways. I'll just give your neck and shoulders a quick rub. I learned a lot about muscle pain when I was on the circuit."

She sat stiffly at first, but gradually he felt her muscles unwind. Being able to touch her, even through layers of silk jacket and blouse, was a gift. The soft material offered little barrier, and the warmth of her skin radiated to his fingers. Her scent, not the cloying expensive perfume he pictured Lesley wearing, teased his nose. Her hair brushed the tops of his hands like gossamer threads.

"Angel said you rode in the rodeo."

"I was a team roper. Different breed of cat."

"Really? Don't they have steer roping in rodeos?"

"Rodeos have a bunch of events. Bronco busting, bull riding, steer wrestling and roping. Team roping has its own circuit. Sometimes ropers'll do rodeos, but if you're roping professionally, you don't have a lot of time to earn the points you need to qualify for the finals. Part of the trick is picking the right events.

"Some ropings, like the BFI—the Bob Feist Invitational up in Reno—take place right after or just before a big rodeo so cowboys can do both and earn a few extra bucks."

She rolled her neck, making her hair whisper across his fingers. "What do you mean by team? A whole bunch of you..."

He chuckled at the image. Few people outside the sport understood it, even though roping had been around for years. "There's two on a team. A header and a heeler. The header tries to get a rope around the steer's horns then turn him so the heeler can catch his back legs. All in about six seconds."

"Wow. Sounds difficult."

"Takes practice. And teamwork and a good horse. The circuit wasn't as big when I was roping, but now it runs from the East Coast to Hawaii. You ante up your entrance fee, and if you're lucky you can win enough prize money to pay your way to the next one."

"Angel said you were one of the best."

He shrugged. "I had a good horse."

She snorted at his humility.

"No, I mean it. Goldy—Hall's Golden Boy—was one

of the best. He took the American Quarter Horse Association's Horse of the Year award twice.''

She rolled her shoulders at his deepening touch. A little sigh escaped her lips. ''Which were you? Head or heels?''

''Heeler. I made it to the Nationals the year before I quit.'' The year Lesley found out she was pregnant with Angel.

''Did you win?''

He ran his thumb alongside the ridge of her spine; her shiver made his heart skip a beat. ''We had it nailed then my steer slipped a hoof—that's a five-second penalty. It wound up being about a fourteen-thousand-dollar mistake.''

She made a choking sound.

''It's a tough business. Ask the losing quarterback the day after Super Bowl and he'll tell you the same thing.''

''Why'd you quit?''

''I got hurt.''

She turned. His hand accidentally grazed her breast. ''Badly?''

A sudden surge of longing made him rise and walk a few steps away. ''I broke my arm. Nothing big. I could still work, I just couldn't throw worth beans. I missed the rest of the season, and when it came time to start training for the next year…it just wasn't there.''

''What wasn't there?''

How could he explain the depth of energy, drive and determination it took to propel a person into the competitive world of professional sports? His disillusionment had been a long time coming; the injury just sealed it. ''I don't know. The drive, I guess. Lesley said it's like getting back on a horse after he tosses you, but it wasn't like that. I still rope for fun, but back then I was—''

She had a thoughtful look on her face. "Burned out?"

"Yeah, I guess. I knew I wanted something else. Put down roots. Stop living out of a horse trailer. I sold Goldy to buy the little house where Miguel and Maria used to live."

"Used to? They've moved already?"

Tom sighed. Fatigue was catching up with him, and it hadn't been easy saying goodbye to the friends he'd grown so close to over the past couple of years. "That's where I was today. I helped them load everything up in Ed's horse trailer. They didn't want the girls to see them leave. They're planning a big housewarming party in a couple of weeks, and I'll take the girls up then."

Abby sat back on the couch and closed her eyes. "So many changes."

He snapped off the overhead light. The new exterior floodlights added a soft shadowy quality to the room. A night-light in the bathroom illuminated the way to the hall. He walked to the couch and held out his hand. "Come on. You're exhausted."

She shrunk back. "I can sleep right here."

He shook his head. "Not if you want to be able to straighten up in the morning. Trust me, it's a lousy bed."

When she opened her mouth to protest, he dropped to one knee in front of her. Her eyes were shadowed, but he didn't need to see them to know her fear. "Abby, it's been a lousy day for all of us. I could really use the company. We won't do anything. We don't even need to get undressed. Come on."

He held out his hand. Two heartbeats later, she put her hand in his.

CHAPTER THIRTEEN

ABBY'S FIRST WAKING thought was: home.

She came to full consciousness by tracking the individual elements of her languor. Tom's arm heavy and secure around her body, his hand tucked innocently below her breast. His warm, even breath tickled the back of her neck in a soothing way. Her buttocks nested against the curve of his pelvis—spoon-fashion, something she couldn't have pictured herself enjoying. She and Landon were individual sleepers who jealously guarded their territory on the bed. Cover thievery and bed hogging were grounds for reprisal in the morning.

Keeping her eyes closed, she savored his scent, picturing it as a magic shell protecting her from the encroaching day. She could drift back to sleep, or turn ever so slightly and start something she was pretty sure Tom wouldn't be anxious to stop. But that wouldn't be fair to him. He deserved more. The truth, at the very least.

Carefully, she shifted to her back. Traces of pink peeked through the curtainless window. She recalled her mother's anguish over not having time to do something about Tom's bedroom. ''He doesn't even have curtains,'' Grace had wailed, as if the idea violated some canon of design law.

Tom awakened. Abby felt a slight tensing of his arm. She turned her head and was rewarded with a smile. Her heart swelled painfully.

It would be so easy to stay here forever.

"Are you okay?"

His first concern was for her. "I'm fine. I didn't expect to sleep, but I was dead to the world. Did Heather wake up?"

He shook his head slightly. "I checked on her a couple of times, but she was fine." A lock of hair fell across his forehead. She brushed it back. She loved the springy texture.

"What time it is?" Out of habit, she'd removed her jewelry before washing her face and brushing her teeth with the cellophane-wrapped toothbrush he'd given her last night. "I buy 'em by the gross."

"O-dark-thirty," he said, his voice husky and full of portent. "Too early to get up, but not too early to be up."

He kissed her, igniting feelings too close to the surface. Her body cried out to respond, but she gently pushed her hand against his chest. His heart pulsed beneath her fingers. She stifled a cry of regret.

He broke off the kiss, cradling her jaw in his work-roughened hand. "Wishful thinking on my part. The girls will be up soon. Go back to sleep."

"No. I have to tell you something."

He stiffened. "Can it wait?"

She shook her head. Now, before she lost her nerve.

He moved away and sat up. He glanced toward the window then back to her. "I'll put on some coffee. I don't know about you, but my brain needs a little kick-start in the morning."

Abby made a quick trip to the bathroom. Her shorts and shell were a mass of wrinkles; she smoothed them as best she could. Fortunately, she'd hung her jacket over the back of a chair and it covered a multitude of flaws. She patted a cold washcloth to the puffy bags beneath her eyes and brushed her teeth. By the time she walked into the kitchen, she could smell the aroma of coffee.

Tom was waiting for her with a red plaid stadium blanket and two steaming cups. ''Follow me,'' he said, leading the way to the back door.

Puzzled, she wedged her feet into her deck shoes and followed. Dew tempered the morning, making it cooler than seemed possible since the afternoon would undoubtedly repeat yesterday's century mark. She smiled as she passed the neatly enclosed washer and dryer room that Al Carroll had salvaged from the former lean-to.

''You haven't seen this, have you?'' Tom asked, drawing her attention to a small, redwood arbor. A simple nook, just four posts with two-by-four joists and one-inch-square redwood crosspieces, housed a sturdy redwood glider.

''Wow. Where'd this come from?''

''Ed and Janey bought the glider. Al helped me build the rest.''

''It's fabulous. I bet you see the most wonderful sunsets.''

''Sunrises, too.''

He used a towel to wipe the dew from the glider then spread out the blanket. As soon as she sat down, holding the two mugs he'd handed her, Tom joined her and pulled the edges of the blanket around them. ''Snug as two bugs in a rug,'' he said, taking his mug.

They drank in silence, watching the pink glow on the horizon intensify. Meadowlarks trilled their happy greeting. The air smelled of earth, animals and butterscotch, from the coffee. If not for her nervousness, Abby would have enjoyed the peaceful moment.

Finally, she said, "Tom, when I told you about Billy, I left out some parts."

He waited, his gaze on her now. In a way, his silence felt like a safety net. He would listen. He wouldn't be able to understand, but she knew he'd try.

"Billy was in a lot of pain. Some mental, some physical. While he was in the hospital, he became addicted to painkillers. When he got out, he bought a bar in Hawaii with some friends and basically stayed stoned or drunk the whole time he lived there.

"When we got together, he wanted to change his life around. I truly believe that, but..." She sighed, remembering the handsome young man with so much potential. "It just didn't work out. Emotionally, he had good days and bad. The worst involved alcohol and drugs."

She rolled her shoulders to loosen up the tension and took another sip of the now-cold coffee. "Remember I told you I left for three days?"

She felt him nod.

"I left because that night he beat me up so badly I barely made it to the hospital before I passed out."

Tom let out a harsh groan. "Oh, Abby."

She gnawed at her bottom lip. "He was a proud man, but he felt so diminished. Not just his leg, but the circumstances of his accident. He told me he felt his whole life was a lie." She pictured herself at that moment—straight home from her psychology class, full of "fix-it" tips, ready to make him all better. "I tried to mother him, I guess. I only made things worse. He grabbed me and threw me against the coffee table. He was very strong. I didn't know how to fight back." She flinched when Tom moved closer. "I think I blacked out from pain."

She forced herself not to double over. "The X rays showed four cracked ribs and a concussion."

"Abby," Tom said, looping his arm round her shoulder. "Oh, sweetheart."

She held up her hand, but its jittery shaking made her curl her fingers into a fist and bury her hand in her lap. They'd stopped gliding. "Somehow, I got to my car. I don't remember driving, but somehow I made it to the hospital.

"When I woke up, my parents and brothers were there. Everybody looked so serious, they told me the police were looking for Billy, but he'd disappeared."

She took a deep breath. "My brothers left when the doctor came in. He told me about my ribs and said I had a concussion and some kidney damage. Then he told me that the baby I was carrying was dead."

She felt a shudder pass through him. "I didn't even know I was pregnant."

He tightened his grip, for which she was grateful. It helped her say the rest. "They told me it would probably self-abort, but they recommended—given my physical and emotional trauma—a therapeutic procedure, they called it. Basically it boils down to an abortion."

She fought to keep her coffee in her stomach.

"None of it was your fault, Abby." His eyes were full of sorrow and sympathy.

"I could have left Billy. I knew how he got. He'd slapped me once before and squeezed my arm so hard he left bruises, but I chose to stay."

"You're a caring person. You were trying to help him."

She made a snorting sound. "That's right. Abby the Magnificent to the rescue." At his look of confusion, she said, "That's what my grandmother used to call me.

She told me I could do anything I set my heart on. And I believed her. I wanted Billy—the hero I'd created—to be real. To be well." Sorrowfully, she turned to Tom. "It was ego. Pure ego. I was positive I knew best."

"You were young."

"But I wasn't dumb. I was in college. Spousal abuse wasn't kept behind closed doors anymore. I knew my relationship with Billy wasn't healthy. I did everything in my power to make him happy. Sometimes it worked, sometimes it didn't. When it didn't, he blamed me. I was too loud, too young, too dumb, a bitch, a nag." She smiled ruefully. "It wasn't until I started working at VOCAP that I learned how powerful a weapon words can be. They can slice to the bone and shred every ounce of self-confidence a person possesses."

"Even knowing that doesn't keep you from blaming yourself. Right?" he asked, his voice low and hard.

"I *knew* Billy was sick. He needed help. If I'd called the police the first time it happened…"

"If, Abby. If. Isn't that one of Donna's trouble words? I read those pamphlets you sent about victims' rights. The one on spousal abuse said, in the past the police stayed out of domestic issues, unless the woman got killed."

"I should have tried."

"Why do you do that?"

"Do what?"

"Beat yourself up about something that happened ten years ago." His eyes narrowed shrewdly. "Is this why you think we can't be together? You think I'd somehow think less of you for this?"

Abby's stomach turned over. "It's part of the reason."

He waited.

Unconsciously, she moved her hands to her abdomen. No visible scars, but...the wounds were still affecting her life. "The abor...procedure was quick and fairly painless. I had some bleeding for a few days but nothing serious. I didn't start having problems—female problems—until two years later. Heavy bleeding. Bad pain. My doctor did a laparoscopy. He said there was some scarring and my fallopian tubes were damaged. He couldn't say for sure why, but he said there was a seventy percent chance I'd never have children."

Tom's arm pulled her close, supportively. He pressed her head to his chest and lowered his chin to the top of her head. "I'm so sorry, Abby. I know how much you love kids."

A fist squeezed her heart; she scooted back, trying to catch her breath. "It's not about me, Tom. When you remarry, you'll want more kids. I've seen how you are with babies. You love babies."

He frowned. "I have two great kids. If you and I had a baby I'd be tickled pink because it was part of you and me together, but that's the least of my worries. I love you, woman, not your tubes."

She smiled, it was impossible to resist his heartfelt pledge. She caressed his jaw, rubbing her palm against the sandpaper bristles. She would treasure this moment forever. "You're the most incredible man I've ever met."

"But?" he said, his blue eyes darkening.

"You say it doesn't matter, but I think it will. Someday. I don't want you to settle for less than you deserve."

He opened his mouth, but whatever he intended to say was lost when a very faint cry interrupted the morning's quiet. "Daddy?"

Tom gave her a long, serious look. "This isn't over, Abby. We can work this out."

Abby wanted to believe him, but she knew in her heart she didn't deserve the life he was offering. He'd come to realize it, too, in time.

TOM AND ED STOOD companionably, elbow-to-elbow, at the gate of the new corral. Tom had unloaded the mares and their offspring in their new quarters earlier that morning. The final heat wave of summer had broken finally, giving a much-needed respite. Animals and humans alike seemed to mellow when the temperature stayed in the eighties. Fall wasn't far off, Tom could sense it. His daughters were halfway through their first week of school. So far, so good. Ed and Janey had returned from Janey's checkup, along with Peter and Maureen. This was the first chance Tom and Ed had managed to find a moment to talk. He sensed something changed in the older man's attitude. Tom was pretty sure he knew what it was.

"Ed, let's cut the pussyfooting. We're ranchers not lawyers. You want Pete back here."

The older man let out a sigh. "Janey wants him home. He's my son. But you know I've come to think of you as a son, too, Tom."

Tom smiled. "My mama might not have objected to that, but I think my daddy would have had some concerns." At Ed's chuckle, he went on. "You know how I feel about you and Janey. We don't have to get into that. I don't want you thinking my feelings are gonna be hurt if you bring Pete into the business. In fact, it's a great idea. Without Miguel around, I practically have to piss on the run. Gets kinda messy."

Ed spit into the dust. "Maybe we need to hire another

hand. Peter's an advertising executive, not a rancher. He turned his back on this a long time ago.''

''He was a boy. Now he's a man. A smart man. He knows about computers, right?''

Ed nodded slowly.

''Well, I got one in my office that isn't even out of the box yet. Maybe you can get him out here and start him doing some of that on-line stuff you were talking about. Why not let Pete handle all the paperwork end of things?''

''And you and me'd handle the real work?''

''You don't think I'd abandon you to a greenhorn, do you?''

Ed's relief showed in his smile. ''That's the best news I've had since Janey's doctor told me we don't have to come back for six months.''

''She's looking good.''

''She's feeling good. The tests look clear and she's started on a drug that they're studying to see if it can prevent the cancer from spreading or coming back. She feels good to be involved in that. Helping other women.''

Tom sighed. ''I'm glad to hear it. Makes what I gotta tell you a little easier.''

Ed's big, freckled hands gripped the barbless wire. ''Oh, Lord.''

''This is gonna look darned ungrateful after you just got done putting a pile of money into that addition, but the girls 'n me are moving out.''

Ed's jaw dropped open. ''What?''

''My house is sitting empty. An empty house is an easy target. Yesterday, I found some beer bottles out behind the barn. Kids partying. Vandalism comes next. Plus, my mares need someone looking after them.''

"Couldn't you rent it out again?"

"I could, but I figure Pete and Maureen are gonna need a place to live when they move back. That new addition would make a real fine master bedroom."

Ed's eyes lit up. "And Pete can keep an eye on things when you're not here."

"And he'll be nice and close to that darned computer you've been trying to cram down my throat."

Ed clapped a hand to Tom's back. "We're gonna get you outta the saddle and belly up to a computer one of these days, son, mark my words."

"I guess so," Tom's voice was less than enthusiastic. Val had given his old computer to the girls. So far, Tom had managed to avoid hooking it up, but once they moved into the three-bedroom house, that might change. In fact, he planned to use the computer to get back into their good graces.

ABBY STARED at a gangly Joshua tree a few feet beyond the low stucco fence separating her parents' Palm Desert home from the desert. How anyone could consider that greenish-gray, bristly, misshapen thing a tree was beyond her.

"Juice, dear?"

Abby spun around. She hadn't heard her mother rise. Grace liked to awaken at her own pace. She called it her reward after so many years of marching to other people's drums. She still worked in the design studio of a local furniture store, but her employers accepted Grace Davis's hours as her own.

"Sure. Thanks. I was going to make coffee, but I got sidetracked."

Grace glided gracefully to the whitewashed cupboards in the compact, artfully spare kitchen—no fussy decorator's clutter for her. A huge ceramic bowl filled with bananas, oranges and apples provided the only color accents.

The house was one of a thousand replicas—pseudo-adobe with red tile roofs and minicourtyards. Two bedrooms, two-car garages. Emergency panic buttons in each of the two bathrooms made Abby think the builders believed those were the only places old people ever got sick.

"Just as well," Grace was saying. "Your father only drinks decaf. I drink hot molasses water in the morning. You should try it. Much better for you than coffee. But I bought these individual coffee bags right after you called." She plopped a square bag on a string into a soup bowl–size mug and added boiling water. "Black, right?"

"Yes, please." While her mother fussed around the kitchen, Abby dunked her coffee bag. The mindless motion gave her time to reflect on the odd turn of events that had propelled her to the desert.

Daniel had shown up at her office door the Monday after her long, emotionally charged weekend with Tom and the girls. She'd spent the better part of Sunday playing board games with Heather and Angel, and even joined the family for a brief horseback ride around the property, but in the end, she left with nothing settled between her and Tom.

Daniel's sudden proclamation shocked her. "Abby, you're outta here."

At first, Abby thought he was firing her, but then he explained an audit of VOCAP's accrued vacation-time records showed Abby was ninety-seven hours over the limit. "Take it or lose it, Abby. New policy."

Since she didn't have a choice in the matter, she'd

called her parents to see if they were between cruises.
"Come tonight," her mother told her. "No, on second
thought, that's a long drive. Start fresh tomorrow. Your
father will be ecstatic."

"Is fruit and toast all right? We only have eggs once
a week in omelets," Grace said pleasantly, bringing her
back to the present.

"Toast is fine. Thank you."

Grace's hand stopped in midair above the toaster. The
smile on her lips seemed wistful. "Your grandmother
taught you such fine manners."

Abby let the observation pass. At the same instant
she realized Grace was only setting two places at the
table. "Where's Dad?"

"Golfing. You have to get out early. This is a desert,
you know."

Their first evening together after her eight-hour drive
was fairly brief. They shared a light meal, took a stroll
around the neighborhood—bringing Abby up to speed
on all the gossip—then went to bed. Abby was asleep
the minute her head hit the pillow.

"It's Wednesday, Mom. How come you're not getting ready for work?"

"I told them my daughter was coming for a visit, and
I wouldn't be in this week or next."

Abby was surprised, and touched. "Really? You
didn't need to do that."

"Yes, I did." Grace looked across the distance separating them. "Abby, do you realize this is the first time
you've come to us for solace?"

Abby hadn't realized her mother read the reason for
her trip so clearly. All Abby had said on the phone was
that she had an unexpected vacation.

Grace went on. "Even after what happened with

Billy, you chose to stay in Welton instead of coming home."

"I had school." A lame excuse considering the depth of her anguish.

Grace carried a plate with four slices of toast on it to the table. She went back for a bowl of pink-grapefruit slices, chunks of banana and juicy-looking slivers of mango. "Let's eat. More water for your coffee?"

Abby refilled her cup from the spotless stainless-steel teakettle. "How did you know I...that I might need...?"

Grace pursed her lips. Without lipstick, they were less youthful. Tiny lines made them look withered. For the first time, Abby had a sense of her mother's age. A peculiar pang knotted in her chest. "Abby, dear, you're my daughter. We haven't been close, but I still feel as connected to you as I did the moment you were born."

The words surprised Abby as much as they moved her.

Grace took a sip of black liquid that looked just like coffee. She selected a triangle of toast and set it on her plate but didn't take a bite. She looked reflective when she said, "I don't want this to sound ungrateful. Your grandmother was a wonderful woman who did an absolutely fabulous job of raising you, but she also had an uncanny way of making it an either-or proposition for me. We never really spoke about it out loud, but I knew if I turned you over to her to care for, I was—in a way— giving you up."

She shook her head and hurried into an explanation to cut off Abby's question. "Maybe it was my own sense of guilt. You have to remember, Abby, back then women had very well-defined roles. Some women were working and raising families, but that was usually because of death or divorce. I was blessed with an understanding husband who wanted me to be happy and fulfilled.''

Abby chewed a bite of toast. It tasted like sawdust. She examined it more closely—crusty, dense and fibrous, perhaps it *was* made of sawdust.

''When I found out I was pregnant for the third time, I wasn't terribly pleased. I truly regret feeling that way, but it's the truth. Then your grandfather died, and although I loved Quincy dearly, I saw his death as a way of being able to have my cake and eat it, too. Agnes needed help, I needed help. We'd help each other.''

Abby shrugged. ''I have no complaints.''

Grace looked at her seriously. ''Perhaps not, but I do. Agnes was from a different generation, and, as much as she loved you, she resented me for not doing my God-given duty.

''I looked at it as a win-win situation. Agnes had meaningful employment. I kept the job I loved. You were cared for in your own home.'' Her eyes looked sad, and she frowned. ''I just didn't figure it would cost me my daughter's love.''

Abby started to protest. ''Mother—''

''Think about it, dear. You were Grandma's girl. When you were sick, she cared for you. When you fell down and skinned your knee, you ran to her. When she died, you grieved so much I was worried sick, but in the back of my mind—God forgive me—I thought, now we'll have a chance to be close. But it was too late.''

Abby's heart squeezed painfully against her rib cage. She hadn't guessed any of this.

An image came to her. She was sixteen. Her first date. ''I remember one time when you came in my room and starting talking to me—girl talk, you called it. I thought you were going to try to tell me about the birds and the bees. In a way I wanted to hear it—that wasn't something Grammy would have talked about, but I didn't want to be disloyal to her.''

Grace nodded. ''I know. At least, I figured as much. I was prepared to be patient. I always figured there'd be time, but then you fell in love with Billy.''

Chagrined, Abby said, ''I really put you guys through hell, didn't I?''

''We were worried about you. I was afraid Billy might turn violent. His father was like that.''

''He was?''

Grace nodded. ''Don't you remember me telling you the reason Billy's mother divorced his father was because he beat her? You didn't believe me.''

''His mother was abused?'' Abby asked, shocked. ''I don't remember that.''

Grace related the story as she knew it. Abby had heard a thousand like it over the years. A pattern of abuse that became generational. ''Such a sad, sad time,'' Grace said. ''We were so happy when you met Landon. I thought he was just the ticket, but your dad said Landon was too 'insubstantial' for your tastes.''

Abby smiled.

''What about Tom?'' Grace asked, causing Abby's bite of toast to lodge sideways in her throat. ''He seemed pretty substantial to me that afternoon I helped the girls with the wallpaper. I was quite impressed that a man who'd just received the brush-off could be that cordial when he drove me to your house.''

''He told you?'' Abby croaked.

''Of course not. Angel said you 'dissed him.' I put my own interpretation on that. Was I right?''

Abby swallowed a mouthful of lukewarm coffee. The

bitterness made her shudder. Suddenly, to her surprise, Abby blurted out, "I love him, Mom. He wants to marry me."

Grace's smile slowly segued to a frown of concern. "I hear a big but dangling."

Abby smiled. Her mother's silly aphorisms were legendary.

"Are you afraid to tell him about Billy?"

"I told him everything," Abby said with a sigh. "He said it didn't matter. Even my tubes—none of it mattered to him. The only part he didn't understand was how I could be so forgiving toward everybody else and not forgive myself."

Grace rose suddenly. "I know the answer to that one. Come with me."

Curious, Abby followed her to the master bedroom. The spacious suite with ivory walls and cathedral ceiling could have graced the cover of *House Beautiful.* Abby took a seat on the bed, sinking into several inches of down. Her heart began beating erratically the second her mother withdrew an old jewelry box from the closet. "Is that Grammy's...?"

"Hopeless chest," Grace finished.

"I'd forgotten all about it." As a child, Abby had been permitted to carefully examine each of the cherished, often whimsical, mementos her grandmother had saved over the years. A single glittery earring. A campaign ribbon supporting Woodrow Wilson. A silver bracelet adorned with tiny charms, including one from Saint Louis.

"Do you remember this?" Grace asked, passing her a small, store-bought valentine card, brittle with age.

Abby studied the precious card. It looked in almost-perfect condition except that it had been ripped in two and was held together with invisible tape—the kind used in modern times, not when it was first given. She traced the slightly raised heart in the middle where a boy and girl sat holding hands. She knew the trite verse by heart, and she knew what she'd see when she opened it up. The elegant inscription read: "To my Aggie. With love and admiration, Quincy E. Davis. Your husband."

She turned it over. The scar looked ugly and mean. "I don't remember it being ripped," she said, puzzled.

"You did it."

The card fluttered to the carpet. "Me?"

Grace picked it up. "The day after Grandma died. It happened so fast. Agnes went into the hospital for exploratory surgery. They removed a tumor in her stomach. They didn't know if it had spread, but they told us she'd probably live another few years, maybe longer. But Agnes went to sleep that night and didn't wake up."

"She gave up. She didn't even try," Abby said in a small voice.

"You always were hardest on the ones you loved the most. You were so mad at Agnes you tore the card in half. You couldn't forgive her for dying."

Abby walked to the window and looked at the distant mountain peaks without really seeing. "I hated her for a while. She left me all alone." Cringing, she realized too late how that must have sounded to her mother.

"I think she was being noble," Grace said, her voice gentle. "Agnes lived through the hell of watching her husband die. She kept him at home for as long as possible then spent every single day with him in the hospital, watching him waste away. Besides the emotional toll, it cost her every penny of Quincy's insurance and all their savings."

Grace shook her head sadly. "She once told me she

wouldn't dream of putting us through that. 'I'll go when I'm called,' she said. 'I won't fight it the way Quincy did.'"

Abby blinked back tears that clustered in her eyes. She had no trouble picturing her grandmother saying that. Looking over her shoulder, she told her mother, "I'm glad she didn't suffer. She would have hated the indignity."

Grace put the valentine card away and closed the lid of the box. "This is yours, you know. She wanted you to have it."

"How come you never brought it out before?"

She shrugged. "I guess I was waiting for a sign from above."

Abby, who'd attended parochial school at her grandmother's behest, didn't consider her mother a terribly religious person. "I beg your pardon?"

Grinning impishly, Grace said, "A little angel called me and said you were sad. She was afraid you might need a little help finding your way home. And since guidance was more your grandmother's specialty than mine, I thought this might be the right time to bring out the hopeless chest."

Abby walked to the bed where her mother was sitting. "An angel, huh? The kind with long brown hair?" When Grace smiled, Abby leaned down and put her arms around her mother—a gesture she couldn't recall doing voluntarily beyond hello and goodbye. "Am I?" Abby asked. "Hopeless?"

"Hopeless?" Grace asked, her voice thick with emotion. "My daughter? Not on your life."

CHAPTER FOURTEEN

"How will Abby know where to find us, Daddy, now that she's back from her trip?" Heather asked, looking up from her coloring. She was stretched out on Tom's bed, using a hunk of cardboard as a base upon which to complete her art project. Homework, Tom assumed.

"Huh, Daddy? What if she thinks we're lost?"

"I'll call her later—after she gets home from work. This is her first day back in the office. I left a message on her machine yesterday but I couldn't remember my damn...I mean, darned, cell-phone number and the telephone company's not coming here until tomorrow."

He decided to upgrade his service with a separate line for the computer, since, with a daughter hitting puberty, he'd never get to use the phone otherwise.

Heather looked up. "You said a bad word."

"I know. I'm sorry."

She frowned, her face suddenly pensive. "Mommy said bad words, too. Sometimes."

Tom lifted a wooden box the size of a large briefcase from the cardboard box he was unpacking. He kicked the empty packing box aside and lowered the weighty burden to his bed. Made of unvarnished pine, the rustic box with poorly mitered corners showed the wear and tear of years of use. His eighth-grade wood-shop project—a gun case for the antique pistol collection he intended to have one day. He raised the lid.

The scent of cleaning oil billowed out like embalming fluid. The royal-blue velvet lining his mother had sewn looked moth-eaten in spots. His father had helped him arrange the layout to accommodate four long-barrel pistols. Three spots were filled. The fourth—his 1847 Walker—had been sold to pay off Heather's hospital bill. *Best deal I ever made,* Tom thought, smiling at the little girl coloring so industriously.

Tom wasn't sure what to do with his collection. The guns were one of the few interests he had shared with his father. He remembered his father telling him, "The history of weapons makes a fascinating study in human nature. Man's inhumanity to man, always looking for a faster, more deadly weapon, pretty much sums up the future, I fear."

A born pessimist who often sought solace in a bottle, Walt Butler also possessed a gift for storytelling and a voice that charmed his listeners. Tom liked to remember the times the two of them shared at Walt's workbench, assembling the pieces of a black-powder reproduction he'd ordered from some catalog.

Walt's pride and joy was an 1851 Navy Model Yanks. "Wild Bill Hickok carried a pair of 'em with ivory grips when he was a lawman in Abilene," he'd say, then burst into song about "the prettiest town he ever seen."

After Tom's mother died, Walt didn't sing much. He told Tom, "Genevieve was my voice. My hope." Walt soon developed a bad cough that resisted all cures.

"Mommy said a bad word at me," Heather said in a small voice. "That night."

Tom looked at his daughter, catching the sadness in her tone. Donna had warned him that as Heather's memory of her mother returned, she'd become more comfortable talking about it. "Honey, sometimes people say things they don't mean," Tom said, closing the case and sliding it beneath his bed.

"But, Daddy, Mommy was mad at me. She said I was bad."

A fist closed around Tom's heart. "Baby, you're not bad. Mommy loved you very much. Maybe she was upset about—"

Heather interrupted. "She was mad because I told her I didn't want to go with her. I wanted to stay at Caitlin's with Angel. I cried and kicked the door. Mommy said good little girls do what they're told, bad little girls had to sit in the back seat until they could be nice." Her bottom lip quivered.

Tom pulled her into his arms. "Oh, sweetness, you're the nicest little girl in the whole wide world. Mommy was angry, she didn't mean it like that."

Tom brushed aside her crayons and sat down, scooting her into his lap. "Did I ever tell you about the time Mommy saved my life?"

Her mop of white-blond curls danced against his chest.

"Well...I'd been at a roping out of town and won the big prize—eight hundred dollars, cash. This was before Angel was born, and your mommy and me were renting a little place over near Chowchilla. Mommy was a waitress at a truck stop, and somebody who came through there told her about my big win.

"On the way home, my truck broke down. A buddy took my horse with him, so I just locked up the truck and started walking. It was real late by the time I got home. I tried to be quiet, but Rosie was tied up by the back door, barking like crazy." Heather's eyes grew wide with anticipation. "All of a sudden, there was this loud boom and something went flying over my head.

"I hit the ground, belly first. That's when I heard your mom laughing. Seems she'd been waiting up with a shotgun full of buckshot because she figured I was out drinking up my winnings and she was gonna teach me a lesson."

Heather frowned. "Mommy tried to shoot you?"

"She wasn't trying to hurt me, only scare me. But you know what? She scared somebody else, too.

"Suddenly, there was this commotion by the garage. Somebody'd been hiding out, waiting to ambush me. That's what Rosie was barking about. Mommy's shotgun blast scared him away and probably saved my life."

Heather's smile lightened the weight on his chest. "Mommy was brave."

"Very brave. Do you know what else she did that was very brave?" Heather shook her head. "Just to make sure her most special little girl was safe, she parked her car under a big light in the middle of the parking lot, even though it meant she had to walk farther to get to the bank. She made sure you were safe because she loved you very much."

Heather tilted her head. "Really?"

He squeezed her tight. "Really."

She wiggled back and looked up at him. "Daddy, when you call Abby, would you tell her I have a present for her?" she asked, leap-frogging to a new subject with the agility of a six-year-old. She reached behind him and picked up the drawing she'd been working on.

As Tom studied the picture his heart swelled in his chest.

"Did I get Abby's hair the right color?"

Tom couldn't say for sure, the tears in his eyes were

making it hard to focus. Before he could regain his composure, Angel appeared in the doorway of the bedroom.

"Goddamn it," Angel said, her voice heavy with disgust. "If it's not one thing, it's another. Where's the cell phone?"

Tom pulled his attention from the paper in his hand to his daughter standing so belligerently, hands on her hips—a pose he'd seen many times in the past two weeks. She hadn't been any more thrilled about the move than Heather, until he promised Angel her own room. She'd agreed with the stipulation Abby's mother would be called upon to help decorate it.

"The phone?" he asked blankly. He wasn't used to keeping track of dental floss–size telephones. "In my jacket pocket, I think. The denim one hanging on the back of the chair." He nodded toward the small desk and chair in the far corner.

Janey had insisted on sending over nearly every spare piece of furniture in her house. The desk, a blond, square thing, reminded Tom of a kid's desk, although the computer sitting atop it looked anything but childlike. In this matter there was no negotiating: the computer was a useful tool, but he wanted it where he could keep an eye on it.

Angel stalked to the desk. He could tell by the set of her shoulders that she was upset. "What's wrong, kiddo? Tough homework assignment?" So far, their teachers had only glowing reports of the girls' transition. He credited a great deal of that to their participation in Tomorrow's Rainbows and the counseling Donna continued to give, although they now only saw her for one hour every other Saturday.

Angel scowled at him. "I'm starting my period."

Tom's heart missed a beat. "Already? Aren't you too young?"

She gave him a dry look. "Gee, thanks, Dad. Make me feel even better."

He flinched. "Sorry. This is a little out of my league. Do you need to see a doctor?"

She rolled her eyes. "I need Abby."

"SAY IT ISN'T SO, Joe," Melina said, her eyes awash in tears. She plopped theatrically into Abby's spare chair—the same chair Tom had used the first day he came to her for help. He'd looked so out of place, and yet he fit. Even from the first, he fit in her life.

"Did Daniel really fire you? The nerve. After all these years. After all you've done for VOCAP. The bastard. We can sue. He's just doing this because you wouldn't date him. We can prove—"

"I quit, Mel," Abby said.

Short and simple. She repeated the speech she'd given Daniel this morning. "I'm burned out. Everybody saw it coming except me. I was in denial, but I realized the truth when I was on vacation. I'm ready for a change and so is VOCAP."

Daniel then broke the news that he'd hired her replacement—a Ph.D. candidate who was looking for a position where she could really make a difference. According to Daniel, she was qualified, eager and married. Why the last made a difference, Abby didn't know, but she wasn't surprised to learn Daniel had already hired someone else. All in all, they parted amiably, her two-week notice a mere formality.

Rocking back in her chair, Abby pushed aside the box into which she'd been sorting the keepsakes and memorabilia that had accumulated over the years. A plaque from the County Community Action Association, a tea caddy from a family whose son had been killed by gang members, a beaded necklace Heather Butler made in Rainbows.

Melina took a tissue from the box on the desk and dabbed at her eyes. "Are you sure? What are you going to do now?"

"I'm going to finish my degree and start grad school. As soon as I have my master's, I'll probably hang out a shingle with Donna."

She and Donna had had a long talk last night when Abby returned from her trip. "I'll take the kids, you can handle their parents," Donna had told her, not the least surprised by Abby's decision.

"What about the Butlers?" Melina asked.

Abby fingered Heather's tiny beads. Her grandmother wasn't overly religious but she did put stock in the symbols of her faith. She'd always kept a strand of rosary beads hanging beside her bed. Abby never knew what kind of sign Agnes expected them to reveal, but now she could appreciate the soothing quality of the motion. She manipulated one bead and noticed for the first time an image on the opposite side of the small, smooth bead. She turned each bead over until she read the message it spelled out: I Luv You, Heather.

Abby missed them so much. She'd sent three postcards from the San Diego Zoo, but she hadn't seen or talked to any member of the Butler family in more than two weeks. Tom's message on her machine last night welcomed her home, but when she tried his number there was no answer. No one answered at the Hastingses', either. Abby had already made up her mind to drive out to the ranch as soon as she finished cleaning out her desk. She had bridges to mend; she only hoped it wasn't too late.

When the phone rang, she answered formally, "Abby Davis."

Melina rose to leave, but Abby stopped her.

"Really?" she said, grinning. "That's great. I'm happy for you. Truly, I am." She had to stifle a giggle working its way up her throat. Finally, the person on the other end of the line said goodbye, and she could release the pent-up laughter.

"That was Landon," she said, hurrying to explain. "He called to tell me he and Deirdre just got back from Tahoe. They got married."

"What?" Melina sputtered. "I thought he was a confirmed free spirit, and she was some kind of psychotic nag."

Abby lifted her shoulders and let them fall. "Who can predict the course of true love?"

Melina sat forward. "Speaking of which, what about Tom Butler?"

Abby thought a moment. How could she put into words all the feelings churning through her head and heart?

Before she could formulate an answer, the phone rang again. "Abby Davis."

She sat up abruptly, causing the bead necklace to fall to the floor. "Angel? Slow down. What's the matter? You what? I'll be right there." She started to hang up but caught Angel's cry and put the receiver back to her ear. "You moved? When? Okay. I got it. I'll stop at Wal-Mart and be there as soon as possible."

Abby hung up. Her heart was beating double time. "She called me, Mel. Me. Angel started her period and she called me.'' Suddenly, Abby gulped. ''What if I blow it?''

''How can you blow it?''

Abby grimaced. ''Do you know what my mother did when I called her at work and told her I'd started? She told everybody in the store—even complete strangers. I was so embarrassed I never went there again.''

Melina looked sympathetic. ''My mother just told me to go talk to my older sister.''

''What do I buy?'' Abby asked, grabbing her purse.

Melina waved off the question. ''They make a zillion products for younger girls. It's really big business. Don't worry, you'll do fine.'' She stood up when Abby did and opened the door. ''Did you say they moved?''

''Angel said they moved into Miguel and Maria's old house. It makes sense, I guess, but I got the impression Tom had some bad memories associated with it. Who knows? We all have ghosts, right?''

Melina looked at her curiously. ''I don't know about that. I think yours are gone, girl. What'd you do? See an exorcist while you were on vacation?''

Abby thought about her friend's question as she drove to the house on Plainsborough Road. For the first time in her life, Abby had enjoyed every moment spent with her parents. She golfed with her father. She hiked to the top of a canyon one morning with her mother and a group of senior hikers. The three of them piled into Grace's urban assault vehicle and drove to San Diego to visit Jarrod and his family.

The two weeks flew by and, despite missing Tom and the girls, Abby left the desert feeling rested and healed. Grace insisted she take Agnes's hopeless chest, and Abby planned to go through it at her own pace, no longer afraid of the memories.

Who could say if Agnes had made a conscious choice to die or if the fear of being ravaged by illness was more than her heart could handle? Either way, while she was alive, she'd given Abby a precious gift: unconditional love. Only after Agnes's death did Abby begin to put restrictions on the love she shared with others.

She'd withheld love from her mother because she was afraid of diminishing the love she'd felt for her grand-mother. She'd dived blindly into a relationship with Billy, sure she could turn hero-worship into love. Poor Landon never had a chance because, by then, Abby was so fearful of losing she didn't even ante up when the game started.

But Tom had demanded her complete participation, and, finally, she was ready to play. As the roofline of the little house came into view, Abby's heart beat faster in anticipation. Such an exciting game, but the stakes had never been higher.

TOM WATCHED the Honda approach. His heart felt lighter knowing she was near, but at the same time weighty. Just because he'd made some changes didn't mean Abby would welcome them. From his perch on the top step of the porch, he watched her get out of the car. She moved with such grace, her carriage proud but not haughty. Her black, double-breasted business suit with crisp white blouse looked too formal for her sur-roundings, but she corrected that by kicking off her high-heel shoes and tossing them into the car.

"Hi, cowboy," she said, her voice light and welcom-ing. Heedless of her nylons, she hopped from grassy patch to grassy patch until she reached the concrete ap-proach at the bottom of the steps. The image reminded Tom of the first day they met.

"Hi, stranger. Long time no see. You've been missed."

"Have I? That's nice to know." Her green eyes lit up. Lingering rays from the setting sun cast her hair in bronze. Her lips, shimmering with a recent application of lipstick, looked inviting.

"Where's the rest of the greeting party?" She held out a plastic bag like a peace offering. "I brought stuff—female stuff."

He'd been dreading this part. He didn't want Abby to think Angel's plea was a ruse to get her out here. This wasn't the way he'd planned it, but he wasn't one to pass up an opportunity when it fell in his lap.

"Janey dropped by right after Angel called you. Ed took Peter and Maureen up to the city to catch a plane and isn't due back till nine or so."

"Are they still thinking about moving out here?"

He nodded. "Yep. They're putting their house on the market as soon as they can."

"I bet Janey's ecstatic."

"She's happy. Ed was a little nervous—he thought my nose would be out of joint about having to work with Peter. I told him it was about time I had some help around there." He paused, not anxious to break the news that he'd abandoned the building in which she'd invested so much time. "Since they'd need a place to live and the bunkhouse was looking so good thanks to you and your mother, I decided I should be the one to move out. This house was sitting empty...so we moved."

Abby eyed the building with a thoughtful look, then said, "I'm so glad. It needs a family."

Pivoting on one heel, she pointed toward the ancient oak tree a hundred yards to the right. "I had a dream about that tree while I was gone. Isn't that crazy? Of course, it's understandable—there are no real trees in the desert,'' she told him with mock seriousness. Her features took on a dreamy quality when she went on. ''One night, I saw that tree with a rope swing, and I was swinging higher and higher until my toes touched the lower branches. I felt so free and happy.''

With a girlish look, she added, ''You were pushing me.''

Tom's heart missed a beat or two. Was there a message in her dream? Did he dare to hope? The planking beneath his butt seemed harder than it had a few minutes earlier. He scooted forward, his elbows resting on his knees.

''Anyway, you were saying…?'' she prompted, pulling him back from his fantasies.

''Janey came by and invited us for pizza. Ed hates pizza—it's been their one ongoing argument for the past fifty-three years. I told her you were coming. I didn't say why you were coming—I didn't want to embarrass Angel, but Heather blurted it out and Janey was so matter-of-fact about it, Angel seemed to shrug it off, too.'' He frowned. ''Janey said they'd stop at the store on the way to the pizza place.''

Abby burst out laughing. ''Do I feel silly!'' She gave the plastic bag a shake. ''You should have seen me at Wal-Mart, agonizing over which product was perfect. That's what took me so long.''

''You're not offended? Angel was pretty upset when she called you.''

Abby tossed the bag on the top step. ''A girl's first period can be a big deal, but it doesn't have to be. I'll be around if she wants to talk.''

Tom dropped the twig he'd rubbed smooth. ''Heather

was afraid you might want to move back with your folks or…''

Abby's hoot made Rosie, who seldom left her spot under the rear porch, bark. Blushing, she covered her lips. ''I had a great time and I love my parents, but good grief! They eat wooden bread and drink molasses, and they're on the go all the time. I had to come home to rest, they wore me out.''

Tom studied her. This was a new Abby. She seemed at peace in a way he hadn't seen before. ''You're healed,'' he said, recognizing the truth of his words.

''Almost,'' she said softly. She closed the distance between them, moving to the bottom step. Tom caught the scent he could have identified blindfolded.

Tom made room for her between his knees and she took it. Eye-to-eye, he met her look, afraid to blink. His heart stalled, waiting to see if his dreams were about to come true or if his imagination had conjured up a wraith that would disappear before his eyes.

''I missed you,'' she said.

He missed her, too. He wanted her more than he could put into words, but he knew he had to be smart this time. There was too much at stake to blow it.

''Abby, I've been thinking—even cowboys do it, from time to time,'' he said, afraid of appearing too serious since that hadn't worked the last time. ''I…'' He hesitated then leaned to one side to extract a piece of paper from his rear pocket. ''I did some research while you were gone.''

He handed her the paper and waited while she unfolded it. He watched her expression turn from curiosity to amazement. ''Tom, these are Web sites.''

Her shock seemed profound. ''Peter gave me a few lessons on the computer and I went on-line. Angel told me I could find anything on the Internet, so I went looking.''

"You did this for me?" she said in a small voice.

"I'd do anything for you, Abby."

She turned, holding the crumpled paper to the light spilling from the living-room window. As she read, he told her about his many hits and misses on the information superhighway. "It's not a complete list, of course, but, Abby, it's amazing how much information there is about new fertility treatments, including fixing up damaged fallopian tubes."

He saw her surreptitiously bat away a tear. "The last one on the list is an adoption hot-line," she said in a small voice.

He put his hands on her waist and pulled her closer. The wool was stiff and formal but she wasn't. "I want whatever makes you happy. If you want a baby, then we'll do whatever it takes to make that happen." He grinned at her. "We haven't even tried the old-fashioned way yet. Who knows? We might get lucky."

Her laugh lifted a load from his heart. "Who could be luckier than me? I love you, Tom Butler."

Instinct told him to kiss her, but he had a whole speech planned about agendas and patience. He wanted her to know he could wait as long as she wanted. "I love you, too, and I'd like for us to get married, but I won't push you, Abby. I know your job is important—"

"I got fired today," she said, interrupting him. "Or, I quit. Depends on whose story you believe."

"Oh, babe," he said, pulling her close, offering comfort. "Are you okay?"

He stroked her back, wishing she wouldn't melt against him quite so provocatively when he was trying to set the record straight about his intentions. Marshaling his restraint, he moved her back far enough to make eye contact. ''I know how much of yourself you put into VOCAP, but you said you were interested in going back to school. Maybe this will work out for the best.''

''Maybe,'' she said, worrying her bottom lip in the most provocative way. His groin tightened, and he had to stifle a groan.

''Whatever you decide, the girls and I will be here waiting until you're ready for an instant family.'' He swallowed against the knot in his throat. ''As long as I know you want us.''

The softening in her eyes was his first clue, the sweet, joyful smile on her lips the second. ''Tom, you already are my family.''

Momentarily stunned, he sat there with his mouth open, until she laughed and threw her arms around him. He had no choice but to hold her tight. And kiss her.

ABBY'S HEART never felt fuller. Tom's arms were warmer, stronger than she remembered. His scent enveloped her, and she couldn't imagine ever not wanting to feel him beside her.

There were things to resolve. Her college plans. Her idea of setting up a practice with Donna. And, most important, the girls.

''What will we tell Angel and Heather?'' she asked, nuzzling the open V afforded by his worn denim shirt. ''We can't let our feelings for each other rush them into something they're not ready for.''

He pulled back, giving himself room to rise. With a tender smile, he reached for her hand. ''Come. I want to show you something.''

A little unnerved by the seriousness of his tone, Abby hesitated just a second then put her hand in his. No limits, no restrictions. She was betting on unconditional love.

At the threshold, he paused, a boyish grin on his face. "This may be rushing things, but…" He bent over and scooped her into his arms.

"Tom. Put me down. You'll ruin your back." Despite her protest, Abby's heart swelled at the romantic gesture. In a way it sealed things more finally than a signature on a marriage license. "I'm not a bride."

"You're my bride, and you will be until the day I die."

Abby blinked back tears, tightening the hold around his neck. "I love you, cowboy."

He opened the door and marched through the portal. Once inside, he kissed her soundly then lowered her feet to the floor. "Wait here," he said, dashing toward the staircase. "If I take you upstairs I'll never let you back down, and the girls will be home any minute."

Suddenly alone and feeling a bit overwhelmed, Abby looked around. Boxes mingled with familiar furnishings. The house was once Lesley's, but Abby couldn't feel any ghosts. Maybe Lesley's spirit sensed Abby had no desire to diminish her daughters' memories of their mother; she only hoped to add her own.

She looked up when she heard Tom's boot steps hurrying down the stairs. In his hand was a piece of paper, which he handed to her like a little boy bringing home a blue ribbon. Abby's first impression was of crayon markings, bright and crude, obviously the work of a young child. She turned it horizontally and studied the drawing.

Tears filled her eyes, blurring the images. "Oh, Tom."

"She made it for you," Tom said, his melodic voice husky with emotion. "It almost made me cry."

Abby blinked rapidly, relishing each image: a square house with a porch, four windows and a big tree in the corner. Standing in front of the house were four figures, two big, two small. She'd labeled each person, printing with obvious care: Daddy, Angel, me, Abby. Abby's name, however, had been crossed out and above it, written in green, was the word *Mom*.

"She was most concerned about getting your hair color right."

Abby cupped his jaw with her free hand. How could one so masculine, a hero right out of a country-western song, be so sensitive? "Are you sure they're ready to let another woman into their lives?" Abby asked, afraid to believe her great good fortune. "It hasn't been a year."

He kissed her sweetly. "Christmas is coming," he said, nibbling a path along her neckline. "They wouldn't have time to feel sad if they were getting ready for a wedding."

Dizzy with desire, she clung to him. "Thanksgiving is sooner."

His warm breath tickled her ear while his teeth playfully nipped. "Too close to Angel's birthday. I already promised her a big slumber party for all her friends. Not my idea of a honeymoon."

She had some honeymoon ideas of her own and didn't necessarily need a wedding to put them into practice.

He pulled back suddenly, leaving her bereft.

"Columbus Day is coming up."

"Columbus Day," she whispered, threading her fingers into his wavy hair, fluffing out the impression of his hat line above his ears. "If it's okay with the girls, you've got a date. Now, kiss me, cowboy."

And, gentleman that he was, Tom obliged his true love's request.

"HAVE WE GIVEN them enough time?" Angel asked tensely, squinting toward the little, white house a quarter mile off the road. She and Heather had put a lot of thought into this plan and she didn't want to blow it.

"Relax, honey," Janey advised. Janey had helped co-ordinate the tactical aspect of getting the two girls out of the house once Angel got Abby to come there. For an old person, Janey had proven to be downright romantic. "You're too young to get an ulcer. Adults have to work themselves into lifelong commitments. They don't see things so black and white like young people do."

Angel sighed, hating the truth but recognizing it. "But it's so obvious, Janey. Dad and Abby are meant for each other. You know what Dad's been like since she left, and when I called Grace, she told me Abby was positively blue, missing us."

"Yeah," Heather said. "Abby's gotta be my new mom because her mom is my fairy grandmother."

Angel rolled her eyes. She'd given up trying to break her sister of the habit of labeling people. Angel liked Grace, too—a whole lot better than her real mom's mother, although she did feel better after taking Donna's advice and writing Ruby a letter of forgiveness. She could understand how upset Ruby was and how she wanted someone to blame for what happened. But Angel knew from being at Rainbows that sometimes bad things happened for no reason, and you had to go forward with your life. You couldn't let it hang over you forever. Angel knew her mother would want her to be happy and have a full life. She'd want the same for her father.

A memory came to her. She and her mother were sharing a plate of Thai food at an outdoor bazaar, and Angel asked Lesley why she'd divorced their dad. "You know, honey," Lesley told her, "your dad is a great guy. One of the best. But he's an old world kind of guy, and I'm a new world kind of woman. It just wasn't meant to be. But someday he'll meet a woman who's looking for that kind of man and they'll live happily ever after."

"Mom would have wanted Dad to be happy," Angel said, her voice sounding kind of funny.

Janey slowed the car to make the turn. "I know, dear. Let's just hope Abby feels the same way."

Nervous, Angel threaded a hunk of hair between her lips and chomped down, but she hastily spit it out, recalling the promise she'd made to her father. He had enough on his mind without worrying about her nervous habits.

Angel glanced at her sister in the back seat. For a little punk, she wasn't too bad. She'd been a good sport about drawing the picture, even though she thought it was a bit obvious.

"Oh, look," Janey said.

As the car slowed, Angel heard Heather's seat belt snap open; her sister plopped over the seat for a better view.

"They're kissing," Heather screeched. "Look, Angel, they're kissing."

"Right on," Angel said, trying to keep tears from coming. She wasn't about to do something as childish as cry.

"They look nice," Heather said.

Angel looked again. They did. The two people framed in the doorway of the little house looked perfect.

"We're home, kiddo," Angel said. And for the first time since she arrived in the valley, she meant it.

EPILOGUE

ABBY'S HEAD was spinning. She couldn't decide if it was from the excitement or the delicious realization she was now and forevermore Mrs. Tom Butler.

"I'd say this shindig turned out pretty darned fine, Mrs. Butler," her husband of two hours said as they danced beneath the pink and white streamers suspended from the rafters of the hayloft. An ocean of organdy, miles of pink ribbon and a small tropical island of potted palms had transformed the Standing Arrow H barn into Cinderella's castle.

"Perfect. Absolutely perfect," Abby said, savoring the sight of her father waltzing with Angel. No father could have looked more distinguished; no grandfather could have been prouder to welcome two new grand-daughters to the clan. "If you'd told me back in September that I'd be dancing in a barn on February fourteenth, I'd have said you were crazy."

Tom grinned. "Who could have reckoned on the Dynamic Duo?"

That was the code name she and Tom bestowed on Grace and Heather. From the minute Abby and Tom announced their intention to marry, those two joined forces to collaborate on all wedding plans—right down to setting the date. "It has to be Valentine's Day, Daddy. It has to be," Heather announced. Until that moment Abby hadn't realized how intractable the six-year-old could be—a trait shared with her grandmother-to-be.

"Of course it has to be Valentine's Day," Grace said when they called her that evening. "You don't for one minute believe I could plan your wedding by, say, Christmas or Thanksgiving, do you?" Abby and Tom both were too embarrassed to suggest their original plan.

"I really can't get over this," Abby said, her heart so full of joy she felt certain she'd either weep or have a heart attack before the party was over. "I swear they made a pact with the devil to get this finished on time."

Tom brushed his nose against her cheek. "Never doubt the power of friendship," he said. "Or Janey Hastings. Since the doctors gave her an all-clear, she's back to being a force to be reckoned with." Abby looked across the dance floor to the buffet where Janey and Ed were heaping great mounds of barbecued beef and Portuguese beans on guests' plates.

She sensed his happiness. The madhouse anxiety of the past few weeks would have killed a lesser man. In addition to wedding plans, he had to deal with Angel's volleyball schedule and hectic social agenda, Abby's college classes and volunteer work at the Battered Women's Shelter, as well as the sale of her house and subsequent move. But the outcome was worth it, especially seeing the triumph on the faces of Grace and Heather.

"You know," Abby said, studying the two who seemed to have forged an unbreakable bond, "I wouldn't be surprised if they went into business."

Tom groaned. "That's all we need—a six-year-old wedding consultant."

As if to banish the thought, Tom whirled Abby in a circle, making the billowy skirt of her pale pink gown twirl like a princess's. Grace, Angel and Heather had purchased the gown on a shopping trip to the Bay area. Abby had been horrified by their audacity. "Pink? I'll look like an upside-down ice-cream cone." All three found that image hilarious.

"It's called champagne-pink. It's the hot new color, Abby. You'll be rave," said Angel, who was Abby's maid of honor. "Besides, it'll look really neat with our bridesmaid dresses."

Her mother delivered the most convincing argument. "It was on sale, dear. We saved your father a thousand dollars." If that didn't win her over, the dress's beaded pearl bodice and soft organdy skirt did.

"Have I told you that you are the most beautiful bride in the world?" Tom whispered. His voice still had the power to make her toes curl, and she couldn't wait to start their honeymoon. Since they both felt strongly about maintaining a certain decorum in their relationship in front of the girls, she'd never spent the night at the house, and he'd only stayed with her a half-dozen times when the girls were at slumber parties or with Janey.

"Are you going to tell me now?" Tom asked, kissing her long and suggestively.

Abby blushed. How this matter of a wedding gift had become such a hot topic, she wasn't sure. Probably her mother's doing. But she did know positively, her gift to him wouldn't be revealed until they were alone. "Not yet."

"Not even a hint?"

Abby pictured the elegantly wrapped box tucked in her suitcase. More symbolic than functional since she'd already used up three just like it, her gift was a home pregnancy testing kit.

"Let's just say it's something you'd never guess in a million years," she said, smiling.

When some odd changes in her body began showing up in late January, Abby attributed them to stress, but her mother had suggested otherwise. "You're pregnant," Grace said, hugging her to the point of asphyxiation. Even three litmus tests couldn't convince Abby, but her doctor confirmed it last week.

Although her first impulse was to call Tom from the doctor's office, she decided to wait for a private moment. There would be time when they returned from their honeymoon to share the news with the rest of the world.

Abby called it a miracle, but her mother was more pragmatic. "You're healed, Abby. From the inside out." That, Abby didn't doubt. Angel and Heather had helped remove any fear Abby had about being a mother. This baby wasn't a replacement for the one she lost so many years before. She'd been given a second chance but it came about through the love of one man, and their child was a gift they would treasure together.

"Are you ready, my fairy princess?" Tom asked, breaking into her reverie.

Abby looked into his twinkling blue eyes and smiled. "I'm ready, my cowboy prince. Don't we need to tell the girls goodbye?"

"Oh, don't worry. They're waiting for us." He took her elbow to guide her toward the double doors, which had been closed to keep out the chilly evening. The sun, which had shone so brightly and warmly during their outdoor wedding ceremony, was long gone.

As if by magic, the doors opened outward and Abby spied her carriage—Tom's brand-new pickup truck, the one she'd insisted they purchase from the proceeds of the sale of her house. Today, the top-of-the-line dually was adorned with a hundred pink and white bows. If trucks could look embarrassed, this one positively blushed.

Her father opened the passenger-side door and helped her up to the running board, where she stood and waved while Tom went around to the driver's side. Being certain to make eye contact with those who mattered most, she smiled and mouthed, "I love you."

Melina, standing beside a handsome young man in a western suit, waved the bridal bouquet she'd triumphantly snagged. Val hoisted Heather up high enough to wave exuberantly. Miguel and Maria stood beside Abby's brothers, holding little Rey. Beside them, Grace and Angel, distributing cups of birdseed, chorused back, "We love you, too." Donna blew her a kiss then wiped the tears from her eyes.

"You done good, sweetheart," her father whispered gruffly, his eyes moist. "Your grandma would have been proud of you."

Abby had to dab at her own tears as the truck pulled away, but she couldn't stay sad for long on the happiest day of her life. She turned in the seat, pushing her voluminous wedding gown out of the way. "So, cowboy, where are you taking me?"

He pulled her into the crook of his arm. "To the sun and stars...just you and me and a couple hundred curious cows. Think you're up for it?"

"Just try and stop me." Abby snuggled close, content beyond imagination yet alive with anticipation.

As they turned on the main road, Tom had to wait for a tractor to pass. He flashed a glance toward the ranch. "The kids are going home with your folks, right?"

Abby smiled and said softly, "Two of them are. We're keeping the new one with us."

"The new one...?" Tom's confusion turned to disbelief. "A baby? Really?"

When she nodded, his eyes filled with tears and he pulled her into a tight embrace. "Oh, Abby, that's the best wedding present in the world. I can't believe it. How...?"

She chuckled softly and whispered, "The old-fashioned way—love."